C000089659

Dark Secrets

Meaghan Pierce

Pierced Soul Publishing

Editing by Comma Sutra Editorial

Cover Design by Books and Moods

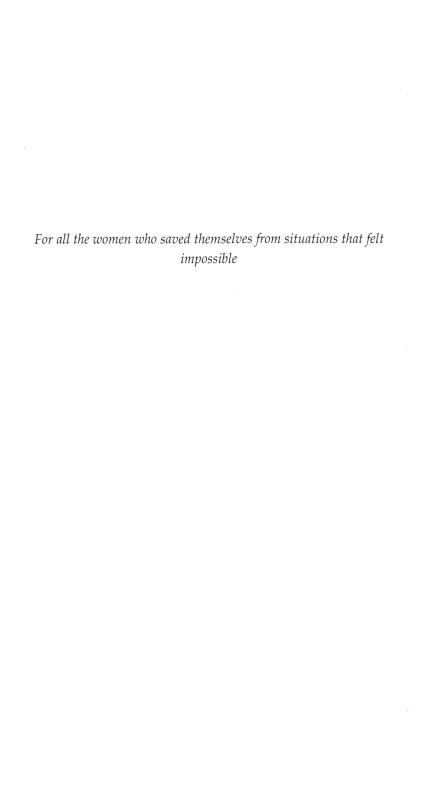

For all the women who saved themselves from situations that felt impossible

Dear Reader,

Please be aware that *Dark Secrets* contains content that may be triggering for some. For a list of triggers, please see the next page.

Dark Secrets contains the following content: domestic violence and attempted rape.

Chapter One

She was in desperate need of a good, stiff drink. Picking her way through Philadelphia's maze of streets in the dark when she was running low on fuel —both for herself and for the beat-up 4Runner that seemed to shudder whenever the wind blew too hard—had a headache creeping up the base of her skull.

Getting gas was the more immediate need even as her stomach grumbled in protest, and she squinted through the haze of blowing snow, looking for a well-lit gas station. She hated getting gas in the dark. It invited far too many unsolicited advances no matter how plain she tried to make herself.

She pulled into a station boasting a ten cents per gallon discount if you paid in cash and cut the engine. Perfect. Cash was all she'd allowed herself for months because cash was untraceable.

She peeled two twenties off her meager wad of bills and stuffed the rest into the safety of her bra. She'd have to find a stopping point somewhere soon and work for a bit to save up more money before hitting the road again.

Glancing out at the parking lot, she took careful stock of the two cars parked at the pumps to her right and the sedan angled haphazardly between two spots by the gas station door. No one seemed to pay her any mind, which was exactly how she preferred it.

Pulling her jacket tighter around her, she hopped out of the car, locking it and testing the door before jogging inside to put forty on her pump. She eyed the sign that said free coffee with purchase and wondered if gas counted as a purchase.

Not that gas station coffee was any good, especially the free stuff. But she'd eaten worse to keep her going over the last year, and it would quell the incessant rumbling in her stomach that was getting harder to ignore.

Once the bored teen behind the counter rang her up, she sidled over to the coffeepot and poured herself a cup, satisfied when no one said anything. Adding as much cream and sugar as she could stand to make it palatable, she took it back outside and used it to warm her hands as much as drink while she slid the nozzle into the tank and pressed the buttons to release the fuel.

She sipped the hot liquid while the gas hissed through the line, grimacing at the bitter aftertaste. After another tentative drink, she tossed it unfinished into the garbage can and shoved her hands deep into her pockets. She'd rather starve than ingest whatever the hell that was.

The wind blew her curls into her face, so she kept her head in constant motion, making sure no one got too close to sneak up on her. The hiss of the pump slowed as the total on the digital readout neared forty, and it shut off with a thunk.

Lifting the nozzle and setting it back in the holder, she twisted the gas cap into place and climbed behind the wheel. Rubbing her hands together to warm them, she decided on her next move.

It was too late to try and make it to another city. The wind was picking up and blowing fresh snow across the roads. Driving in near white-out conditions in the dark didn't appeal, especially when the internet on her shitty prepaid phone was spotty at best.

She was hungry, but she had practice ignoring that sensation when other needs were more pressing. Right now, finding somewhere to sleep for the night that was relatively safer than the confines of the rusted Toyota was the more immediate problem to be solved.

Unwilling to waste gas driving around looking for a motel, she used the station's free Wi-Fi to look up some possibilities. Anything that looked halfway decent would completely wipe out what little money she had, and she needed something to get her to wherever she would rest for a few weeks to build her reserves back up.

There was a motel out near the highway, but the fact that it rented rooms by the hour was a sure sign it attracted a lot of sex workers or drug dealers. Or both. She'd learned that the hard way back in Idaho.

Ultimately she found one that didn't look too terrible. She'd long since stopped turning her nose up at peeling wallpaper and dirty carpet. As long as it didn't have bugs or mold, she could make it work. And this place was only fifty bucks a night.

Easing out of the parking lot, she followed the curt directions of the GPS as it sent her through the heart of Philadelphia to the other side of town. She nearly missed a turn when the internet stalled the monotone order to take a right but made it just in time. Waiting for this shitty GPS to recalculate anything made her want to scream.

The traffic had thinned in this part of the city, and she gripped the steering wheel while she followed the barely discernible tire tracks in front of her, easing away from the center line as a snowplow came toward her from the opposite direction.

She was reaching for her phone to turn up the volume when she noticed the flare of headlights and the sedan barreling toward her, impatient to escape the plow. Forced to slam on her brakes, she fought against the urge to jerk the wheel when the car fishtailed on the slick of compacted snow. The asshole had the nerve to honk at her as he whizzed past.

Breaths coming in sharp pants, she pulled even with the curb and took deep, steadying lungfuls of air. What the hell was wrong with this city? At the sound of laughter and conversation spilling out into the dark, she glanced up to see people haloed in soft light. She could just make out the warm wood tones of a bar filled with people before the door swung shut.

Tallying up the bills tucked against her skin in her head, she decided one drink wouldn't put her too far behind. She'd still have enough for a couple nights in that motel, some food while she picked a new destination, and the gas to get her farther south and out of this goddamn cold.

Liquor might be a bad idea on an empty stomach, but maybe she could grab a quiet seat at the end of the bar and nurse a soda or something. Just to get out of the snow for a bit and let her nerves settle.

Cutting the engine, she carefully picked her way over the snowy sidewalk. The door was heavy, and it took some muscle to pull it open against the wind. The noise of the place assaulted every sense as soon as she stepped inside.

It was packed; people shoved in wherever they would fit against the bar and crowded around the tables lining the walls. A single waitress in jeans and a black t-shirt with the words The Black Orchid emblazoned across the chest scurried from the swinging kitchen door to the bar to the tables and back again so fast it was a wonder she wasn't dizzy.

A man, tall and lean with the shadow of dark stubble over his jaw, worked the bar, rapidly pulling beers from the tap and mixing drinks. The hard set of his mouth told her he'd been at this for hours. She thought about turning around and leaving, but then he glanced up and, impossibly, met her gaze across the room.

Instead of retreating, she pushed forward, around a couple making out by the door and past a table of what looked like frat boys and claimed a spot that freed up at the end of the bar. He finished the cocktail he was mixing and set it down on a black napkin, adding the money to the till and smiling politely at the woman who flirted with him.

When he made his way to her end of the bar, something funny fluttered in her chest.

"What can I get for you?"

His voice was deep and warm, and that funny flutter kicked up a few notches. What was wrong with her? Men did not make her flutter. At least not in a way that wasn't fear.

"Club soda with lime, please."

She watched him reach for a tumbler and a bottle of lime juice, acutely aware of the way he kept glancing at her face. Maybe she was fluttering because he made her nervous, fixing her with those intense blue eyes.

"Is it always this busy?" she asked as he added club soda to the glass from the nozzle sprayer.

"On a Friday, yes." He set the drink on a black napkin and slid it toward her. "That'll be four dollars."

She felt her cheeks heat as his eyes dipped down to where she reached into her bra for the money, then quickly back up to her face.

"You look like you could use a little help," she said, fishing out a five and handing it over.

"We could." He moved down the bar to stuff her money

5

into the register and bring back her change. "Why? Are you volunteering?"

She blinked. Was she? More money was always better than less, and she wouldn't mind a bigger cushion while she figured out where to go next. Something in her face must have given her away because he immediately moved in to capitalize on her hesitation.

"I'll pay you ten dollars an hour in cash, plus whatever tips you make if you can stay until the crowd thins or we close. Whichever comes first."

The jingle of a bell signaled another group entering the bar, and she stuck her hand out. "Deal."

He grinned, giving it a firm shake, and reached under the bar to hand her an apron and an order pad. "I'll take your coat and put it in the back."

She slipped her phone into her back pocket and tied the apron around her waist, wrapping the string twice to secure it. Taking a deep breath, she leapt into the fray.

It was easy to fall into a rhythm, dancing between tables and the bar. They had an actual food menu, but since she didn't have a code for the ordering system, she handed everything over to the waitress and shouldered the load of running food instead.

"You're a godsend," the waitress said, catching her in the kitchen and grabbing a bowl of what looked like beef stew and a basket of warm bread off the line. "I'm Clara, by the way."

"Delaney," she replied. "And I'm happy to help."

Delaney flashed a quick smile before shouldering her way back into the bar. The pulse of customers eased from standing room only to comfortably full, and after a bit longer, most of the tables sat empty.

When a young couple got up from their two top and made for the door, she bussed it, splitting the tip in half to share with Clara, who'd been responsible for putting in their food order, and pocketing her portion.

The right front pocket of her apron felt nice and thick from the bills she'd stuffed there, and the thought made her giddy. Maybe she'd splurge on the good motel after all.

"I really appreciate your help."

She yelped, spinning around and clutching her chest like her wildly beating heart might burst through her skin. On instinct, her eyes darted around for the quickest escape, and she took a shaky step back for the comfort of distance.

He watched her for a beat and then took his own step back, shoving his hands into his pockets. She felt her cheeks heat when she realized several people had turned to look in their direction.

"I didn't mean to scare you."

"You didn't," she lied.

Never show fear. Never show weakness. The words repeated like a mantra in her head.

"Well, I do. Really appreciate your help, I mean. I had someone call in sick, and we were swamped, as you could tell. I think I can cut you loose if you're ready to settle up."

Only a few people remained pushed up to the bar, and he didn't seem concerned with them as he pushed a button to open the register and started counting out bills.

"Six hours plus a refund on the drink you never finished. And a bonus for doing me such a huge favor."

She blinked at the amount of money he handed her. Too afraid to count it with so many people watching, she quickly slipped it into her bra and untied her apron. She'd have preferred to do this somewhere private. No one was watching her, but she felt exposed having this much money out in the open.

"I split the cash tips since all I did was run the food."

7

He cocked his head when he looked at her. "Why did you split them?"

"Because Clara is the one who put all the orders in."

"Did someone complain?" Clara wondered, stopping at the sound of her name and pushing her cornsilk hair off her face.

"No," Delaney shook her head. "I was just saying I split the cash tips so you can have half."

Clara's eyes went wide. "Really? You don't have to do that. I got a ton of tips from credit cards, and James likes to keep everything fair, so I'm not worried." She gestured at the man still watching their exchange. "You keep that. You earned it, and you kept me from drowning."

Clara turned back to James. "You really should fire Maizy. She's fucking useless."

With a toss of her hair, Clara turned and disappeared back into the kitchen. Before anyone changed their minds, Delaney dug the bills out of the apron pocket and stuffed them into her jeans.

She'd tried to keep a running total in her head, but it had been so busy. If she had to guess, there was probably a couple hundred dollars in tips. Added to the money James had handed her, it was more than enough to keep her comfortable on her journey south.

"Well," Delaney said, suddenly feeling awkward. "I'm glad I could help. It was nice to meet you."

She slipped into the jacket he'd laid on the bar and turned toward the door. When he caught up with her, he moved into her line of sight before speaking.

"I didn't catch your name before."

"It's Delaney."

"Are you looking for a job, Delaney? Because," he continued when she didn't answer, "I really do need to fire Maizy, and you obviously have more than a little experience waiting tables. It's supposed to be a busy weekend. You'd really be doing me a favor."

She hadn't considered staying in Philadelphia for this next stretch. She'd been eyeing North Carolina to get out of the worst of the cold, but if she wouldn't have to waste time looking for a job, it could be a good option.

"You don't have to decide now. If you—"

"I'll do it," she said before she could change her mind.

The smile he sent her had that little flutter dancing behind her sternum again.

"Great. Can you come in tomorrow at two? We can go through all the necessary paperwork and get you set up in the system. I can give you a schedule then too."

"Yeah. Two is fine. See you tomorrow."

She reached for the door, steeling herself against the blast of icy air that washed over her face. For a split second, it felt good against her cheeks, heated from the busyness of the bar. Then it knifed through her, and she shuffled quickly to her car, jumping in to shield herself from the wind.

Well, that was the most impulsive thing she'd done in a very long time, but if the money was always as good as it had been tonight, it would be worth it. She could roll out of Philadelphia in a few weeks with enough to last her a long time if she was careful with it—and she was always careful with it. She had to be.

Chapter Two

The hardwood was cold under his stocking feet as James padded down the stairs and into the kitchen. The light filtering through the windows was dim, the snow holding the city in somber gray even though it was nearly ten.

He tugged open the refrigerator in search of the iced coffee he preferred no matter the season and grabbed a bottle, twisting the top off and tossing it on the counter before taking a deep pull. The jolt of caffeine felt like liquid electricity and started clearing out the first of the cobwebs from his brain.

Plenty to do today, even if he was getting somewhat of a late start. He hadn't been able to fall asleep last night, his mind taunting him with images of dark eyes and smooth brown skin. She'd stepped into his pub and drawn his attention like a siren's call, mysterious and forbidden.

It had been a long time since anyone had drawn his attention like that. His wife had. Six years ago, she'd somehow stopped being his cousin's wife's best friend, and he'd really seen her for the first time. Loving her had been a joy. Losing her had nearly broken him.

After Maura's death, he'd spent months closed inside the house where they'd planned to build a life together. Until one day his sister-in-law came over, picked her way through the wreckage of pizza boxes and empty beer bottles, and told him to get the fuck over himself. Reagan was blunt like that.

She'd been right, though. Maura wouldn't want him to mope around in his own filth, blaming himself for not getting there sooner, for not being able to save her. So he'd done his best to get back to his life. He'd stopped canceling the house-keeper's weekly visits, he'd learned how to do more than reheat day-old pizza, and he'd eased himself back into syndicate duties.

The one thing that helped knit him back together again had been opening the pub. They used to stay up late into the night talking about opening a pub one day. Maura loved to plan and plot and scheme. A year after her death, on their wedding anniversary, he bought the building that would become The Black Orchid and used all her notes to bring it to life. The pub she'd always wanted, named after her favorite flower.

Far beyond his work with the syndicate as a Callahan, The Black Orchid was the one thing that was only his. Not that he resented supporting his family's centuries-old seat of power over the criminal underworld of Philadelphia. Far from it. He'd been raised in this life; he knew what it demanded of him.

The Black Orchid was simply his opportunity to be the one issuing orders rather than another cog in the wheel serving at the pleasure of his cousin Declan. Everyone had something outside the syndicate to keep them grounded. The pub was his.

Rather than hiring a manager to run it, as Brogan did with his rental properties, James loved to put in the work to make it thrive, to keep his finger on the pulse of what the Orchid needed. Even if it made balancing his work with the family and keeping the pub going a challenge some days.

That was why he only employed people from one of the twelve families. They understood why he'd randomly slip out for a few hours or show up at odd times with bruised knuckles. They didn't ask questions that were none of their business.

Now he'd broken his own rule. Extending a job offer to the woman with silky black curls and a lithe dancer's body had been nothing but impulse. Born of an unspoken desire to pull her closer even though he'd be forced to keep her at arm's length. There was an unspoken rule about family rela- tionships. No outsiders.

It wasn't expressly forbidden. Evidenced by the fact that Brogan had fallen in love with a Mafia princess and Aidan's marriage to another Mafia daughter had been neatly arranged to cement an alliance. But it was hardly encouraged.

This life was hard. It was messy; it was complicated. They needed partners who knew what they were getting them- selves into. Partners who wouldn't go to the cops when their lovers came home covered in blood.

Anytime one of the family strayed outside the syndicate, things inevitably didn't go well. His own grandfather had found that out the hard way, dating and almost marrying an outsider who nearly cost the family everything they'd spent decades building and protecting.

The risk was unspoken, but it was no less real. Don't endanger the family by getting seriously involved with someone who wouldn't understand. Declan's generous contributions to influential politicians and the syndicate men and women they had on the police force could only do so much to protect them.

It was why when James recently decided to dip his toe back into the dating pool, he'd kept it strictly to the twelve families. Fuck knows there were plenty of women to choose from—the syndicate had grown prolifically in the last century and a half—but none of them tugged at him. No one had tugged at him in a long time. Not the way Delaney did last night.

He finished the last of his iced coffee and tossed the bottle in the recycling bin with an irritated huff. There was no use wasting time and energy wanting a woman he couldn't have. No matter how tempting.

James's phone signaled, and he dug it out of the pocket of his jeans. A reminder from Declan about the meeting tomorrow to discuss the updates being made to their delivery systems and a note about something new Evie wanted to discuss. Intriguing.

Grabbing an apple from the fruit bowl the housekeeper kept stocked on the counter, James slipped into the boots he'd left by the front door and abandoned his apartment for his office in the pub.

Originally the apartment over the pub had been a respite from the memories that swirled around the house he'd shared with Maura, filling every crevice. It was as much an escape as the Orchid had been a memorial. Now he enjoyed the convenience of it, even though Reagan claimed it had turned him into a workaholic. She was hardly one to talk.

When he reached the bottom of the stairs, he veered away from his office and toward the sound of thumping bass coming from the kitchen. Stepping into the opening, he saw his line cook, Addy, blue hair held back by a wide band, bobbing her head to the heavy metal pumping from a Bluetooth speaker fixed to the wall.

She was chopping something on the stainless steel surface in front of her, but her hands were obscured by the ingredients stacked beside her, and he saw only the rapid movement of the knife. He moved further into the kitchen, and she glanced up, immediately reaching over to turn down the music she knew he hated.

"Hey, boss."

"Early, aren't you?"

"Yes, but I wanted to get everything prepped because I have a new dish I want you to try before we open."

He leaned his hip on the counter. Onions. She was chopping onions and scooping them into a prep container.

"Is it going to be better than that fish thing you made me try last month?"

Addy rolled her eyes and sliced a second onion in half before peeling it and adding the skins to what she called a garbage bowl. Not that she threw it in the garbage. She usually made stock or soup out of it. Addy hated waste, and she was very good for his bottom line.

"It's not my fault you have an unrefined palate. Clara liked that one."

"I think she was just being nice," he replied, hiding a grin when Addy pouted.

"This one is beef. You like beef. You're practically a carnivore."

Taking a bite of the apple he'd forgotten in his hand, he raised a brow. "Have you heard from Maizy?"

"No." Addy fixed him with a pointed stare. "Please tell me you're going to finally fire her ass now."

"I am." He ignored her little victory wiggle. "I hired a new waitress last night. She starts today."

The knife stilled, and Addy's brows shot up. "Already? That was fast."

"She helped us out in a pinch and seems like she'd be a good fit."

"Wait. You hired Delaney? The girl from last night?"

James's brows drew together. "I did. Why? Is there something that happened while she was working I should know about?"

"No, she was great, but…"

"But?" he prompted when she resumed chopping the onion and didn't continue.

"She's an outsider. Is Declan okay with that?"

James's spine straightened, and his eyes narrowed on Addy's face. "I wasn't aware Declan made the hiring decisions around here. What else should we be calling him about?"

Addy's head snapped up, the knife falling to the cutting board at his sharp tone. "That's not what I meant. It's just that you've never hired someone from outside the syndicate before."

"So you don't trust my judgment."

Addy winced, but her voice was firm, and he could tell she was annoyed with his temper. "I didn't say that either."

He pitched the half-eaten apple into the trash with more force than he meant to, watching the empty can wobble before settling back on the floor. He didn't like that Addy had voiced the concerns he'd had only moments ago himself.

"I do generally seem to know what I'm doing. It'll be fine," he said, more to convince himself than Addy. "As long as everyone can keep their mouths shut and not discuss syndicate business in the walk-in."

"We'll do our best, boss," Addy said, the usual cheerful note in her voice returning. "But sometimes the gossip is so juicy. Surely even Delaney can indulge in innocent gossip."

James chuckled. "There's nothing innocent about you or Clara, or Mike, for that matter—especially when you're gossiping."

"You're just jealous because you don't know Molly Maguire is engaged to Kyle Murphy but pregnant with some unknown man's baby."

James halted in his retreat to his office. Damn. He'd known Molly Maguire since diapers. He'd never have suspected her of doing something like that.

"She's what? How could you possibly know that?"

"My cousin Sarah heard it from her sister-in-law Elena, who heard it from *her* sister Mary Kate, who's married to Kyle's sister Hannah. You went to Mary Kate and Hannah's wedding two summers ago."

James rubbed at his temple. Syndicate gossip could be as exhausting as it was scintillating. "Addy. That sounds more like a game of telephone than reliable information."

"I didn't say it was reliable. I said it was gossip. I'm not *The New York Times* over here. I leave the fact-checking to the professionals. All I know is what Sarah heard from Elena, who—"

"Heard it from Mary Kate, who's married to Hannah," he finished for her. "I know. Just, yeah, keep that kind of shit to a minimum around Delaney too. God forbid she pick up any of your bad habits. Like that terrible music you make me listen to."

Addy pointed the knife at him and grinned. "Secretly you love it. I keep you on your toes."

He shook his head with a chuckle. "I'll be in my office. Try not to make my ears bleed."

James had barely closed the door when the music began blasting over the speaker again. At least the wood and glass kept it muffled to a low thrum, and he couldn't hear the incessant screaming Addy swore passed as music.

He took himself through the rote of his normal routine. Reconcile the receipts from the night before, reset the amount of cash and change in the till, check alcohol inventory and adjust the purchase order he'd put in on Monday as needed.

Tomorrow Addy would slip him a list of things she needed for the kitchen, and he'd use that to make a purchase order from their restaurant supplier on Tuesday. Serving food alongside alcohol had been Maura's idea, and it had done well for them since opening a year ago. Thanks in no small part to Addy's genius in front of a stove. Her kitchen creations were magic disguised as pub fare. Save for that fish thing.

Once the usual was done, he shifted to pulling together the documents he'd need to bring Delaney on as an employee, though part of him wondered if she might appreciate an offer to work for cash under the table instead. She seemed like a runner, someone trying to live under the radar.

He'd watched her last night; he hadn't been able to help it. His eyes followed her around as if they were independent of the rest of his body. Her constant vigilance had struck something in him.

The way she stood with her back to a solid surface whenever possible, the way her eyes roved over the room every few minutes, the way she yelped when he'd come up behind her. She'd lied about being scared, as if the admission of fear would have somehow gotten her in trouble.

In that moment, he'd had the sudden, overwhelming urge to know everything about her, what she loved, what she hated, what made her afraid, but he'd shoved it down. It didn't matter how appealing she was or the ridiculous and unexpected way she pulled at him. She was off limits. Both because he was bringing her on as an employee and he had a very strict personal rule not to mix business with pleasure and because she wasn't in the syndicate.

Addy was right. Not about needing Declan's permission —that still rubbed—but about it being a potential risk to have her here on a permanent basis. It would be even more of a risk to get involved.

Except he shouldn't even be thinking about getting involved after spending next to no time with her. He needed to chill the fuck out. Maybe get laid so he'd stop having these ridiculous thoughts about a woman he'd just met.

James scrubbed a hand over his face and shoved the last of the paperwork he needed her to fill out this afternoon into a folder. Whatever her past, Delaney was good at her job, and after the hell Maizy had been putting him through for months, James needed someone reliable.

And if that reliable someone had kept him up half the night wondering what her mouth tasted like, then that was his own shit to work through.

Chapter Three

"Need me to warm up your coffee, hun?"

Delaney glanced up at the waitress in the bright yellow A-line dress and white apron and tried to remember if coffee refills were free. Shit.

"Um."

"They're on the house," the woman added.

"Yeah. That would be great. Thanks."

"No problem. Your food should be up in just a minute. Sorry about the wait."

Delaney smiled as the woman moved away. The diner she'd found near her motel might have been a greasy spoon, but it was busy when she'd walked in for an early lunch. The wait and the free Wi-Fi had given her time to do some research on her phone.

First she looked up short-term rentals. If she was going to be in the city for a while, she wanted something with a better lock than the flimsy motel room door. Carpets that didn't smell like vomit would be a huge bonus. She shivered. She might never get that smell out of her nose.

Everything even remotely close to the pub sat well beyond

her budget. Unless this job paid *really* nicely, housing costs would eat up all the money she was trying to save. The only things she could afford were across the river in New Jersey, and when you factored in time and gas for the commute, it hardly made the savings worth it.

She sighed. This was precisely why it was easier to hunker down in a small town. Everything was dirt cheap. Even if small towns came with their own set of problems in the form of nosiness. Plus, as a Black woman, she stuck out like a sore thumb with her medium brown skin and tightly coiled curls.

She'd take a big city's anonymity over a small town's curiosity any day. Which still left her dealing with higher prices. Maybe the motel wasn't so bad. She could ask to be moved to a different room or buy a bunch of candles or something.

When the waitress came back with her food, Delaney's stomach grumbled. She'd eaten a granola bar that had been set out on the check-in desk at the motel the night before and another one this morning, but nothing else in nearly twenty-four hours. She was pushing her limit to how long she could go without eating.

Which is why she'd treated herself to what the diner menu called the Sunrise Sampler. A little bit of everything. The smells spiraling up to her nose made her mouth water and her stomach cramp in anticipation.

She ate slowly, partly because she wanted to savor every bite and partly because she knew from experience that eating too fast after not having anything in her stomach for so long could lead to throwing everything back up again. Then it would be a waste of food and money.

She cut into a sausage link and popped the bite into her mouth, sighing as the spice and fat exploded on her tongue. A year ago, she never would have been caught dead in a diner like this, salivating over pancakes and sausage. Now, it was the best thing she'd ever tasted.

Her phone beeped, and she frowned. No one had her number, so she had no one to text or call. She flipped the phone open to read the small display and saw the search alert notification.

She'd set up several to go to her email, and every day some faceless bot on the internet combed the headlines for the parameters she'd set and let her know if it found anything related to her specs. So far it hadn't hit on anything relevant. Usually they were similarly worded, but nothing about her. For that she was grateful.

She clicked the link in her email and opened the news article. **Local Woman Found Drowned**, the headline read. Not about her, not even local to Philadelphia. She scanned the article. Mother of two drowned while swimming. Left behind a loving wife, devoted parents, and one younger brother.

Just another senseless accident, the article declared, but Delaney allowed herself to wonder if that was true or if something more sinister had taken place at the pool where the woman lost her life. She shook the thought from her head and spooned up a bite of egg, smiling when the waitress refilled her coffee again and left the bill.

The bill. Even though she had the money to pay it and leave a nice tip, parting with cash always made her feel a little unsteady. Managing her meager funds had been the hardest part in the beginning. She'd spend too much on things like hotels and food and then not have enough money to fill up her tank with gas.

The first night she had to sleep in her car in a parking lot in New Mexico had been eye-opening. She'd never let her funds get that low after that. Something always had to give, though. Her three biggest needs were housing, gas, and food, and without fail, one of them always got the short end of the stick. Usually food.

So today she would pay the bill and be grateful and hope this new job paid enough to keep her fed and warm. All she needed was enough money to fund her trip south and out of the cold. And the sooner, the better because all Philadelphia did, shrouded in clouds and snow, was remind her of home.

Checking the time, she shoved the money for the check into the folder and left it next to her plate before slipping out into the cold. The wind had died down, but it was starting to snow, and she was grateful she'd traded in her used sedan for the SUV back in Ohio. Even if it did take a little coaxing to start when temps were below freezing.

She patted the wheel and whispered encouraging words as she cranked the engine and held her breath through the clicks until it finally roared to life.

"Good girl," she crooned, giving the dashboard a gentle pat.

She had time to kill and had spotted a library in her perusal of the area. She wanted to know more about her new boss, and while she could do the research on her phone, reading anything on the tiny screen for more than a few minutes gave her a headache.

She took a ticket for the private parking lot to avoid the meters and reminded herself to ask if they validated parking. The lot was mostly empty, but she parked at the back anyway, angled away from the security cameras she'd spotted on her way in.

At this time of day, the library was filled mostly with parents trailing behind young children and older people who were escaping the cold and the boredom. The atrium echoed with her footsteps, and she followed the signs to the bank of computers on the second floor.

She took one at the far end near the wall, shifting her chair slightly so no one could walk up behind her, and keyed up the search engine. She didn't know his last name, so she typed in the name of the bar instead, blinking in surprise when dozens of articles came up about it.

Most of them were older, talking about when he'd opened it a year ago. She clicked into one from the local paper and skimmed it. James Callahan had opened The Black Orchid pub in memory of his wife, who'd been killed in a terrible accident shortly after their wedding. That was sad and also kind of sweet.

Another article linked him as cousin to someone named Declan Callahan, one of the city's wealthiest and most influential men, and she felt her palms go sweaty. James had seemed like such a nice, down-to-earth guy last night, but she knew looks could be deceiving. She'd have to be careful around him.

Most of the articles she clicked through were more of the same. The reason he'd opened the Orchid, his connection to Declan Callahan, his desire to create a legacy in his wife's memory. Then, at the bottom of one article, almost like a footnote, was a mention of how he donated a percentage of his first year's profits to a local woman's shelter, which intrigued her. Immediately, she wondered if he did it because he was kind or because he felt guilty about something.

Glancing at the clock in the corner of the screen, she cleared her browser history and keystrokes and closed the window, winding back down the stairs and through the atrium. Almost at the doors, she spotted a little machine to validate her parking and slipped her ticket inside.

The snow had kicked up, and she hunched inside her jacket, drawing the only scarf she owned up over her mouth and nose while she walked as quick as she could to the back of the parking lot.

She did the pleading dance with her car again, sighing

when it sputtered to life. The longer it took to catch, the more nervous it made her. A big repair could set her back months or, like it had in Michigan, leave her completely stranded.

She popped her validated ticket in the machine and eased out of the parking lot, following the directions of the GPS. She hated this stupid phone. They made nicer prepaid ones these days, but she'd found those to be a theft risk. No one ever looked twice at her flip phone.

The drive to the pub was free of plows and idiots eager to get around them, and she pulled alongside the curb by the front door again. The neon open sign was lit, and she let herself in, smiling at Clara, who waved. It was busy for this time of the afternoon, and she realized the press coverage was obviously more than just hype. People seemed to love this place.

"You're back!" Clara said, stopping in front of her with her hands on her generous hips. "James said he made you an offer. Need me to go get him for you?"

"He said to meet him here at two. I guess I'm a little early."

"He likes punctuality. You can wait at the bar if you want."

Delaney lifted herself onto a stool and watched a man who wasn't James mix a cocktail before pouring it into a martini glass with a flourish. She grinned as the already intoxicated girl in front of him clapped. He flushed as bright red as his hair before moving down the bar toward her.

"Hi, there. Can I get you anything?"

"No thanks." She waved a hand in the air. "I'm waiting to talk to James."

"Are you Delaney?"

Delaney's eyebrows shot up, panic instantly flooding the back of her mind that a stranger would know her name.

"Clara was talking about you this morning. Said you were

a real natural. Welcome aboard." He smiled, moving away as the door to the kitchen swung open and James trailed into the pub behind Clara.

He smiled when he saw her, and she had to wrestle that stupid flutter again. He still had the stubble she remembered from the night before, and his eyes were that same clear blue. They looked even more striking when she had the chance to study him, standing out against the pale tones of his skin and his dark hair. So dark it was almost black.

"You came."

She tilted her head at the surprise in his voice. "Did you expect me not to?"

"I had considered you might come to your senses after the adrenaline wore off. But if you're still game, I've got all the paperwork I need you to fill out in my office."

He gestured toward the kitchen door, and she hopped off the stool, noticing how he stepped back so she could have plenty of free space to walk ahead of him. He had maybe six inches on her five-seven, and he was lean like a swimmer with narrow hips and broad shoulders. Everything about him appealed more than it should.

The kitchen pulsed with movement and heat. A woman with blue hair stood shouting orders on the line while men scurried around her. Delaney couldn't remember her name from last night, but the searching look she sent them was familiar.

"Don't mind Addy," James said once they were inside his office. "Her bark is worse than her bite."

He left the door open and crossed to the desk, motioning for her to sit in the metal chair beside it. Once they were both seated, he pulled a folder off the top of a stack and handed it to her with a pen.

"The usual. Name, birthdate, social. All that fun stuff." He watched her for a beat before continuing. "Then I'll need to make a copy of your license or passport."

She hated this part. The part where she handed over her documents and waited to see if they raised alarm bells. He got up to make a copy of her license, and she quickly filled in the details it had taken her weeks to memorize. The copy machine on a shelf under the desk whirred and then fell silent, and when he handed her license back, it was slightly warm.

He scanned the pages she'd filled out and seemed to accept that everything was in order. If he ran a background check with that information, it would come back clean and say she was the daughter of a dairy farmer and his wife from Lincoln, Nebraska. She'd spent weeks memorizing those details too.

"Pay starts at twelve dollars an hour."

"Twelve?" she asked, mouth hanging open.

"Yeah. Why? Did you want to make more?"

"No." She shook her head. "I've never had a waitressing job pay more than two or three an hour plus tips."

His mouth thinned into a hard line. "Yes. I've heard that. It's still twelve dollars an hour. With tips. Thanks to Maizy, I've got an immediate opening, and if you're free tonight and tomorrow, I can give you the hours right away. Otherwise you can start on Wednesday."

"I'm free."

He swiveled in his chair to tug open the bottom drawer of a wide filing cabinet and pulled out a fresh apron, an order pad folder, and three t-shirts. He handed them all to her.

"I pegged you for a small, but if you need a different size, I probably have them. Unless you need an extra small. I'd have to order some of those."

"Small is fine."

"I'm still finalizing the schedule for next week now that

Maizy is gone, but I'll have it worked up by the end of tomorrow's shift. And we're closed on Mondays and Tuesdays, so you'll have those to yourself anyway."

His eyes roamed her face before he asked, "Any questions?"

When she shook her head, he pushed to his feet, and she did the same, but he didn't make a move to leave the office, so she turned to go instead.

"Oh wait, the ordering system?"

"Right." He snapped his fingers and reached into the top desk drawer for a plastic card with the pub's logo on it. "I'll get you set up in the system, and Clara can train you on it this afternoon. We'll be busy tonight, so I'm hoping you're a quick study. But if not, give a shout, and someone will pitch in."

She could feel eyes on her as he created a profile for her in the system, keying in her details and swiping the card to sync them, and she glanced up to see Addy watching her from across the room. Delaney didn't get an uneasy feeling from the woman, but definitely a sense that Addy was planning to monitor the situation closely and then decide what to make of her.

The feeling was entirely mutual.

Chapter Four

J ames pulled into the parking lot of Reign, Declan's nightclub, and waited while Aidan pulled in beside him. Marriage and fatherhood looked good on his youngest cousin, despite how much Aidan had originally hated the idea of being married at all, let alone in an arranged deal to a woman he'd never met.

"Tired?" James asked once Aidan had joined him for their trek across the lot.

"Siobhan has decided sleeping at night is not fun anymore. Viv thinks it's just a phase, so she doesn't want to hire another night nanny. But she's pregnant, so she gets to catch up on her sleep during the day," he grumbled.

"Viv's pregnant?"

"Shit. I'm not supposed to say anything. She's planning this big announcement. That's privileged information if you value my life."

James chuckled while he pressed his thumb to the biometric lock guarding the syndicate's basement offices from the main floor of the club. When the light went yellow, he punched in his six-digit code and waited for the lock to open with a click.

"Your secret is safe with me."

"How about you?"

"I am, thankfully, not pregnant," James said as he led the way down the stairs, the lights clicking on as they neared the bottom. When Aidan snorted, he grinned.

"I thought you said you had a date last weekend. How'd it go?"

James scrubbed at his chin and shrugged out of his jacket. "It was fine. Aisling Donahue is very nice."

"Uh oh," Aidan replied. "That's what you say when you never want to see them again."

"There wasn't any…" He searched for the right word. "*Thing* there."

"Sometimes you have to wait for the thing to develop."

"Sweet Christ," James groaned, stepping into the conference room at the rear of the basement and slinging his jacket over the back of a chair. "Have you been married so long you're giving relationship advice now?"

"God help us," Declan mumbled, and Brogan chuckled.

Aidan dropped into a chair and rolled it toward the table. "Two years and counting, and I seem to be doing just fine."

"Only because Viv has the patience of a saint," Brogan assured him, sporting his own brand new wedding band.

It was good to see his cousins finally settled down with good, strong women who made them happy. The family had been through a lot in the last three years. Pushed to the brink and forced to adapt in ways that had only made them better, stronger.

The syndicate was more profitable than ever thanks to the Mafia alliance Aidan had secured with his marriage to Viv. Life was good, and Declan was slowly making plans to expand operations beyond Philadelphia.

James's father, Sean, had been tasked with wooing contacts in Boston and New York, leaving James in charge of logistics. A role he liked since it played nicely to his strengths to find and fix all the holes in a problem before they caused any damage.

Moving hundreds of millions of dollars' worth of illegal weapons and goods through Philadelphia's harbors under the nose of politicians shouting about corruption while rubbing elbows with Declan was an art form. He enjoyed every fucking second, even if it meant he was doing less hands-on work these days.

"Evie is running late." Declan set his phone on the table. "We'll start with what she already knows. I talked to Sean this morning. Negotiations are going well in New York, but the Bratva are making waves."

"Apparently the Russians are a pain in the ass everywhere," Aidan said.

"They think they can intimidate me into abandoning a deal with the Irish and doing business with them."

James chuckled. "They'll find out the hard way that isn't true."

"Exactly." Declan grinned. "It'll be fun to watch them try. Brogan, Sean is going to send you some names of the Bratva leadership. I want every fucking thing you can find on them, down to their mother's blood type."

"If it's in a hackable database, I'll find it," Brogan assured him.

"Prioritize any connections they might have with other organizations in New York and then expand to Boston and Philadelphia. They usually like to work alone, but I wouldn't put anything past them either."

"Is Ivankov behaving himself?" James wanted to know, and Brogan tensed across the table.

"He is," Declan replied. "Men tend to do that when they

lose a finger for disobeying me. I can't imagine he wants to lose another one, or worse, by conspiring with someone else to undermine me."

"Leo said the Russians seem to really enjoy the casinos now that all of them are fully operational," Aidan said of his brother-in-law. "They're partial to betting on hockey and European football."

"Good. Falcone and his men can keep an eye on them too. How's the deal with Anderson going?"

"It's closed," Aidan said. "For double the amount."

Declan's eyes gleamed. "Perfect. I still want to—"

At a noise from the hall, they all glanced up to see Evie appear in the doorway. She startled a bit to find every pair of eyes on her before moving up the table to take the empty chair to Declan's left.

"Sorry I'm late," she said, dropping a quick kiss to Declan's lips before claiming her seat. "Avery is getting her molars in, and she's not happy about it. What did I miss?"

It struck him sometimes how much Evie looked like her sister. For the most part, James had reconciled what Evie's sister Nessa had done to Maura a long time ago. But every once in a while he'd see Nessa's face in Evie's, and it would throw him. Yank him back to the day he'd rushed in to find Maura's lifeless body on the floor of that warehouse, to the despair he felt when he realized he was too late.

"James?"

"Yeah. Yes." James cleared his throat. "What were you saying?"

Evie watched him with a knowing frown but said nothing. She didn't need to. She knew where his mind had gone, and he knew the guilt ate at her just as much.

"I said," Aidan replied, "is the inventory cleared for delivery on the Polish deal?"

"Yes. It's ready to be loaded as soon as you give the go-ahead. I expanded the team for that one since it's a bigger shipment. Rory will lead with Mick in second. Full escort."

They went through the rest of the shipments slated for delivery in the second half of the month. You wouldn't think January in Philadelphia was an ideal time to run weapons, but the weather made good cover, and people sick of snow and ice were apathetic enough to look the other way.

Not that they ran into many civilians who knew what they were about. Declan made sure syndicate men were strategically placed in jobs around the city where they needed them most. His own sister-in-law Reagan worked for PPD as a forensics tech.

"Last thing before we wrap up," Evie said. "Now that the syndicate has its first female heir"—she glanced at Declan, who smiled—"we want to offer more positions to women."

"We have women working in the syndicate already," Aidan pointed out. "Reagan and Aisling both work for PPD."

"Can you name any others?" Evie cocked her head while she watched Aidan think. "I didn't think so. We lost our ED nurse..." Evie's eyes slid to James, and she gave him a sad smile, clearing her throat. "Almost three years ago, and we haven't put in anyone new at any hospitals in the city."

She leaned forward, resting her clasped hands on the tabletop. "But beyond that, beyond all the opportunities we can give to women who want them, I don't want my daughter rising to lead a bunch of men when we have several decades to lay a solid foundation and do things differently."

Leaning back again, she gestured to Aidan. "Or your daughter. Or Cait's. Or Brogan and Libby's kids, if they have them. Those are the people who will be sitting at this table in another forty or fifty years. I don't want them to be starting behind."

"What did you have in mind?" James wondered.

"Reagan knows some women who are already interested in taking a more active role," Declan said.

"And I have a few in mind too," Evie added. "So, I want to approach those women directly."

"But beyond that," Declan continued, "I want to call a meeting of the twelve families. Take their temperature on this." Evie snorted. "My wife doesn't agree with me on that."

"It's not that I don't agree it's the right thing to do," Evie said. "It's the fact we even have to do it."

"I know, love. But if I learned anything from the changes I started making five years ago, it's that some of them need to be eased in slowly. So we'll meet with the heads of the families first. Figure out who's going to be a pain in the ass about it."

"And then?" Brogan said.

"And then I think we can start with simple self-defense and tactical classes. We've got a group of boys coming of age. They can train together."

"You think that's wise? The training is pretty tough."

Evie shot Brogan a searing look. "Yes. I think it's wise."

Brogan held up his hands in defense. "I'm not saying this isn't a good move. Libby has been whispering in my ear about it for weeks, so I know it's been on your mind. I'm only asking the question."

"We'll gauge interest," Evie said. "See how they measure up, where we can use them best. We have to start somewhere."

"Any questions?" Declan wondered. "I want the family to be on the same page about this. I know we're going to get pushback from some of the older heads, and I want to be a unified front. So if any of you have something to say, say it now."

"Mick Donahue is going to be a real prick about this,"

Aidan said. "Remember how he threw a fit about Aisling becoming a cop?"

"Mick Donahue can and will answer to me if he has that much of a problem with how I'm running things," Declan replied.

"I'm on board," James said, and the rest of the room agreed.

"Thank you," Evie murmured to James as the rest of the room readied to leave.

"For what?"

"Agreeing to this. You're the one who runs hand-to-hand in these trainings."

"You're right, Evie. Avery deserves to grow up seeing the kind of syndicate you dream about. And Maura would have loved it."

Evie's eyes filled with tears, and she blinked against them. "She would have, wouldn't she?"

He nodded, chest aching a little at the thought. "Besides, I've seen you with a gun in your hand. You're almost as good a shot as Brogan. The syndicate needs more women like you, and we've got them waiting right under our noses."

He shoved away from the table when Evie did, slipping his arms into his jacket as he trailed the group to the stairs. There would definitely be pushback from some of the men on this, the ones who still felt a woman's place was in the home and the kitchen, but Declan had done a lot of work to drag them into the twenty-first century, and Evie was determined to drag them even further.

Emerging from the dark of the windowless club, James shielded his eyes against the sun peeking through the clouds for the first time in days, turning the piles of snow to diamonds. At this time of day, Addy would be finishing up prep, Mike would be double-checking the bar's inventory, and Clara would be gossiping while she rolled silverware.

The drive across town was quick, and he pulled into his usual spot next to the employee entrance beside a very beat-up Toyota SUV. The thing looked like it was one bad winter from collapsing in on itself.

Movement out of the corner of his eye caught his attention, and he turned in time to see Delaney emerge from the back door of the restaurant and cross to the SUV. She unlocked it and pulled open the rear driver's side door, the upper half of her body disappearing inside.

He allowed himself the briefest of moments to admire her ass in the jeans she wore before climbing out of the car and crossing to the door. He waited beside it to hold it open for her, frowning at the way she jolted when she turned and saw him standing there. He didn't like that she was so skittish around him.

"I should have figured that was your car," she said, pointing at his Porsche SUV. "It wasn't here before."

"I had a meeting this morning. Settling in okay?"

"Yeah," she said with a smile. "Everyone is really nice."

She crossed to the door cautiously, and he forced himself to remain rooted in place while she skirted around him to get inside. Someone or something had caused her to be terrified of everything around her, and he had the sudden, over-whelming urge to find out exactly what so he could make sure she was never scared again.

Chapter Five

He spread the pages he'd printed off the ancient computer on the desk in front of him. News articles, opinion pieces, comment threads from social media sites, photos. All of it was fanned out on the dirty surface, and he'd been busy shuffling it into some semblance of chronological order for the better part of two hours.

There was plenty of stuff to be found about her until it abruptly cut off. Like she'd ceased to exist. Irritation flared in his gut, and he clenched the paper in his hand so hard it wrinkled. It was better when he could find out recent information about his targets. Always easier to get a bead on them when he could study their habits and patterns.

People liked to think they weren't predictable, but every human was a creature of habit, and those habits sunk you every time. The way you go to the grocery store at the same time every week or the fact that you pick up your dry cleaning every Thursday or how you set aside every third Wednesday for girls' night. Predictable got you one of two things: caught or dead.

He enjoyed the research phase of the hunt almost as much as the hunt itself. Almost. Gathering data was an essential part of his work, and he'd learned the hard way in his early years not to neglect it in favor of brute force.

Not that he didn't also enjoy the brute force, the blood and the pain of it. Bringing a target to their knees in some misguided attempt to beg for mercy wasn't necessary, but it certainly made the entire experience more enjoyable.

He traced a finger over her face in the black-and-white photo. She was prettier than the people he was usually paid to hunt. Knowing that sent a little thrill through him. Finding her was going to be fun.

The money he'd been promised to locate her didn't hurt either. It was the kind of money he could retire on—if he didn't love the thrill of what he did. He relished the feel of a gun in his hand, the paralyzing fear he always saw in their eyes when he found them. It fed the darkest parts of him.

He took the quick, easy cases to pay the bills. A husband wanting to catch his cheating wife to beat the prenup or a father who seemed a little too interested in who his daughter might be fucking. He took these bigger cases, the ones that required hours of research and weeks or even months of recon, to appease the part of him that needed to hunt.

He hadn't taken a big case in months, and he was getting restless. Despite his impeccable record—a one hundred percent success rate—his methods weren't always in line with the crowd who could afford his fees for this type of work. Finding someone who didn't want to be found wasn't always a pretty process. Sometimes it couldn't be tied up in a nice little bow so the rich and the powerful didn't have to associate with someone who got their hands dirty.

He pushed back from his desk and stalked to the little mini fridge he kept in the corner, retrieving a can of Coke and downing half of it where he stood. He peered through the dingy windows to the busy street below, curling his lip at the potent smell of spices wafting up from the food cart some asshole had insisted on parking at the corner. Christ, he hated this city sometimes.

He might not choose to retire on this payout, but maybe he could upgrade his offices and get off this street. Too many foreigners were moving in. Besides, he deserved a hefty reward not only for taking this job, but for keeping his mouth shut about it.

The client wanted absolute secrecy, and that shit wasn't cheap. That's why he'd doubled his fee. The fucker hadn't even blinked.

He strode back to his desk and finished the rest of his Coke, tossing the can toward the trash, not caring if it actually landed or not. His eyes focused on her photo again, her perfect smile exposing even white teeth and the expensive dress clinging to every inch.

She'd be easy to catch. How long could a pampered princess like that really survive on her own? She'd already made one mistake; odds are she'd made more. She'd probably gotten sloppy, gotten bored, holed up somewhere entirely too predictable, and hoped no one bothered to look.

Well, no one had bothered to look. Until now. As soon as he got confirmation from his contact and the deposit check cleared, he'd be on the road, searching, tracking, hunting. He'd find her. He always found what he was looking for.

Maybe he'd take his time with her before turning her over. The idea sent another little thrill through him. He rarely got invested in the targets he was after, but there was something special about her.

He shuffled to an older photo he'd pulled off the internet when she'd been younger, rounder, full of promise and dreams and life. A sinister smile split his too-wide mouth as his eyes traced her profile, the swell of her breasts, the curve of her hips.

He wondered what she'd sound like when she screamed. Would she beg for her life? Cry? Would she try to make a deal? He'd find out soon enough.

Chapter Six

Delaney did a final sweep of the room to make sure she'd packed up all her stuff. Satisfied, she zipped up the large duffel bag and slung it over her shoulder. She could hardly remember a time when she would have left all her belongings in a hotel room and not even thought twice about the maid service coming in to clean and make the bed.

Then again, some junkie breaking into a suite at the Plaza hoping to find something to pawn was highly unlikely. The only junkies she'd known then were prim housewives popping pills prescribed by their doctors.

She'd paid for the entire week up front for the discount the motel offered and because it meant she wouldn't have to interact with the creepy manager as much. The way he stared at her out of sunken eyes the color of mud set her teeth on edge.

On her way out the door, she hung the do not disturb sign out even though she had everything she owned in the bag on her shoulder. The morning sun had started to melt some of the snow that had fallen over the last few days. The most recent storm system had moved on, but not before dumping another three inches on the city. Hopefully the weatherman was right, and they would get a break.

The old 4Runner was constantly grumbling in protest at the frigid temperatures, and she really couldn't afford to have it go belly up. Not when she'd amassed what felt like a small fortune in the week since taking the job at the Orchid.

It paid so well and tips were so good she might not even have to stay as long as she'd originally planned before she could start heading south. She'd found a few smallish towns in North Carolina that looked promising. Even some along the South Carolina border that might do if she dared go that far.

She held her breath as the SUV sputtered to life and then coughed. That was not a good sound.

"Come on, baby. A few more weeks. Then I promise to take you somewhere warmer."

Pulling out of the parking lot, she followed the flow of midmorning traffic, already knowing which streets to take to avoid the worst of the high-volume areas. One thing that had served her well in this long stretch of life on the run was her memory.

She could memorize and recall almost anything. Lists, maps, faces, details, patterns. Sometimes it was a blessing, like being able to remember multiple routes to and from a location so she wasn't always driving the same way twice. Other times it was a curse, like at night when she relived her past in her nightmares.

They'd gotten better. But they never strayed far, always there to swoop in and remind her why she was running, why she couldn't stop yet. Why she would probably never be able to stop.

That thought depressed her. That she might have to keep doing this for the rest of her life. Moving from place to place every few months, always looking over her shoulder, always wondering if they would find her.

When she'd first made this plan, she hadn't thought beyond the immediate need to get away, to be free, to find safety. Anything beyond the next right decision hadn't even entered her mind. If it had, she would never have been able to leave, rooted in place by the sheer number of choices she'd be faced with, to say nothing of the difficulty of those choices.

The employee lot behind the Orchid had been freshly plowed and sprinkled with ice melt, and Delaney wondered if James did that himself or hired a company to do it. He had to hire someone. She couldn't picture the man who drove a brand new Porsche SUV and wore expensive clothes, casual as they were, out here doing that kind of manual labor in the cold.

She parked at the corner of the lot, a few spaces from the door, and tucked her duffel under a blanket on the floorboard of the backseat. She preferred to bring it inside with her, but they didn't have employee lockers, so she'd had to satisfy herself with her second option.

The security the blanket afforded her was as much an illusion as anything else. If someone really and truly wanted what you had, they'd find a way to take it. But at least the car would look empty if someone peered into the windows.

She wrapped her scarf around her neck and shoved her hands into her pockets to dash to the door, knocking on the employee entrance and squirming against the wind that cut through her jeans and sent goosebumps flooding over her skin.

Addy's smile was as bright as her mermaid blue hair when she opened the door. "Right on time as always. You can settle the argument we're having."

"We wouldn't be arguing at all," Clara called from the

back of the kitchen where she sat rolling clean silverware into napkins, "if you would admit that I'm right."

"I can't," Addy said, returning to her task of prepping ingredients for the lunch crowd. "Because you are decidedly not right."

Delaney chuckled as she unwound her scarf and slipped out of her jacket, hanging both on a peg by the door. They reminded her of sisters, though they were technically cousins through some complicated family tree she still didn't quite understand.

She liked them both with their quick teases and inside jokes they were more than happy to explain. It had been a long time since she'd worked with women close to her own age. Most of the waitresses who worked in the greasy spoon diners where she could get temporary jobs were old enough to be her mother.

She carried her apron to the table where Clara was rolling silverware and started to help.

"Okay," Delaney said, reaching for a black napkin and folding it into a triangle. "What are you arguing about this time?"

"We're not arguing," Clara grumbled, setting her finished roll into a bus tub. "We're having a spirited discussion."

"That's usually code for there was yelling right before I got here."

"We hadn't quite reached yelling yet," Addy assured her. "But Clara thinks Batman is the best superhero, and she is obviously incorrect because the best superhero is Captain America."

Clara snorted and rolled her eyes. "Captain America is an obnoxious goody two shoes."

"Maybe, but that doesn't diminish his superhero capabilities."

"You didn't say we were picking them based on abilities, just who was the best overall."

"Right." Addy dumped the shrimp she'd been deveining into a container and covered it with plastic wrap. "And the best is Captain America."

"The best is Batman because he doesn't even have super strength! He doesn't have any powers at all! He fights bad guys because he knows it's the right thing to do."

"Please."

Addy stomped to the walk-in with the shrimp and yanked open the door hard enough to make Delaney chuckle. She had no dog in this fight, but watching them spar over something so trivial was definitely the most entertainment she'd had in months. It felt good to laugh again.

"Batman is a bored billionaire. It's not like he'll move on to clean up the next town when Gotham is all sorted."

"Of course not. Captain America isn't exactly traveling the world looking for bad guys." Clara pointed a knife at Addy before adding it to the napkin with a metallic clunk. "Also, wasn't the guy in a coma for seventy years or something?"

Addy sniffed. "He was frozen. I don't see what that has to do with being the best superhero."

"He was literally sleeping on the job for *seven decades*!"

"At least he was BORN!"

"What in the hell is going on in here?"

All three women jumped at the sound of James's voice from the doorway. He was dressed in dark jeans and a black sweater, the sleeves pushed up to his elbows, revealing muscled forearms. That was certainly something she shouldn't be noticing. Or appreciating.

"Addy was informing everyone—loudly—of her wrong opinion about Captain America," Clara said with a toss of her long blonde hair.

Addy mumbled a string of curse words under her breath.

"Delaney was supposed to be settling it for us. Well?" She pinned Delaney with an expectant look when she didn't immediately respond.

Delaney's hands fumbled with all three sets of eyes on her, and she felt heat flood her cheeks. "I'm sorry. I haven't seen any of the movies. I'm no help."

"What?" Clara's eyebrows shot up, and Addy's mouth hung open. "You've never seen a single superhero movie? Not even an old one?"

Delaney shook her head and started rolling silverware again. "I don't really watch much TV." Hadn't been allowed to.

"But these are…are…"

"Classics," Addy finished. "You have to watch them. You should come over on Monday, and we'll binge as many as we can."

"Oh, you don't have to do that."

"It'll be fun!" Clara insisted. "We can watch them all in chronological order for maximum effect."

"I'll make pizza. My homemade pizza is to die for."

"It really is. I bet I could get my sister to make brownies too."

In a finger snap, they had gone from fighting to plotting, making a list of which movies were more important and which were fringe, and Delaney could barely process the switch. James caught her eye from across the room, lifting his shoulder and giving her a casual smile.

"Excuse me for interrupting," he said, a little louder than their animated conversation. "Thanks so much for your time."

Delaney's lips twitched at the sarcasm.

"I'm heading out for a few hours. Mike should be here soon to man the bar and run food."

"Oh, that's right. Today's the first day of the tr—" James

cut Addy off with a sharp glare. "Thing," Addy said instead.

"What thing?"

Addy shared a long look with Clara until understanding finally lit her green eyes. "Ohhh. Right. That thing. My dad was telling me about it the other night. I think it's great."

"You two try and behave yourselves," James said, slipping his arms into his coat.

"Us two? What about Delaney?" Clara fixed her painted mouth into a pretty pout.

James met Delaney's gaze and held it for a beat longer than necessary. "Out of the three of you, she's the least of my worries. I'll be back before the dinner rush."

Without another word, he slipped out the back door, and she heard the deep growl of his engine as he pulled out of the lot.

"So rude," Addy mumbled. "It really is a pretty big leap for...everyone."

"I heard Evie was pushing it hard."

There was a lot of respect in Addy's smile. "I heard that too. I knew she'd be good for the family. Are you going to go?"

Clara slid a look at Delaney, choosing her words carefully as she rolled the last of the silverware. "I think so. Reagan said they were going to stagger them to fit different schedules and gauge interest. I figure it can't hurt to at least check it out."

"You think parents are going to freak out about it?"

"Weirdly enough, my mom is the one who has the biggest issue with it." Clara rolled her eyes. "I'm still going to go, though. But." She cleared her throat. "Back to our superhero movie marathon. I think we should start with the Batman universe, then move on to Captain America."

They were deliberately talking in code because of her, and the secrecy of it had worry twisting in her belly. She could feel the life being squeezed out of the few timid tendrils of trust that had blossomed over the last week.

This is why trusting people was so often a wasted effort. Everyone had secrets, herself included, and it would always be easier to avoid getting involved with people and their pasts than wading into the mess and be in danger of drowning.

Chapter Seven

J ames pulled into the half-full parking lot of the squat beige building where they ran their training drills and killed the engine. It was more like a training compound than a warehouse, and he loved this part of his role with the syndicate more than anything else.

Declan purchased the large piece of property on the outskirts of Philly almost a decade ago after convincing his father to better train their men. Over the course of a few years, they'd gone from scrappy, old-school fighters to well-trained, cohesive units.

The opportunities to put those skills to use had been legion in the years since instituting these training policies, including regular drills and training new groups as classes. The syndicate had become untouchable in nearly every way.

A wide strip of cleared land ran the length of the building between the warehouse and the trees, and they used it both for target practice and to run outdoor drills. They didn't bother with the drills in the winter, but target practice was always a must no matter the weather.

He let himself in through the side door and was surprised

by the number of people already inside. They were clustered in groups, talking low, but their voices echoed into the tall rafters. He spotted Reagan standing at the edge of the crowd with Brogan and Holt and wound his way toward them.

"Good turnout," he said, and Brogan nodded.

"I know," Reagan breathed, eyes bright with excitement. "Look at how many women came."

He turned to get a better look at everyone and noticed that women made up at least 50 percent of the group. And most of the men were really boys somewhere between sixteen and eighteen who were eligible for the next training cohort. Existing units trained separately.

"I doubt this is even everyone interested," James said.

"It's not," Reagan replied. "Evie and I talked about offering some self-defense classes at different times and on different days so people could fit it into their schedules. Around jobs and childcare and whatever."

"Self-defense and not full-on training?" Brogan wondered.

"Yeah. An opportunity for them to get their feet wet, I guess." Reagan shrugged. "This is more than I thought we'd get for a full training group. We should have done this years ago. God bless Evie," she sighed.

"Speaking of," James said, "is she not coming today?"

"She said she was when I saw her this morning," Brogan replied.

"She texted me." Reagan held up her phone before setting it on a table with her coat. "She'll be a little late, but she's coming."

"Better get started, then."

James glanced at Brogan, who motioned for him to go ahead. Shrugging out of his jacket, James tossed it on the pile they'd already made and stepped up in front of the crowd.

"Today we're going to put you through your paces and see what kind of shit you're made of," James said once the talking had stopped. "Most of you know how we run this. Holt trains on tactical ops thanks to his time in the PPD, Brogan on firearms, Reagan and me on hand-to-hand."

He surveyed the group, noting the mix of apprehension and excitement. "We're going to run this the way we always do. Split you off into groups and measure your skill level. By the end of today's session, you'll be sore, and we'll have a better idea of where to put you and what you need to learn. Any questions?"

A woman with short brown hair and deep blue eyes raised her hand. "What happens if we do really well?"

"Assuming you pass the training," Brogan said. "You'll get put into the rotation for regular assignments wherever your skills are strongest. As with anyone, you'll start at the bottom and work your way up."

"Assuming you pass," a blond boy with freckles sneered, and the boys around him snickered.

James moved to stand in front of him, making sure he was close enough that the boy had to tilt his head up or take a step back to meet his gaze.

"You're a Donahue, aren't you?"

The boy nodded, eyes filled with challenge. "Brian."

"Ah," James said with a knowing grin. "Mick's youngest. I know how your father fights. I'll be sure to keep an eye on you."

The boy's face went red, and James took a step back. "Today we'll start with hand-to-hand. If you've got a basic skill level, everything from knowing nothing to being able to land a decent punch, you'll work with Reagan."

He waited while about half the women and a couple boys moved over to stand next to Reagan, who beamed. "Moderate skill level is knowing a few different punches, some experience with fist fighting. You'll be with Holt and Brogan."

After this group self-selected, James was left with about

ten people—eight boys and two women. "All of you would rate your skill level high?"

He eyed the woman who'd spoken when she nodded, noting that Brian had put himself into this group as well. Not surprising. His father was a brutal teacher, and most of his kids came knowing how to throw more than a few punches. Not much form or discipline, but they could hold their own in a fight.

"I'm not training with a bunch of girls," one of Brian's friends spat.

"Name," James said, his voice razor sharp.

"Timmy McBride." The kid's chin ticked up a few notches in challenge.

"I know your brother," Brogan said.

"And?" Timmy's voice carried the defiance of youth and hubris.

"And I know he doesn't suffer fools."

Timmy snorted. "Training with women is bound to get someone hurt, and working with them is going to get someone killed. Just because Rory's the head of our family doesn't mean he knows what's best for everyone."

"That's an interesting sentiment," Evie said from the side of the room. Timmy flinched and took a quick step back when Evie approached. "Are you saying you don't respect the chain of command in this organization? Because your participation is entirely optional."

The tone of her voice had Timmy's eyes snapping to her face and widening. "I didn't say that."

"Then please"—Evie spread her arms out to her sides—"enlighten me." When he didn't speak, she continued. "Your place in the Callahan syndicate is a privilege, not a right. If you don't like how Declan or I run things, you are welcome to make your own way in the world, devoid of whatever protection this organization could afford you."

She took a step back to address the whole group. "That goes for any one of you. If this is the hill you want to die on, by all means, there's the door."

When no one moved, she turned to James, smile bright. "Sorry to interrupt. Please continue."

He chuckled under his breath when she moved to stand near Reagan. "This last group is with me."

He took them through a routine, testing their skills and their ability to adapt to a partner. How fast did they learn a partner's habits or tells? How good were they at evading a punch instead of trying to win with sheer force and power? Did they advance more than they assessed?

Not surprisingly, the women were far more patient than the men, and more than once, the brunette had Timmy flat on his ass. He was determined to bring her down with brute strength, and every time they sparred, he underestimated her ability to turn his strength into his weakness.

The fourth time he was on his back, breath wheezing from his lungs, James crouched over him. "Quit thinking you can beat her just because she's a girl and start studying her."

He helped the kid to his feet and put them into another match. This time Timmy danced at the edge of her range instead of going right for her, but he was still impatient, lunging while she danced out of his way and brought her knee up into his gut and her elbow down between his shoulder blades. He dropped to the floor on his hands and knees.

James shook his head and rotated partners, making mental notes on each one. Some of the boys would have to be moved down, but both women were solid. He'd be able to teach them a lot. Already his mind was spinning with how best to utilize both of them, wondering what their other skills were.

As they finished up, he could almost hear Maura's excited

giggle in his ear. Since they had no brothers, her father had raised Maura and Reagan like boys, teaching them how to shoot and throw a punch. Maura was better with a gun, but she could hold her own in any fight and then walk you through all the first aid you needed to patch yourself up after.

He rubbed at the bittersweet ache in his chest as the trainees filed out and joined Evie and the rest at the center of the room.

"That was fantastic," Reagan said.

"A better turnout than I expected," Evie added. "What are everyone's initial impressions?"

"The women underestimated themselves."

Holt nodded at Reagan. "By a lot."

"The boys overestimated their abilities. Especially the ones who put themselves at a high skill level."

Reagan laughed. "I saw the brunette put Timmy McBride on his ass more than a few times."

Brogan snorted. "He deserved it. His form is terrible."

"And he figured he could beat her just because she's a woman," James added.

"So I'm not totally out of my mind with this plan?" Evie met each gaze in turn.

"Absolutely not," Reagan assured her with a bolstering pat. "I've talked to at least a dozen women who couldn't make it today, and they're all planning on coming to some of the other self-defense classes we have set up. This is long overdue. Aisling, me, my sister, we've been in the minority for far too long, and we don't need to be. Not when so many women are willing and able to make us even better than we are."

Evie nodded. "The meeting with the family heads went worse than I expected, even if Declan didn't seem as rattled by it as I felt. It seemed mostly split along generational lines, except for your dad," Evie said to Reagan. "Mick Donahue was a very vocal dissenter."

"We expected as much," Brogan reminded her.

"I know." She took a deep breath. "Anyway, I've got to get going. I can't make the next training, but I'll be at that self-defense class this weekend, Reagan."

"She's really worried about this," Holt said once Evie had slipped out.

"There's a lot to worry about," Brogan replied. "But change is messy, and if Declan really didn't think he'd be able to pull this off, he wouldn't have let it get this far. He puts the stability and longevity of the syndicate above everything else. Not even Evie could talk him into something he didn't see as a long-term benefit."

"That's true," James agreed. "And Reagan is right. There's no need to leave this resource untapped, especially not with Declan's expansion plans gaining ground in New York."

"I love being right." Reagan grinned when James rolled his eyes. "Now, let's re-sort these groups so we can get out of here."

It took them close to an hour to shuffle the groups based on actual skill level and set up a proper training schedule. They'd run similar drills on shooting and tactical skills at the next session, and then James could really sink his teeth into the meat of what he was best at. Hand-to-hand combat.

Reagan's skill lay in using knives or other close combat weapons, but he held all his power in his fists. Winning a fight was about the expert use of your body, exacting the right amount of force at the right moment, and reading your opponent. Fighting was a dance, and in another life, he might have been a boxer.

The sky was already tinged with pink when he stepped out of the warmth of the building and into the biting wind. At least it wasn't snowing. He checked his phone for the first time all day, satisfied that his lack of missed texts meant nothing had blown up at the pub.

Beyond the focus of today's training, he could let his mind drift to Delaney. She'd looked so comfortable sitting there while Addy and Clara argued over superheroes of all things. It was the first time he'd seen her really relaxed instead of her normal hyper-vigilance. It was nice.

Until he ruined it by announcing his presence. He'd caught all of them off guard, but only Delaney's walls had gone all the way up. She was always watching him as if he might come unglued at any moment and attack.

Then Addy and Clara had pushed it a step further by nearly running their mouths about syndicate business, the one thing they were not allowed to run their mouths about, right in front of her. Delaney's whole body had gone rigid, and her eyes had filled with fear when he'd silenced Addy with a look.

Just when he thought he was getting somewhere with her. Not that he should be getting anywhere at all. But just because he shouldn't didn't mean he didn't want to.

Chapter Eight

Delaney scooped a ten-dollar bill off the table she was bussing and shoved it into her apron pocket with a smile. Saturdays were gold most anywhere in the restaurant business, but here in Philadelphia, or at least at The Black Orchid, they seemed to be magic.

There was some kind of ball game on tonight—she had no idea which one—and they'd been packed since six. Her feet might hurt, and her back might be a little sore from carrying tray after tray of drinks and food, but her apron pocket was full of cash tips, and more in credit cards waited for her at the end of the night.

Tonight would easily put her close to a thousand dollars in savings. She felt almost antsy to be carrying around that much money, but she liked to feel the weight of it tucked against her heart. So far Clara hadn't even blinked at her request to trade smaller bills for larger ones.

She cleared the rest of the plates and glasses from the table into the bus tub and gave it a quick swipe with her cloth before shuffling the salt and pepper shakers to the back of the table with the laminated drink menu. No sooner had she set the tub on her hip and stepped away than a party of four claimed it, and she bit back another grin.

"Having a good night?" James wondered when she stepped up to the bar after ringing in a drink order.

"A very good night." She watched him pluck the ticket from the printer and slap it on the bar as he grabbed a shaker glass and a bottle of rum. "Are you putting something in the drinks to make people so generous?"

He grinned. "No, but I might consider it. You seem to be settling in okay. I know I haven't had much chance to chat this last week. Need anything?"

The sincerity in his voice threw her a little, and the intensity of his gaze caused that flutter behind her ribs that she'd started associating with only him to beat a quick rhythm. No other man had ever made her flutter like that—before or after she'd run.

"No. Everyone has been so great. I even managed to sit through a whole day of superhero movies and not die of boredom."

He placed a top over the shaker, and she tried not to watch the flex of his forearms as he mixed the drink and then expertly poured it into a glass without spilling a drop.

"Have you decided, then?"

"What?" She dragged her gaze back to his face, unable to tell if he'd seen her staring at him or not.

"Batman or Captain America."

"Oh." She laughed, and he smiled. "I don't have the heart to tell them I think I'm team Dr. Strange."

"He is far superior to both." He set a beer on the tray next to the cocktail and selected a tumbler for scotch. "The man is a wizard *and* a superhero, for fuck's sake."

She smacked the flat of her hand on the bar and pointed at him. "Exactly! Plus he's a doctor. An actual doctor."

He added the scotch to the tray and slid it toward her. "Into doctors, are you?"

"Well, I much prefer them to lawyers."

As soon as she said the words, she wished she could grab them back, but he didn't seem to register the words themselves as much as her reaction to having said them. This was the problem with getting too comfortable.

She gave a weak smile before lifting the tray and carrying it back to the table, setting drinks on napkins and taking their food order. When you got too comfortable, you let things slip. And while he may not have put it together today, that didn't mean he wouldn't put it together tomorrow or the next day or the day after that. Then she really would have to leave Philly sooner rather than later.

She kept herself busy for the next few hours, avoiding any more conversations with James while he prepared drinks and only pausing long enough in the kitchen to ask for some extra ketchup or a side of pickles. The mood in the pub as the game apparently went well kept her feet moving.

Cheers rent the air when the right team won, and she couldn't help but smile, even if she still had no fucking clue who was playing or what. Finally, as the restaurant cleared out, she allowed herself a minute to lean against the end of the bar and catch her breath.

"Why don't you take five?" James said, sliding a glass of water toward her and indicating an empty stool.

"I'm still on the clock."

"I won't tell the boss."

She smiled and dropped into the chair, sighing with relief. He looked about to speak when the front door opened and drew his gaze. She shoved away the disappointment that she didn't have his attention anymore. She shouldn't want his attention. It was better if he was focusing it elsewhere.

"Well, look at what the cat dragged in."

James wiped his hands on a towel and shifted to lean his elbows against the bar as a woman with coppery red hair swinging to her shoulders claimed a stool a few seats down. Another woman with long blonde hair and startling green eyes sat beside her, and two more women stood at their backs.

"Double date?" James wondered.

The redhead rolled her eyes but grinned. "No. Just hanging out tonight."

"Well, you're always welcome. What can I get for you?"

"That depends. What kind of family discounts can I get?" the redhead asked, tongue tucked into her cheek.

Delaney blinked in surprise. She hadn't met any of James's family yet. The fact that she wanted to stay and learn more about whoever the redhead was to him was exactly why she pushed away from the bar and moved to take her water to the kitchen.

"Oh, Delaney, wait."

James's words had her retreat grinding to a halt. She took a breath and plastered a smile on her face before turning back around.

"The infamous Delaney." The redhead replied, eyebrows raised in question as she shot a quick look at James, who pretended to ignore her.

"I didn't realize I was infamous," Delaney said, extending her hand.

"Clara has told me a lot of things about you." Delaney's eyes widened. "Good things. I'm Reagan, by the way. This oaf is terrible at introductions. Apologies for his poor manners."

Delaney cast a furtive glance at James to see if Reagan's jab had upset him. He appeared to be the picture of calm, but she knew that for the facade it often was.

"Reagan is my sister-in-law."

"His favorite one." Reagan grinned.

"My only one."

"Oh. I didn't realize you had remarried."

She kicked herself as soon as she said it. Great. Now he would know she'd researched him, that she knew he'd been married before. Why did this man make all her common sense fly right out the window?

"I haven't," James said, eyes searching her face. She still didn't see anger there. He must hide it well. "She's hard to shake, this one."

"You need me," Reagan protested. "Remember when you tried to cook that chicken on wax paper and nearly ruined your oven? Who saved you then?"

James sent her a dry look. "Wax in the bottom of the oven would hardly have been the end of the world."

"Sure," Reagan replied. "But what about that time you exploded eggs in the microwave?"

James scratched his eyebrow with his thumbnail. "Remember when we talked about the way you overshare? This is one of those moments."

Reagan beamed while the blonde with her chuckled. "I am undeterred by your brotherly grumpiness." She leaned across the bar and gave James a loud smooch on the lips. "We'll take four beers and whatever Addy wants to feed us."

"Coming right up," Delaney said, eager to get away from whatever explosion might be coming.

She spun on her heel and gave Addy their food order through the window. Addy's face lit up when Delaney mentioned Reagan's name. At least people seemed to like Reagan, though Delaney knew just because someone liked you didn't mean they would rush to your aid in a crisis. God knows plenty of people who claimed to be her friends never had.

She spent the last hour of her shift bussing tables and cutting people off while Clara went through closing duties, all the while keeping a close eye on James. He hovered close to Reagan and her group of friends without inserting himself into their evening. He seemed amiable enough; there was no glint of calculation in his eyes, no gleam of ways he was thinking of making Reagan pay for embarrassing him.

She expertly avoided his gaze once he'd ushered out the last guests and locked up while she sat at the bar reconciling her receipts. He didn't speak, but she could feel him watching her as much as she'd watched him. He didn't push her for conversation, but his eyes followed her even while Clara chatted in his ear about some family thing.

She wished his gaze didn't have desire sliding through her belly. She didn't know what to do with desire. It had been so long since she'd felt any, and it hadn't led her to very good places in the past. Plus, she'd only known him for two weeks. She had no idea who he was or what he was capable of.

When Clara hopped off her stool, Delaney did the same and followed her through the kitchen to the employee lot. She waved when Clara pulled out and rested her forehead against the steering wheel for a brief minute while fumbling the key into the ignition.

She was grateful to have a day off tomorrow. Maybe she could catch up on the sleep that had evaded her for most of the last year. It wasn't likely, but it was nice to think about.

Finally sliding the key home, she turned it, and the engine clicked in rapid succession, coughed, and then went silent. No. No, this couldn't be happening. She shoved down the rising panic, took a deep breath, and tried again. It was the same.

When it rained, it fucking poured. Naturally when she'd finally gotten a healthy amount of money saved, she'd have to drain it to fix the damn car. She allowed herself thirty seconds to wallow in self-pity before pulling out her phone and deciding on her next course of action.

She could call a cab. Although, the idea of being stuck in a car with a stranger at this time of night and being driven to that part of town hardly appealed. Clara was gone, and Addy left as soon as her shift was done for a date. Which left her with only one choice. James. He was the only one still there. She might be wary of him, but at least he wasn't a stranger.

Steeling herself, she pushed out of her stupid, traitorous car, hunching into her jacket on her way back to the door. She banged on it with her fist and barely swallowed a yelp when it opened almost immediately.

"Hey." James looked her up and down. "Did you forget something?"

Most of the lights in the kitchen were off, meaning she'd probably caught him just before he went upstairs to bed himself. She felt bad asking him for this favor, but it was too cold to sleep in her car.

She gestured over her shoulder. "My car won't start."

His eyes didn't leave her face. "Do you need a ride?"

That's exactly what she needed, but still she hesitated. She couldn't help it. Every instinct she'd honed over the last year told her that getting into a car with a man she barely knew was a terrible idea, but getting into a cab with a total stranger would be even worse.

"I'm not going to hurt you, Delaney."

He didn't say anything more, didn't try to force any other platitudes or assurances. It was a simple statement, and even if she'd heard it before, she'd never heard it laced with the honesty his voice carried.

"Okay." She held his gaze while her heart beat a wild rhythm in her chest. "I need a ride."

He grabbed his jacket off the hook and tugged his keys from his pocket, pressing a button for the remote start while they crossed the lot. She retrieved her bag from the backseat of her truck and locked it out of habit. Not like anyone would be able to drive off with it.

The thought of having to jump through all the hoops to get it fixed had a bone-deep weariness settling over her, and she was grateful for James's silence as she navigated them away from the pub and toward her motel. Sometimes this life was too much, this constant existence in a state of fight or flight. In her darkest moments, she asked herself if going back would really be all that bad.

"This is where you're staying?"

His voice wasn't angry or disgusted. It was...shocked. Like he was genuinely surprised she'd stay somewhere like this dirty, rundown motel. She tried to muster the shame that normally swept over her, but she was too tired.

"Only until I find something a little more permanent," she lied.

He didn't even pretend to believe her. "Are you sure I couldn't put you up in a hotel? Or maybe my cousin has somewhere you could stay. He owns a bunch of rental properties."

"You don't have to go to that kind of trouble. The rooms here are clean." Another lie. "And it's mostly quiet. It's only temporary." At least that last one was true.

The lies rolled easily off her tongue, but they woke a long-buried emotion. Guilt. She hadn't felt guilty about lying to get what she needed in a long time. It felt like a relic of a bygone era. Back when she'd had morals and hadn't needed to do whatever it took to stay alive.

"I can call the pub when I figure out what to do with my car. I promise I won't let it sit in the lot for too long."

He pursed his lips when she reached for the door, like he was debating whether he would let her out. Her pulse quickened until finally she heard the thunk of the automatic locks.

"Do you need me to come pick you up tomorrow?"

"I'm off tomorrow. I'll call around to some mechanic shops and see if someone can come look at it. Or tow it or whatever."

"I know someone who can—"

"I appreciate that. But I've got it. Thanks for the ride."

Before he could say anything else, she slipped out of the car and jogged toward the motel, letting herself in the side door closest to her room. When the door was locked behind her and the chair from the makeshift desk shoved under the handle, she crossed to the window just in time to see his tail-lights fading into the dark.

She let the curtain drop with a sigh and sank onto the edge of the bed. Just when she thought she was getting ahead, the powers that be found a way to slap her back down and put her in her place. And to make matters worse, she was feeling far too many unfamiliar things about her boss and his crystal clear blue eyes and strong arms.

Chapter Nine

"**E**xplain to me again why I'm out here in this weather replacing the starter in a car you should probably sell for scrap anyway?" came Aidan's muffled voice from under the beat-up 4Runner.

"Because," James said when his cousin appeared to toss aside the old starter and reach for the new one he'd purchased yesterday, "you're the only person I know who works on cars, and you owe me for keeping your secret about Viv and the new baby."

Aidan's eyes narrowed. "Well, I don't like the reason, but it's a reason. And this piece of shit is hardly a '65 Mustang."

Aidan slid back under the car again, and James heard the clang of metal as he fitted the new part into place. He'd already been toying with the idea of fixing her car when Delaney had called the day before and said she was still searching for a shop. She'd promised to have it dealt with by the beginning of her Wednesday shift, but he'd been busy forming a plan.

He'd called Aidan out to take a look, hoping it was a

simple fix. Aidan made no promises that the starter was the definite culprit since they didn't have the keys to try and turn it over, but it looked corroded enough that he suspected it to be the issue. James would have paid to rebuild the entire engine if that's what was necessary, but the starter was an easy part to buy, even for a car this old.

He heard Aidan swear, and he chuckled to himself. "I really appreciate you doing this."

"You should," Aidan said. "Are you going to tell me who I'm doing it for?"

"One of my employees." He'd been hoping to avoid this line of questioning completely. "She needs a working vehicle."

James knew he'd said the wrong thing as soon as Aidan slid out from under the car and sent him a curious look, one eyebrow raised.

"You do this for all your employees who need working vehicles?"

"I would if it was necessary." He wasn't sure if it was a lie or not, but Aidan didn't seem to believe him either way.

"Who is she?"

"I told you." James shoved his hands further into his jacket pockets while Aidan wiped his on a towel. "She's an employee who needed a favor."

"Oh shit." Aidan threw the towel on top of his toolbox and shut it with a clang. "You like her."

"Contrary to your own personal experience, cousin, it is possible to be nice to women without wanting to bang them."

"Okay, well, that right there is proof you like her. You only deflect with sarcasm when you're avoiding telling the truth."

James turned and stalked back toward the kitchen door to the pub, jabbing his key into the lock and yanking it open. "Marriage has made you perceptive. I hate it. Do you want some coffee?"

Aidan set his toolbox down by the door. "Yeah, coffee's good."

James led his cousin upstairs to his apartment. No need to dirty the pub's kitchen when they weren't even open today. He didn't normally drink hot coffee, but he had the stuff on hand and one of those pour over contraptions. He kept his hands busy boiling the water and setting up the filter in the pour over.

"So?" Aidan said while the kettle hissed its way to boiling. "Who is she?"

"You don't know her."

Aidan scoffed. "I know everyone in our age bracket in the syndicate. You didn't vibe with Aisling, so I imagine you didn't try for another Donahue. You're too decent a guy and wouldn't want to make things awkward."

The kettle whistled, and James turned to pour the water over the grounds, watching intently as the coffee dripped down through the tip of the cone and into the glass mug. "She's not in the syndicate. She helped me out in a pinch when Maizy was a no-show, and I offered her a job."

When he turned to set the cup in front of Aidan, his cousin was staring at him. "You can't do that."

"I'm not doing anything." James pulled milk and an iced coffee for himself out of the fridge. "I hired her. I fixed her car. That's it."

"I know you, James. I know"—Aidan gestured up and down James's frame with his finger—"this. You like her."

"I barely know her." James twisted the top off his iced coffee and slowly placed it in the recycling bin to avoid his cousin's gaze. "You're reading entirely too much into a friendly gesture."

Aidan stared at him for a long moment. "You know you can't be with someone who's not in the syndicate."

James raised a single brow. He didn't need every

goddamn person reminding him of what he couldn't have, what he shouldn't want.

"Viv wasn't in the syndicate last I checked."

On a sigh, Aidan added milk to his coffee and stirred in some sugar. "As much as I love my wife, you know why that's different. She was chosen for me, and she was born into this life, same as us. You can't bring a civilian into our world. It's a recipe for disaster."

"I'm not bringing her into anything. I know the unspoken Callahan rule as well as anyone else. Dad drilled the story into me from the first moment I told him I had a crush on some random girl at school when I was ten. But like I said, I barely know the woman, so you have nothing to worry about."

Aidan studied him over the rim of his coffee mug and, seemingly satisfied, changed the subject. "I heard the training went well the other day. That little Timmy McBride got his ass kicked by a girl. Rory seemed pretty pleased by the news."

James snorted. "Kid deserved it. An asshole in the making who needed to be put into his place. Bonus points that it was a woman who did it without even trying. How's Evie doing with all of it?"

"More worried than I've ever seen her about anything. More worried than Declan even."

"Declan's worried?"

Aidan shook his head. "Not really. If he didn't think this would end well, he wouldn't have allowed it."

"Brogan said about the same." James leaned back against the edge of the counter. "Still, it's a heavy thing to turn things upside down."

"Most people think she's turning them right side up. My wife included. Evie's right. It'll be our daughters sitting at that table in forty years. They deserve to lead a syndicate that doesn't look down their noses at them because they're women."

"There will still be challenges. Push back."

Aidan set his mug on the counter and shrugged. "There always is. Doesn't matter what we change." He turned for the door and paused. "James? Don't do anything stupid."

"Wouldn't dream of it."

Alone, James scrubbed a hand over his face and pushed away from the counter. He knew the risks and the unspoken rules, and he had deliberately kept his distance from Delaney for precisely those reasons. That and the fact that she would barely make eye contact with him most days.

Irritated with the whole situation, he set the dishes from the coffee into the sink and went downstairs to grab Delaney's number from her file. He'd thought about saving it in his phone the way he had every other employee's number saved there, but something about doing that with hers felt like crossing a boundary.

He pulled her file out of the cabinet and laid it open on his desk. He'd run her background check, the name and details she'd given him coming back to a sweet old couple in Lincoln, Nebraska. He didn't believe it for a second, but he'd stopped short of asking Brogan to run a deeper search.

She'd gone to a lot of trouble to hide her identity because her documents were very convincing knockoffs. If anything, it served as a reminder that he knew nothing about this woman and that keeping her far away from him and the syndicate was the right thing to do. She could have her secrets, and he could have his.

He punched in her number and pressed the phone to his ear. Her voice was filled with nerves when she answered.

"Delaney, hey, it's James."

"Oh," she said, surprise filtering through the apprehension. "Is everything okay?"

"Yeah. Everything's fine. Sorry to bother you on your day off, but I was wondering if you'd gotten any update on your car situation."

He heard her expel a breath before she said, "I've called a few places. I'm sorry it's taking so long."

"No, it's not that." He'd been rehearsing this part since he'd decided to fix it for her. "I was thinking it might be the battery. We didn't try to jump it the other night. I have cables in my car."

She was silent for a beat. "I didn't consider it might be as simple a fix as jumping the battery."

"If you're free today, I can come pick you up, and we can try it out. If it doesn't work, I can help you figure something else out."

He heard the reluctance in her tone, but she finally agreed. "I'm free all day. So whenever is good for you."

"Oh, great." He tried to infuse his voice with as much nonchalance as possible. "I can be there in about twenty minutes."

As soon as he pulled up, she shot out the side door he'd watched her disappear into two nights ago, that big, heavy duffel bag slung over her shoulder. He wished, not for the first time, that this woman wasn't such a tempting mystery he wanted to solve.

She climbed in and rubbed her hands together in front of the vent, and he wondered if that fleabag of a motel had working heat. He'd thought about offering to put her up at a hotel again. Or at least make up the difference between what she was paying here, but he knew she wouldn't accept a kindness like that. Kindness made her uneasy.

That's why he'd devised this plan to pretend it was the

battery that needed a jump and leave her none the wiser that he'd paid to have the starter replaced. Assuming it was the starter causing the issue and the car would actually start. If it didn't, he'd have to default to plan B. And he had no idea what the fuck plan B was yet.

They rode in silence, her fingers tapping a nervous rhythm on her thigh. For the first time in weeks, she wasn't wearing a Black Orchid t-shirt and instead had on a poppy-red sweater that brought out the warm tones of her skin. Her black hair framed her face in tight coils, and she sucked her bottom lip between her teeth when she caught him staring.

"Sorry to drag you out on your day off."

James couldn't help but chuckle. "I'm the one who dragged you out."

Her smile was sheepish. "If not for my mess of a car, you'd be free to do...whatever it is you do when you're not working."

"It's no trouble. Really." He pulled into the parking lot and angled the nose of his car as close to hers as he could. "Why don't you wait in here where it's warm until I have everything hooked up?"

She nodded when he expected her to refuse, and he tried to hide his smile as he got out and retrieved the jumper cables from the trunk. He fumbled with the latch on her hood and popped his own, pressing the remote start to turn his car off before hooking the cables up.

Once he had everything secured, he restarted his car and let it run for a few minutes before motioning for her to get out. He schooled his face into a mask of concentration.

"Okay, give it a try."

He saw her take a deep breath before turning the key in the ignition. She groaned with relief when the car immediately turned over, and he smiled.

71

"Oh my God. You're a lifesaver. How did you know that would work?"

James disconnected the cables and started winding them into a circle. "I didn't. Just a hunch. My cousin likes to work on old cars, and sometimes I pay attention when he rambles."

"I don't know how to thank you."

When he glanced up at the catch in her voice, she had tears in her eyes. The look on her face shot straight to his heart.

"No thanks necessary."

"Let me give you some money." She reached into her duffel bag and pulled out a small change purse. "It's the least I could do."

"Absolutely not," he said, and she jerked. "I'm not going to charge you for the two minutes it took to jump your car, Delaney. I'm glad I could help." Her brows knit together. "Really."

She stuffed the purse back in her bag and nodded, blinking rapidly. She still didn't trust him, not all the way, but that was fine. He didn't require praise for doing a good deed, and she'd either figure out that he had no ulterior motives, or she'd move on to a new city and he would never see her again.

"You probably want to let that run for a good twenty or thirty minutes to make sure the battery is nice and charged," he said, breaking the heavy silence between them.

She nodded and lifted her bag from the front seat of his car before sliding it into her own and climbing behind the wheel.

"I really do appreciate your help," Delaney said, though she didn't sound convinced.

He smiled and nodded. "Any time."

She closed her door but held his gaze through the wind-shield for a beat before backing out of the spot and maneuvering around his haphazardly parked SUV in the small lot. He watched until her car turned the corner and disappeared from view.

He wouldn't do anything stupid. He shouldn't. Couldn't. But fuck if he didn't want to.

Chapter Ten

Delaney deftly picked her way through the poorly plowed parking lot and let herself into the thrift shop she'd found online the night before. Scouting good thrift shops had become a sad but thrilling kind of hobby.

Find one in the right part of any city, and you were bound to uncover a treasure trove of expensive items for pennies. Rich people who clear out their closets, kitchens, or basements and donate their designer, name brand, barely worn, barely used items to the less fortunate. She'd been that person once.

She'd first learned this trick in Boise after spending hours looking through thrift store after thrift store and finding nothing but matronly tops circa 1982. Someone had taken pity on her and directed her to a shop right on the edge of Hills Village. For the first time in months, she'd run her fingers over designers she recognized.

There was a balance to be struck, though. It was dangerous to be caught at a fleabag motel wearing Prada, no matter how little you paid for it. It made you an easy target.

After learning that lesson the hard way, she stuck to simple tops and jeans, donating what she was replacing so someone else could get some life out of it. Today she was in the market for some new sweaters. The ones that had lasted her through early winter in Ohio felt thin now that February loomed.

She wanted some color to chase away the gloom. Her desire for some brightness was in no way influenced by the way James had looked at her in the red sweater she'd worn the other day. She'd felt him watching her when he picked her up, his brilliant deduction about the battery saving her hundreds if not thousands of dollars in repairs.

He confused her. The man she saw with her own two eyes was at complete odds with the man she expected him to be. He was slow to anger. In fact, she'd never seen him angry at all. Not at drunk and belligerent customers, not at his staff, not at women who flirted with him openly. If it was an act, it was the best she'd ever seen.

Still, the evidence went against every sharply honed instinct. Not just from all these months on the run, but from the years of experience before that. Experience that told her people acted one way in public and another way in private, and the only mistake was assuming they wouldn't.

She wished he didn't call out to a part of her she thought she'd buried a long time ago, the part of her that was lonely and sad. She thought she was over needing to be held, to be touched, to be wanted. Apparently she wasn't, and that pissed her off.

Getting attached to anyone, even Clara or Addy, would only serve to do her more harm than good. This was the choice she'd made when she decided to run. She'd known it then as much as she knew it now. She'd adapted. Only the loneliness persisted. But there were worse things than loneliness.

"Let me know if I can help you find anything!" the young man behind the counter said with a smile.

She gave him a little wave, and he went back to adding price tags to the plates stacked in front of him while she went back to rifling through the hangers, looking for her size. She found a thick cable-knit sweater in her favorite color and tossed the bright pink shirt over her arm. In another life, she'd have spent weeks searching for the perfect shade of lipstick to match.

She grabbed another sweater in blue—definitely *not* because it reminded her of James's eyes—and two long sleeve shirts in case she needed to layer them to keep warm. Despite complaining multiple times to the skeleton that passed for a manager about the heat, it never seemed to get any warmer in her room.

She'd taken to sleeping fully clothed and was seriously contemplating splurging on a nice warm quilt. Something she could easily keep in the car when she was out.

The man paused what he was doing to ring her up, and she was grateful when he avoided making polite conversation. She hated talking about the weather, and she knew absolutely nothing about sports. Once outside, she added her purchases to her duffel and slipped the t-shirts she was donating into the donation bin.

The key to survival was packing light. Well, one of the keys to survival. It hadn't taken her long to discover what was actually essential and what was unnecessary dead weight. Hair care products were essential. She still had a few hours before her afternoon shift started, and she wanted to pick up some replacements for her stash.

Of all the things she missed about her old life, good hair care products were probably the biggest. She'd never lug around all the tools necessary to maintain her old routine, too much dead weight, but she'd grown to love her natural curls and the process of taking care of them. It gave her something to keep her mind and her hands busy. A mindless task to get lost in when things felt overwhelming.

Now was as good a time as any to replenish the stock she used sparingly. She had more than enough money to feel comfortable spending this much on shampoo and conditioner and curl creams. She snagged a new silk pillowcase on her way to the register and politely smiled and nodded through a conversation with the cashier about the upcoming winter storm the news was calling for.

They'd been wrong about the last one, but he was hopeful they'd gotten it right this time, and maybe his grandkids would get a day or two off school. Before he could launch into a mind-numbing retelling of the blizzard of '96, she grabbed her bag from the carousel and told him to have a great day.

The salad she ordered for lunch felt decadent, not because it was fancy, but because it was expensive. She so rarely allowed herself to eat well, and since she could only stomach so much fast food, she skipped more meals than she consumed. The result had been a sharp loss of weight on her already thin frame.

She'd finally started to put some back on in recent weeks thanks to James's policy that staff eats for free, but even then, she felt guilty showing up before her shift just to eat. Especially when Addy and her line cooks were busy serving customers.

They rarely let her miss dinner, though. If James wasn't making her take a break to eat, Addy was. It felt foreign to have someone concerned for her welfare after so long as a ghost, slipping in and out of people's lives before anyone really had the opportunity to get attached. She preferred it that way.

Their kindness and attention and insistence she get

enough food rattled her. Most of the time, she didn't know whether she should feel grateful or suspicious. The battle inside her own mind over it was exhausting.

The kitchen was a flurry of activity when one of the cooks let her in. She slipped into the bathroom to change out of her sweater and into her Orchid shirt, tucking the long tail into the waistband of her jeans. She really was too skinny. She missed the ample curve of her hips and the way her ass used to fill out a good pair of pants.

Giving her curls a quick fluff and running chapstick over her lips, she darted into the hallway to clock in and ran head-long into James's broad chest.

"Whoa."

He reached up with strong hands to steady her shoulders, and she leaned into them before realizing what she was doing and stepping away.

"Sorry," she said. "Didn't want to be late. I just need to run this out to my car really quick." She held up her sweater.

His eyes dropped to it and then back to her face. "Of course."

She could feel his eyes on her all the way down the hall, which sent a little zing up her spine. She really needed to get ahold of herself. She was already too attached to this place and its people.

She'd been over to Addy's twice now to watch movies she enjoyed with women who made her laugh. They'd gossiped and chatted without the usual air of barely veiled secrecy they so often had when talking at work. It was nice to have something that resembled friends, even if she didn't know how long it would last.

It was steady for a weeknight, and customers were friendly. Whatever marketing magic James was wielding, he should bottle and sell it. He could easily make a fortune teaching people the secrets of The Black Orchid's success.

She dropped a plate of fries off at one of her tables and moved to the next one, a youngish couple who'd been staring at their menus for longer than was usual. Something about the guy put Delaney slightly on edge, but he hadn't been outwardly rude or dismissive.

"Did you two decide on what you'd like to drink?"

The man's smile was easy and quick and had the hair raising on Delaney's arms. She turned to the woman, whose smile was forced, her eyes a little wary.

"We'll both have the winter lager and burgers cooked medium well. I'll have fries, and she'll have a side salad with fat-free dressing."

Delaney made eye contact with the woman, imploring the blonde to trust her. "Did you want anything else?"

She hesitated, gaze flickering to her date's face before she said quietly, "Could I also get an angel shot? On the rocks, please."

Delaney had no idea what she was talking about. She felt like it was some kind of code she was supposed to understand but didn't. James would know, and if not him, then Clara. She smiled and nodded.

"Absolutely. Let me go put that right in."

She didn't rush from the table like she wanted to but kept her pace easy while she skirted the bar where Mike was mixing drinks and went to the kitchen.

"Addy," she called over the noise. "Where's James?"

Addy gestured toward James's office, but he was already making his way down the hall at the sound of his name. When he saw her, his face pinched into a frown.

"I'm here. What's wrong?"

"There's a couple in my section, table six. There's something about the guy he...he gives me a bad feeling." James didn't look like he was prepared to tell her she was overreacting or being ridiculous, so she kept going. "She ordered an angel shot on the rocks. I have no idea what that means, but I think she needs help."

James squeezed her arm before moving quickly to the kitchen door and peering out into the restaurant. "Is that them? The woman with the long blonde hair and the guy with the military style cut?"

Delaney stepped up beside him, pushing onto her toes to see through the circular window. "Yeah. That's them. Do you know what her drink order means?"

"Yes." He nodded. "It means whoever the fuck that guy is, he's making her uncomfortable, and she needs us to call her a cab and get rid of him."

"He's had her hand in a vise grip since they sat down." Delaney's eyes dropped to the way the guy still had her hand clutched on top of the table, and she shivered. "How do we get her away from him without making it obvious?"

"Did they order anything else?"

"Burgers and a couple of beers."

James turned to her. "You feel safe going back over there?"

She was surprised he was thinking about her safety and comfort right now, but she nodded.

"Okay. Take them their beers and tell them her angel shot is on its way. See if that prompts her to get up and head for the bathroom. I'll make sure he leaves. Delaney"—she paused on her way to the bar to ask Mike to fill the drink order— "stay away from that guy until he's gone."

She gave a weak smile before pushing through the swinging doors, James right behind her. Mike poured the beers, eyes darting to the couple while James explained the situation. When they were ready, she pasted a smile on her face and carried them to the table.

"Your burgers shouldn't take long, and your angel shot is coming right up. Let me know if I can get you anything else."

Delaney held the woman's gaze before turning away.

"I think I'm going to use the bathroom," Delaney heard the woman say right before the scrape of a chair against the hardwood.

At a look from James, Delaney veered off course and headed for the bathrooms, following the woman inside in time to see her leaning both palms against the counter, head hanging down between her shoulders.

When Delaney stepped all the way in, the woman jumped as if she'd expected the man to be standing right behind her. If he had, Delaney wouldn't have been surprised.

"We're going to take care of him. Are you safe?"

The woman nodded and then burst into tears. "I just met him online last month. Right before New Year's Eve. He came on so strong and so fast, and I didn't know how to stop it."

"Does he know where you live?"

The woman shook her head. "No. I always had him pick me up from a random address near my apartment."

Smart. Even though this woman would beat herself up about letting this happen, however briefly, she'd eventually realize her instincts had been right all along. Next time she'd be more likely to trust them instead of brushing them off. At a noise from the pub, they both jumped. Her date didn't seem interested in leaving quietly.

"What's your name?" Delaney asked to distract her.

"Kylie. Kylie Reynolds."

"It's nice to meet you, Kylie Reynolds. Do you have someone you could maybe stay with tonight? Just in case?"

Kylie nodded and dug her phone out of her pocket, punching in a number and holding it to her ear. "Hey, Dad. Do you think you could come pick me up from this restaurant in Center City? Yeah, the guy I'm out with is a real jerk." She laughed even though tears gathered in her eyes. "Thanks, Dad."

She ended the call and pressed her fingertips to her eyelids. "He's on his way. God. I feel so stupid."

"You shouldn't," Delaney said, placing her hands on Kylie's shoulders. "Don't tell yourself this is your fault. Men like that are good at pretending, at making you doubt what you see and what you feel. Now you know better for next time."

Kylie smiled through her tears, and they both flinched at a knock on the door.

"He's gone." James's voice was warm and strong, an anchor in her sea of nerves. "I need an address so I can call a cab."

Kylie moved to the door and yanked it open, flinging herself into James's arms and hugging him tightly. "Thank you so much. I called my dad. He's going to come get me. I'll pay for the food."

"You won't. It's on the house. You can eat at the bar while you wait for your ride."

Swiping at a tear that escaped down her cheek, Kylie wandered off toward the bar, and Delaney was alone with James in the narrow hallway. They both spoke at once.

"That was—"

"Are you—"

Delaney smiled. "You first."

His eyes searched her face. "Are you okay?"

"Yeah." She nodded, and her heart squeezed at the softness in his eyes, the relief. Why did this man have to seem so good? "I'm okay."

"What were you going to say?"

"That was amazing. What you did for her."

"I'd do it for anyone."

He said it so casually, but she believed it deep down to her core. That he would do it again and likely had before. They still hadn't moved, and she felt his nearness much more acutely. Her heart pounded with it but for the first time it wasn't fear. It was something else entirely.

Chapter Eleven

James sat holed up in his office, catching up on the paperwork he'd been avoiding. The training sessions this week had kept him busy. They'd finally separated all the different skills into groups, and he was already seeing improvements from the handful of people he'd been working with, as well as working on form and technique with the less experienced groups.

Brogan had a couple women who had the makings of really excellent marksmen—a skill that was always in demand in their line of work. Reagan was still giddy over the progress, wholly undeterred by the bad attitude of some of the boys she was training in weapons fighting. He could tell she enjoyed drilling them extra hard when they let their mouth engage before their brain and said something stupid.

The more they improved, the easier it was to see where everyone would fit into the organization when they were ready. Being able to train even more people to bolster the ranks of the syndicate would make Declan's expansion into New York and then Boston even easier, leaving enough people to cover ground here in Philadelphia while also covering the other cities as emissaries and muscle so they could maintain a regular presence and protect their interests.

All of that, exciting as it was, along with his regular duties of managing syndicate inventory and shipments and deliveries, had left precious little time to do the paperwork required by the state of Pennsylvania to run a legitimate business. So he'd shut himself up in his office while the lunch rush raged outside the door, determined to get caught up.

When his phone buzzed on his desk, he sighed. He should have put the damn thing on silent.

"Hey, Aidan," he said, tossing his pen on top of the pile and leaning back in his chair.

"Hey. Busy?"

James surveyed the stack he still had to get through. "Only marginally. What's up?"

"I need a second for my meeting today."

"Don't you usually take Rory?" James leaned his elbows on the desk. "You two have a fight?"

Aidan chuckled. "No. Bridget went into labor."

"Oh, shit. Isn't she early?"

"Late. But that means Rory is at the hospital, and I need a wingman to watch my six. Up for doing a little business with me?"

James was already out of his chair and reaching for his jacket. "Absolutely. Send me the address. Addy," he called when he pulled open his office door. "I'm going out for a few hours."

"Sure thing, boss," Addy replied, not bothering to look up from the steak she was plating.

His phone signaled with the details, and he took the fastest route to the rundown deli, pulling into the mostly empty parking lot. Aidan had taken over as Declan's right hand two years ago, inheriting the role from his brother, Finn, who'd been killed by Italian thugs during a raid. Aidan carried it well, both his position and Declan's high expectations.

Aidan had made the syndicate a lot of money in the last two years. As good as Finn had always been at the politicking, Aidan had a unique style that didn't leave room for bullshit and often brought in multi-seven figure deals. James didn't know what kind of deal his cousin was closing today, but it was likely a smaller one based on the meet location.

Aidan's truck was already there, and James pulled in beside him, meeting him at the tailgate to check his weapon.

"Thanks for coming."

"Of course," James replied. "What's a little tax evasion when you can help sell millions in illegal weapons?"

Aidan's smile was wide, and he clapped James on the shoulder. "This guy is more like tens of thousands. According to Finn's notes, we did business with him a few years ago. But Brogan can't find much on him in the time since, so I remain skeptical he's good for it. Ready?"

When James nodded, they made for the front of the deli. The smell of cured meat and sweat was overwhelming. Aidan scanned the cramped space with its single row of booths pressed against dirty windows. There was only one customer in the entire place.

The man had a gut that hung over his belt buckle when he stood and waved them over. His hairline was receding, and when he sat, James glimpsed a thinning patch of hair at the back of his head. He smelled like the pastrami sandwich he was eating.

Aidan took a seat, and James did the same, eyes scanning the restaurant and the parking lot beyond while Aidan patiently waited for the man across from them to speak. Finally, the man broke.

"I heard what happened to your brother."

James felt Aidan tense beside him.

"Lots of people heard what happened to my brother."

"Of course," the man drawled around a bite of pastrami. His accent placed him as a southerner, somewhere in the Deep South if James had to guess. "That is, I mean to say he was a fair man, and I'm sorry for your loss."

"I'm sure you didn't ask me here just to extend your condolences, Ralphie. We haven't done business in a long time. So what do you want?"

"Right down to the point." Ralphie gave a curt nod. "Just like your brother. I like that about the Callahans. I've been out of the game for a while," he continued when Aidan only stared, uninterested in the small talk. "I'm looking to get back in."

So that was why Brogan couldn't find anything on the guy.

"What did you have in mind?"

"I want to start small. A few hundred handguns I can run south."

"And why are you buying in Philly?" Aidan leaned back in his chair. He looked relaxed, but his gaze was sharp. "You sound like you're a long way from home."

"Mississippi. We can't get the same kind of quality down there. You can mostly buy from local gangs and street thugs. Get something that hasn't been reported stolen if you're lucky. I'd rather travel where the quality is."

Aidan shot James a look, and James lifted a shoulder. Sounded legit enough. They didn't tend to care where the weapons ended up. Only that they didn't get screwed in the process. Nothing could be traced back to the syndicate unless a buyer squealed, and it had been a long time since that happened. People feared Declan more than they feared the cops.

"When?"

Ralphie leaned forward. "How soon can you get them?"

"How many and what type?" Aidan asked.

"9mm. Hundred fifty of them."

James ran through his mental files when Aidan looked to him for confirmation. "Forty-eight hours."

"That's one oh five in cash," Aidan said. "We get the cash before you get your product. I'll be in touch with details for pickup." Aidan pushed to his feet. "If you aren't good for it, you won't make it to the edge of the parking lot."

Ralphie paled but nodded. "I appreciate you doing business and meeting me out here. The pastrami is the best I've ever had outside New York."

Aidan's lip curled in disgust, and James bit back a smile as light glinted off the windshield of a dark sedan pulling into the lot.

"Aidan," James said, drawing his cousin's attention. "Time to go."

"Anything you want to tell me, old man?" Aidan wondered, hand moving to the waistband of his jeans as two men emerged from the car and advanced on the building.

Something told James they were here to cause trouble. He clocked a shoulder holster on one of the men and assumed the other one had it tucked into his jeans. The restaurant had gone eerily quiet.

Aidan rounded on Ralphie and yanked him out of his seat. "You son of a bitch. Tell me why I don't just shoot you myself?"

"If you kill me, you don't get your sale."

Aidan barked out a laugh, spinning Ralphie so he acted as a shield between him and the two guys who burst through the door, guns drawn. "A hundred five is a slow Tuesday in my world. Who are they?"

James moved to flank his cousin, gun aimed at the chest of the man closest to them.

"That fucker isn't worth protecting," the taller one said. "He'll shoot you as soon as look at you."

"Your father had it coming," Ralphie spat. "That arrogant bastard thought he could get one over on old Ralphie, but who's the one who laughed all the way to the bank?"

Aidan shoved Ralphie away from him and leveled his gun at his back. "See, Ralphie, I hate double-crossers. They always come back to bite you in the ass."

"Aidan, no. Wait!"

Ralphie spun around, but his protestations wouldn't have made much difference. Before he even choked out the words, he had bullets flooding his body from the two men at the door, and he dropped to the floor like lead, eyes wide and glassy.

"And you two." James brought his aim back to one man's chest as Aidan did the same. "You'll join him if you don't explain. Fast."

"We don't have any beef with you," the tall one said. "We've been tracking Ralphie since he shot our father and stole our stash a few months ago."

Aidan cocked his head, considering. "If I ever see your faces in Philly again, you'll leave in body bags. And Callahan eyes are everywhere."

The men exchanged a wide-eyed look before shoving through the door and peeling out of the parking lot. James tucked his gun back into its holster, and Aidan heaved a dramatic sigh.

"I hate when I'm taking care of bodies when I expected cash."

James shook his head and dug out his phone. "I'll call McGee to come clean up. What about the employees?"

Aidan shook his head. "It's Mafia owned. They won't talk. But I'll call Leo to make sure he knows what went down."

By the time McGee pulled into the parking lot with his

white panel van and descended on the scene to scrub it clean of evidence, the day was creeping toward twilight. Satisfied that everything was handled and the Falcones knew what had gone down on their turf, James followed Aidan out of the gravel lot and turned left where Aidan went right.

Brogan would do a little more digging on the two men once McGee got him some fingerprints from the front door, make sure no one would come looking for them and make a bad deal worse by starting a skirmish they'd have to finish. No one wanted to waste time and resources settling out-of-town scores with strangers who couldn't bother to keep their petty squabbles in their own cities.

James pulled into the lot of the pub and cut the engine. When he reached for his keys, he noticed a faint smattering of blood over the back of his hand. He rummaged in the glove box for a napkin to wipe it off before he went inside.

A normal person might have felt guilt or shame at seeing a man killed and being prepared to kill two more. But defending his family and their interests had never caused James to lose a moment's sleep. It wouldn't tonight either.

He looked up through the windshield when the kitchen door opened and watched Delaney carry a bag of trash to the dumpster. Her smile was bright when Addy opened the door to let her back in, mouth moving fast as they chatted about something.

The lack of guilt, the knowledge that he'd kill a hundred times over, sell guns to more killers, do whatever it took to maintain the Callahan reign over Philadelphia was exactly why he could never let himself get as close to Delaney as he wanted to.

It didn't matter that he couldn't sleep for dreaming about her. He was as dangerous to her as whatever she was running from.

Chapter Twelve

Delaney was dead on her feet as she dragged herself out of her car, hauling the heavy bag on her shoulder to the side door of the motel. Their swing shift help had called in sick with the flu, so Clara stayed late while Delaney came in a little early. She was looking forward to a couple days off her feet, even if she was stuck spending it in this dump.

She glanced at the faded keypad that was supposed to keep out anyone who wasn't a paying guest, but it had stopped working long before she'd checked in, and the door was used freely by pretty much anyone who wanted to. She consoled herself with the fact that her room was at least around the corner and felt bad for the people whose rooms sat right next to the door.

She dug her key out of her back pocket as she turned down the hall for her room, slipping it into the slot and waiting for the light to go green. When it stayed stubbornly red, she rolled her eyes. Come on. She wanted a shower and a bed and the leftover steak she'd brought back from the Orchid.

Tugging the key out, she wiped it on her jeans and jammed it back in hard, a trick that worked at least half the time. The light finally went green, and she turned the handle. She knew something was wrong as soon as the door cracked a scant inch.

She always left the light on by the door. In fact, she left most of the lights on along with the old TV nearly 24/7 so it always sounded like someone was there. The TV flashed blue into the room, but the lights were off.

She'd started to back out of the doorway when suddenly someone yanked it open from the other side. His grin was wide and revealed several missing teeth, the rest rotting right out of his head. Throwing the box of food at him, she leapt away, but he was faster, and he grabbed for her wrist.

"We've been waiting for you."

The single sentence sent an icy chill down her spine, and she kicked at him, struggling against his impossibly strong grip when he tried to haul her into the room. She didn't know what the fuck he wanted, money or something she was even less willing to give him, or who the mysterious 'we' were, but she was not going to let them get her behind a closed door.

"Stop struggling, you bitch. You know you want what we're gonna give you."

His hand found her breast and squeezed, and she gasped, flailing out with her arms until her elbow connected with his nose. His head snapped back, giving her a jolt of satisfaction, but it was short-lived when she saw the violence in his eyes.

"Stop being such a cunt. You've been playing hard to get around here for weeks."

She recognized the voice that came from further inside the room. The manager. The creepy one who always stared at her too long, his eyes lingering on her breasts or her ass.

"Get off me, or I'll scream."

The manager's laugh was a wheezing cough. "Go ahead and scream, slut. Who's gonna rescue you?"

No one would. They both knew that. Screams for help in this place would go ignored more than if someone screamed fire. She had to get the fuck out of here with her body intact. The junkie who held her in a vise grip struggled to pull her inside, and she went limp in his arms, hoping to catch him off guard.

When he loosened his hold, she spun to face him, kneeing him in the balls until he doubled over and backed away. She lunged for the door, yelping when the manager flew at her and grabbed her by the hair. She fought against his grip, but he slammed her forehead into the doorframe, and she felt the warm trickle of blood over her skin and into her eyebrow.

Caught somewhere between hysteria and deadly calm, she actually laughed. He would have to do worse than that if he expected her to stop fighting.

"Come on, girl," the manager whispered in her ear, his stale breath making her gag. "You know you want this big cock."

If she could distract him enough to get close... Hands shaking, she reached back to run her hand over his crotch, nearly retching when he ground it into her palm. She could hear him fumbling with his zipper, the other man still laying on the floor clutching his battered prick, and when she slipped her hand into the manager's pants and found the length of him, she wrapped her fingers around it.

His hold loosened on her hair, and she used his momentary distraction to squeeze his dick as hard as she could. He screamed and dropped to his knees. When he looked up at her, she kicked her foot up into his face and delighted in the sickening crunch of bone.

She didn't wait to see if he would get up, pivoting and scooping her bag off the floor along with the takeout box—

she didn't want this fucker to be able to find her—and ran back out to her car.

She threw herself into the still warm SUV and locked the door, shoving the key into the ignition and groaning with relief when the car started right away. She could see his silhouette in the doorway as she yanked the gearshift into reverse and flew out of the parking lot.

Her hands shook as she weaved through traffic, but she willed herself to keep it together, using the adrenaline still pumping through her to keep her going. She could call Addy or even Clara. Either one of them would let her crash on their couch for a night or two. But she knew there was only one place she'd feel truly safe tonight.

The floodlights were on in the employee parking lot. Enough light for her to see by as she grabbed her bag off the front seat and tossed the to-go container into the dumpster on her way to the door. She prayed he was still awake as she pounded on the door with her fist. Please let him still be awake.

The minutes felt like hours before the door cracked open.

"Delaney?" His eyes narrowed on the cut on her forehead and the bruise she knew was forming. He took quick steps forward until they were nearly touching. "Who did that to you?"

"The manager. At the motel. He...he was..."

"Come on. You can tell me upstairs. Let me clean that up."

He bent for her bag and reached for her hand, lacing their fingers together as he led her through the kitchen to a door that opened onto a narrow flight of stairs and spilled into a lofted apartment.

He set her bag by the door and pulled her gently through the kitchen to a small table tucked under large windows. Easing her into a chair, he retrieved a first aid kit from under the sink and sat in front of her.

His eyes were angry, but his hands were gentle as he used a sterile wipe to clean the blood from her face. She winced as the alcohol hit split skin.

"What happened?" His voice was low, hoarse, like he was afraid he might yell if he tried to speak any louder.

"It was such a long day. I wasn't paying attention."

"Don't do that." She jumped at the sharpness in his tone, and when he spoke again, his voice was gentler. "Whatever the fuck happened wasn't your fault. Don't accept any of the blame for this when you tell me the story."

She pressed her lips together and nodded. "It *was* a long day," she said, and the corner of his mouth quirked up before firming into a hard line again. "I got back to my room and realized all the lights were off. I always leave the lights and the TV on when I'm not there."

He used a cotton swab to dab antibiotic ointment on her forehead, nodding for her to continue. "I was going to leave. It happened so fast. He jerked the door open."

"Who?" His voice was a low growl.

"I don't know. I'd never seen him before. But the other guy. He's the manager of the motel." She shivered. "He's always creeped me out, always staring at me whenever I pay. They were going to… He said they were…"

Her breath hitched, and she pressed her fingertips to her lips to hold in the sob that wanted to escape. "I kneed the first guy in the balls, and he crumpled. The second guy, the manager, he grabbed me by my hair."

She reached up to rub a hand over the tender spot at the back of her scalp. James's hands were steady when he unwrapped a bandaid and pressed it against her forehead with gentle fingers.

"Do you want to tell me the rest of it?"

She nodded and blew out a breath. "He had such a tight grip on my hair I couldn't move enough to get good aim to hit or kick him. So I-I played along. I ran my hand over him, into his pants."

James's hands clenched into fists on his knees, and she shivered. "When his grip loosened on my hair, I squeezed as hard as I fucking could. He dropped to his knees like a boulder, and I kicked him in his ugly face. I didn't stay around to see what happened after that. I didn't know where else to go," she finished in a whisper.

That wasn't true, but she couldn't tell him the real reason she'd run straight to him. What good would it do anyway?

His voice was rough when he said, "I'm glad you came here."

He was so close she could feel the heat of him. His muscles were tense, and she could tell he was angry. But she didn't think he was angry at her. She wanted to lean in and touch him, so instead she looked around the space.

The apartment looked the same size as the floor plan of the bar, the first level anyway, so the kitchen and dining area were large, with new appliances and a generous island counter.

A big flat-screen TV was mounted on the wall in the living room, and it was separated from the rest of the space by the biggest sectional she'd ever seen. She imagined the wide windows inlaid into the exposed brick wall would let in plenty of natural light during the day.

"I guess I didn't think far enough ahead to what came after you rescued me."

"You rescued yourself, Delaney."

His voice was quiet, and when she glanced back at him, he was studying her intently. His hand twitched in his lap, and he sat back, putting distance between them. She wondered if he wanted to touch her as much as she wanted to touch him.

"I hope your couch is comfy. Unless you don't want me to sleep there."

"I don't."

Her heart sank, and she nodded, pushing to her feet. "I understand. I didn't mean to come here and cause you trouble. Thanks for the Band-Aid and everything."

He stood with her and reached for her hand. He pulled her to the door, but instead of opening it to go back down to the kitchen, he picked up her bag and turned toward a set of floating stairs, leading her up. The open loft at the top was dominated by a pool table and a couple of leather armchairs pushed up against the near wall.

He led her to the left and down a short hallway that ended at a bathroom with a door on either side. He opened the one on the right and motioned for her to step inside. It was a bedroom.

A queen-sized bed draped in a dark blue comforter and piled with pillows sat in the middle of one wall, flanked on either side by white nightstands. A dresser with a small flat screen TV on top of it stood opposite the bed, and a door in the corner led to what she assumed was a closet. She turned to face him and saw he was still standing in the hallway.

"I thought you didn't want me to stay here."

His expression was soft, a light crease between his brows the only hint of what he might be feeling. "I said I didn't want you to sleep on the couch. Not with an extra bed with clean sheets right here. There's only one bathroom, but this door locks." He rapped his knuckles against the wood. "And I can crash at my cousin's place so you're not crowded."

When he stepped away, she rushed to the door. "Wait. I...I don't want to be alone."

The words left her in a rush, and she could tell they surprised him as much as they did her. She couldn't take them back. They were the truth anyway. She didn't know why, but she knew she'd feel safer behind her locked door with him across the hall.

His eyes searched her face, lingering on her forehead where her cut was beginning to throb behind the bandage, and he nodded.

"Let me get you something for the pain."

She slumped against the door frame when he disappeared into the bathroom, leaning her temple against the cool wood. She heard water running into the sink before he reappeared holding two pills in his outstretched palm and handed her a glass. She popped them and chased them with a deep drink, shifting so their bodies were nearly touching.

Her heartbeat fluttered, and when she looked up at him, his eyes were on her again. If she reached out, she could touch him. If she eased up onto her toes, she could press her lips against his. She had the sudden overwhelming urge to kiss him, to see what he tasted like.

He didn't move when she shifted again, her arm brushing against his stomach. It was like he was holding his breath, locked in place and waiting for her to make the first move, giving her all the control to push forward or pull back.

When she looked up at him again, time slowed. Their faces were so close she could feel his breath warm against her cheek. She pushed herself ever so slightly onto her toes, her hand reaching out to brace against the hard plane of his chest. Then the shrill ring of his phone cut through the charged air.

She jumped back with a gasp, splashing water over the rim of the glass and onto the floor. His eyes never left hers as he dug it out of his pocket and accepted the call without looking at the screen.

"What?" he demanded, voice tight. "Now?" He listened intently to whoever was talking. "Yeah. Fine. And Brogan? I need your help with something after. Twenty minutes."

He disconnected the call and slid his phone back into the

pocket of his jeans. "I'm sorry. That was my cousin. I have to run out and meet him for something real quick. Are you going to be okay on your own?" He dragged a hand over the stubble on his jaw. "I could call Addy to come sit with you."

"Are you...are you coming back?" She hated the way her voice shook.

"Yes. Of course. I'll be gone an hour. Two max."

"Okay." She nodded as much to agree as to reassure herself she'd be fine.

He started to step away and paused. "There are four locked doors between you and the outside. You're safe here, Delaney."

He didn't wait for a response before stalking back out to the loft. She heard his footfalls on the stairs and the sound of the front door as it closed. Easing the bedroom door shut and locking it, she leaned back against it and heaved out a huge breath.

It was the adrenaline that had made her almost do something so stupid. She should never have come here in the first damn place. She should have called Addy or Clara or tried to find another motel. This was only temporary, staying here. She'd allow herself a day or two to find something else.

Or she could pack up and leave now. She had enough money to last her long enough to settle somewhere else. Remove the temptation to make terrible choices from her life completely.

She eyed the bed with its comforter and soft pillows. It smelled so clean, and it was so quiet. One night. She'd stay one night and then leave Philadelphia first thing in the morning. It was the only smart thing to do.

Chapter Thirteen

J ames knew the moment she was awake. He was alerted by the sound of her feet on the floor just before the creak of her bedroom door and then the bathroom. He could hear the rush of water through the pipes when she turned on the shower.

She'd slept with the lights on. He saw the glow under her door when he got home from helping Brogan move some shit between rental properties. Why the hell they'd needed to do that at midnight, James would never understand. Brogan had repaid him by helping deal with the manager and his junkie friend who dared lay a hand on Delaney, leaving her bruised and terrified.

Neither one of them would ever bother another woman again, and she'd be none the wiser because there was no way in hell he was letting her go back to that place. She could stay here, or she could let him put her up in a nice hotel, but he would make sure she was safe.

He removed a waffle from the iron when it beeped and ladled in more batter as the shower stopped. The door creaked open, and he heard her dart across the hall before her door closed with a snap. Coffee was dripping through the pour over into a big mug when her feet padded down the stairs.

Her eyes were wide when she saw him in the kitchen, but she only hesitated for a second before crossing to stand on the other side of the island. Her sweater was bright pink today, and her feet were bare. He wondered if she was the kind of woman who might paint her toes if she had the time and the freedom to do it.

The iron beeped, and he slid the still steaming waffle onto a plate, added some bacon, and carried the plate and the mug of coffee to the table for her. When she only stared, he took a step away.

"I have iced coffee if you prefer that instead."

"No. Hot is fine. Thank you."

She crossed the kitchen so slowly he took another step back and waited for her to sit before he moved to unplug the waffle iron and set dishes in the sink. He leaned back against the counter to give her plenty of space while she ate.

She drizzled syrup over her waffle and then peeked at him over her shoulder. "Are you not hungry? I feel weird eating by myself."

Hiding a smile, he filled a plate for himself and carried it to the table, leaving a space between them. She'd looked so scared last night he didn't want to spook her.

"How's your head?"

She reached up to run a fingertip over the bandage and winced slightly. "It's a little sore. Thanks for leaving the painkillers on the sink."

"You're welcome."

They ate in silence, though it was hardly comfortable. He had a million things he wanted to ask her, to say to her. He wanted to convince her to stay so he could make sure she was okay. But he said none of it.

"Do you think I should call the police? About what happened last night?"

His hand froze with his fork halfway to his mouth. Shit. He hadn't banked on her wanting to call the cops. If she insisted on it, they had a guy, no, two guys, who worked the beat he could call. And Holt was a detective, albeit with organized crime. Still, he was a resource if James needed it.

"Do you want to call the police?"

Doubt flashed through her eyes, and eventually she shook her head. "Not really. They never seem to care about helping anyway."

He relaxed and tucked the bitterness in her voice away to explore another time. "Did you sleep okay last night?"

She sighed, and it sounded almost wistful. A smile teased at the corners of her mouth. "That was honestly the best night of sleep I've had in a really long time. I'm trying to figure out if I can feasibly sneak the mattress out of here and into the back of my car."

"No need to sneak it." He chuckled. "You can have it if you can make it fit. What?" he asked when she stared.

"I'd laugh, but you actually mean that."

"I do."

He bit into a slice of bacon, his eyes dropping to her mouth. When she captured her bottom lip between her teeth, he had to swallow a groan and look away. Having her across the hall all night had hardly helped quell the dreams he'd been having about her.

"I don't want to overstay my welcome, so I should probably get going today."

He swallowed the bite of bacon that had suddenly gone to sawdust in his mouth. "Leave to go find a different place to stay or leave Philadelphia?"

"I... I'm not sure. I appreciate everything you've done for

me. Last night, the job. But I should go before I cause any more problems."

With a huff, James shoved away from the table and carried his plate into the kitchen. It took every ounce of willpower he had not to hurl the damn thing into the sink at the idea of her leaving town altogether. She was right. It was probably what she should do. It wasn't what he wanted her to do.

He wanted her in his house, safe from whoever or whatever might hurt her. Better yet, he wanted her in his bed, but that was still a line he couldn't cross. It already felt dangerous to have her here, but that didn't mean he wanted her to leave.

"You can stay as long as you want. Don't rush out on my account." He hoped he'd pumped the right amount of sincerity and calm into his voice.

He felt her presence at his side more than heard it. That sweet scent he'd come to associate with her clinging to her skin and wrapping around him. It made him want to pull her close, so he shifted away, leaning back against the sink opposite her and crossing his arms over his chest.

"I'm not rushing out because of you. I don't want you to think that. But about last night. When we… When I almost…" She fumbled with the sleeve of her sweater. "I didn't mean to make you uncomfortable."

James barked out a laugh. "Is that what you thought you made me? Uncomfortable?"

Before he could stop himself, he stepped closer, watching her for any signs that she needed him to move back. Standing this close, he could feel the heat of her body and see the amber flecks in her eyes. He should step away. He didn't want to.

"Delaney." He expected her to tense, but she relaxed against the counter, her eyes never leaving his. "I felt a lot of things last night. Uncomfortable wasn't one of them."

He didn't really know who closed the gap between them, but suddenly, finally, his mouth was on hers, and he knew exactly how she tasted. He didn't touch her; he wasn't entirely sure he could control himself if he gave in to his desire to skim his hands down her sides and around to the small of her back, so he pressed his palms flat to the counter on either side of her hips while he explored her mouth with his tongue.

She didn't touch him either. He thought she was kissing him back, her tongue teasing against his, but an alarm bell went off in the back of his head. One that said shy, scared, quiet Delaney might not resist even if she didn't want it.

He broke the kiss, and she gasped. The sound knifed into him and twisted guilt into a knot in his stomach. Her eyes were wide and her breathing ragged when he chanced a look at her face.

"I'm sorry. I shouldn't have—"

She didn't let him finish, her arms circling his neck and tugging him forward until their lips met again. He touched her then. He couldn't have stopped himself if he wanted to, groaning against her lips when he slid his hands around her waist and pulled her against him.

She felt so delicate in his arms. Breakable. Precious. He wanted to hold on to her and never let go. That thought alone should have had him ending the kiss, backing away from her, offering to take her anywhere but the spare bedroom in his apartment. But he didn't. He couldn't.

For the first time in over two years, a woman had ignited something in him he wasn't sure still existed. She was a spark that set him aflame, and even if just for this singular moment, he wanted to take from her whatever she was willing to give while they were both barefoot in his kitchen.

He swept his tongue against hers, and she sighed. She tasted like syrup, and her arms tightened around his neck. The only thing that stopped him from lifting her onto the edge of the counter and seeing just how far they were both willing to go was the reverberating ring of his goddamn cell phone.

She buried her face against his neck, her breath hot and panting against his skin. It sent shock waves straight to his cock while he dug his phone out of his pants pocket.

"Doesn't that thing have a mute button?" she wondered, and he couldn't help the laugh that rumbled through his chest.

"I hope someone is dying," he said into the phone.

"And a good morning to you, cousin," Declan said a little too cheerfully. "I need you to come to Glenmore House Friday night."

"Is there a meeting I forgot about?"

James toyed with the hem of Delaney's sweater, his fingertips occasionally brushing against the smooth skin of her hip.

"No. Your father will be back by then," Declan said. "We'll debrief over dinner. It's been a while since we had the whole family together. Seven," Declan added and hung up.

James dropped his phone onto the counter and looked into her eyes, cupping her cheek in his palm.

"If you're about to apologize again, please don't," Delaney said when he opened his mouth to speak.

He smiled. "I was going to say I didn't invite you to stay here as some kind of master plan to kiss you or…"

"Or?" she prompted.

"Or get you into my bed." He glanced over her shoulder to steady himself and blew out a breath. "I want you to stay, Delaney, only so I know you're safe. But if you want to leave, then you should do that. I won't stop you or try to talk you into doing anything you don't want to do."

"I think…I think I'll stay. For a little while longer."

He nodded, pressing a lingering kiss to her forehead because he didn't trust himself not to drag her down to the kitchen floor if he kissed her anywhere else. His phone signaled an incoming message. A shipment had arrived and was being loaded for delivery to one of their warehouses.

"I have to go to work."

"But the pub is closed today."

He eased himself away from her and tucked his phone into his pocket. "My cousin is Declan Callahan." He figured she already knew that; she was likely to have done her research. "Callahan Corporation is kind of a family thing. Are you okay here on your own today?"

She turned to watch him cross to the door. Wrapping her arms around her waist, she nodded.

"If you want to go out, don't worry about locking this." He gestured to the front door, stuffing his feet into his boots and bending to tie them. "No one should be coming by today anyway, and the kitchen door downstairs is secure enough. I'll be back later tonight. I'll bring something for dinner."

He lifted his coat off the rack and jogged down the stairs before he changed his mind and tasked someone else with handling the shipment. Plenty of men were just as capable as he was of logging inventory. At least this way, with a little distance between them, he could pretend he wasn't already planning on sleeping with her. Consequences and unspoken rules be damned.

Chapter Fourteen

"Excuse me, I hate to trouble you, but have you seen this woman?" He flashed the homemade missing persons poster and offered what he hoped was a sad, endearing smile.

The old woman slipped bifocals out of her front pocket and held them up to her face to glance at the photo. "No, sorry. Can't say I have."

When she turned to walk away, he jogged after her. "Are you sure? She would have been here around the end of November. Maybe she worked for you?"

The woman didn't even give the paper in his hand a second look. "She definitely didn't work here. We're full up with college students that time of year. Sorry."

She turned to help a nearby customer, and he had to force himself not to crush the paper into a ball and lob it at the back of her head. This was his fifth business just today, and still he was getting nowhere. Either the bitch had gotten herself a new face, or the client's information was bad, and she'd never been in Ann Arbor in the first place.

He pushed out of the yuppie clothing store and hunched

into his jacket against the wind. It didn't help that the weather in this godforsaken state made pounding the pavement with her photo absolutely miserable.

The last two shops on this block were equally unhelpful, though one man did click his tongue and offer up some sympathy for his pretty young wife. It had been a trial not to roll his eyes at that. People saw what they wanted to see, though, and the more sympathetic he could make himself, the better.

Climbing back into his truck, he folded the flyer and shoved it into his pocket. When he arrived, he started with the businesses closest to the spot his client gave him, showing her picture to all the store owners and managers in the vicinity. He'd come up empty.

It hadn't been that long since she'd been there according to his client, only a little less than two months. But it was a busy college town, and with the holiday rush and people's memories notoriously shit at things like this, nothing was popping. After the first few days, he'd drawn a grid over the area and meticulously visited each shop and restaurant, trying to find someone who recognized her.

If this was where she was spotted on foot, odds are she was coming from somewhere nearby. If he went with his gut —which he often did because it rarely steered him wrong—he would hazard a guess that she worked in one of these shops. He'd find her eventually.

Pulling away from the curb, he kept his eyes peeled for a place to eat. He needed to cool his heels somewhere with a cold beer and a good burger and regroup before he tried again this afternoon.

On the corner of the next block was a bar and grille, and he pulled his truck into a parking spot between a Prius and an ugly orange hatchback with bumper stickers like *Save the Earth: She's the Only One We Have!* plastered on the back.

His lip curled as he got out; it took every ounce of willpower he had not to ding the door. No need to draw attention to himself just because he was frustrated. Jumping the curb, he held the door open for a couple coming out and claimed a seat at the bar.

While he waited for the barman to finish up with a group at the other end, he dug a map out of his inside pocket and spread it out on the bar. As convenient as people said GPS was, it got him lost more often than not. He preferred working with a hard copy map and finding his own way around.

He used a red pen to tick off the stores he'd struck out on today. The list was dwindling, and he really didn't want to go home to his client empty-handed. It wasn't a fucking option.

"What can I get you?"

"I'll take whatever you got on tap. But none of that light shit."

The barman chuckled and moved down to pour his beer, setting it on a napkin before offering a menu. He waved it away. "If you have anything resembling a regular double cheeseburger with bacon—nothing fancy—and fries, I'll take that."

"I can do that for you," the man said, keying in his order. "You doing a food tour or something?"

He looked up and saw the man staring at his list marked with red pen. "Looking for someone."

"That's a lot of looking."

"It's very important that I find her." He could tell his tone was rougher than he meant it to be when the man's eyebrows shot up, and he fixed his face into a look of sympathy. "It's my kid sister. She went missing, and my mom is worried sick. I'm trying to find her, is all."

The man leaned his elbows on the bar and nodded at the map. "And you think she was here?"

He shrugged. "Someone said they thought they saw her in this area, so we figured it was worth a shot to have somebody drive up this way and check it out."

"But you're not from around here."

"Good ear." He forced a smile. "I'm from down south a ways. But maybe you've seen her?"

He dug the flyer out from his pocket and unfolded it, holding it up for the man to see. The man took the paper and squinted, glancing up over the top of it.

"That's your sister?"

"Since the day she was born. Do you recognize her?"

The man studied the photo a bit longer before slowly setting it down on the bar. "She worked here a couple weekends at the end of November, beginning of December."

He perked up. Almost a week of searching in the freezing cold, and he happened to wander into the exact restaurant he needed just to grab a beer. "Do you remember her name?"

The man frowned. "You don't know your own sister's name?"

Fuck. "She's gone missing before. Sometimes she gives a fake name."

"Maybe if she's giving a fake name, she doesn't want to be found."

"I understand what this looks like, but my sister is severely mentally ill. When she has a prolonged episode like this, she can end up doing real damage to herself."

The man rubbed a hand over his jaw and nodded slowly. "She seemed fine when she worked here. Said her name was Amy something."

He impatiently tapped his pen on the scarred wood. "Parker, maybe?"

The man thought for a minute. "That sounds about right."

"Thanks. That's a name I can give when I call local hospitals. You said you haven't seen her since December?"

"Yeah." The man eyed the photo again. "She said she needed to make some extra cash to fix her car. We didn't put her on the books, just let her wait some tables and keep the tips. I think she said she was heading down into Indianapolis next."

"Indianapolis?" He scribbled it down on his paper.

"Said something about trying to get away from all the snow." The man chuckled. "I told her she'd be better going out to California for all that."

He forced a laugh. "Too true. I don't know how y'all do it up here."

"Oh, you get used to it. Your food will be up shortly. Let me know if you need anything else."

The barman moved down the bar, and he gave himself a triumphant pat on the back. They always ran their mouth one time too many. It wasn't a rock-solid lead, but it was a piece of the puzzle and a step in the right direction.

He'd find her. A spoiled brat like that could only hide from him for so long.

Chapter Fifteen

Delaney cleared the breakfast dishes from the table. The steady pulse of bass from whatever music James listened to while he was in the shower drifted down the stairs. Three days. That's how long it had been since he'd kissed her in the kitchen.

Her eyes lingered on the spot where he'd backed her up against the counter and boxed her in and sent electricity racing down her spine when their lips met. It was something that should have terrified her—being that close to a man—but it didn't.

It had unsettled her, though. As soon as he left her alone in the kitchen, she lurched for her phone and immediately started looking up other places to stay. Motels in better neighborhoods, vacation rentals that gave discounts for long-term stays, and even a few short-term lease apartments.

All of them were fine; she'd obviously stayed in worse places, but she found a reason to shoot down every single one. They were too rundown or too expensive or too far from the Orchid.

By the second day, she'd convinced herself that leaving

Philly altogether was the smart thing to do. She had more than enough money to make her way down to one of the Carolinas and ride out the rest of the winter there. If she slipped into a smaller town, she could even rent something cheap and not have to work for a month or two. She'd saved up enough to lay low for a bit and get her bearings.

Except every time she tried to convince herself to leave, she lost against the voice that argued that it was safer here, that she felt safer here. Every sharply honed instinct told her men couldn't be trusted, yet she couldn't ignore the fact that James didn't put every survival sense she had on high alert. She'd never even heard him raise his voice.

It confused her that she felt safe here, that she felt safe with him. A huge part of her wondered if, after a year on the road, her loneliness had finally surged beyond the fear and the anxiety of being hurt again.

It would be laughable if it wasn't so pathetic. That her need for affection was beginning to outweigh her survival instinct. Maybe she was as incapable of taking care of herself as she'd always been told.

She wiped the now empty table with a damp cloth and carried it to the sink to rinse before draping it over a little bar hanging on the wall. Pushing her sleeves up to her elbows, she decided to skip the dishwasher and wash the dishes by hand. She wanted something to keep her hands busy.

She filled the sink halfway with hot, soapy water and submerged the pan he'd used to fry up some potatoes. Another oddity about the man. He could cook and cook well. It was something else she couldn't reconcile about him in her mind.

She set the first glass on the drying rack and heard James and his music on the stairs. He silenced his phone before he reached the bottom and smiled at her when she peeked over her shoulder at him. He hadn't touched her again since the morning he kissed her, but just looking at him made her chest tighten.

Not in fear. She was familiar with that sensation. This was something else entirely. It had been much easier to pretend he didn't affect her when she didn't know the taste of him, when she couldn't recall with crystal clarity the way his hands felt skimming along her hips or pressed against the small of her back.

"You didn't have to do those. I would have gotten them when I got home later."

He meant it too. Another thing about him that surprised her. He lifted his jacket from the hook by the door and slipped his arms into it.

"You did the cooking. I don't mind doing the washing up." When he lingered, she dried her hands on the towel and turned to lean back against the sink. "Early meeting?"

"Yeah, I have to meet my cousin to go over some paperwork."

"Declan?"

He smiled. "No. Different cousin. Declan's brother Aidan."

"Oh. How many cousins do you have?"

She bit her lip as soon as she asked the question. It was none of her business how many cousins or siblings or nieces or nephews or whatever else he might have. She didn't want him asking those questions about her, so she shouldn't be asking them of him. He didn't seem particularly put off by it, though, answering her easily.

"Three surviving. Finn died in an accident a few years ago."

"I'm really sorry to hear that. Were you close?"

"Yeah. We all grew up together. It was hard losing Finn so close to losing Maura."

Maura. Was that his wife? The articles she'd read about

him at the library had only ever called her his wife; they'd never mentioned her name. He looked as if he expected her to ask more questions, but she'd pried enough for one morning. She'd shoved her way into more than his family tree in the last few days, taking up far too much space in his life.

"Well." He drew out the word. "I shouldn't be gone all day unless something wild and crazy comes up." He said it like it was a distinct possibility. "You going to be okay working with the new girl?"

"I thought I was the new girl?"

He grinned, and there was that familiar flutter deep in her chest. The one he'd been giving her since the night they met.

"She's the new new girl. She's been training mostly under Clara for the swing shifts, but I think she's solid on her feet now. I trust you to show her the ropes."

"James," she said when he turned to go. "I've been looking at motels and stuff." His smile faltered, but she ignored it and what it might mean, pushing forward. "I'm trying to figure out my next steps. You've been very generous, but I'm sure you aren't interested in a roommate."

"I meant what I said about you not rushing out of here on my account, Delaney. I don't want you staying somewhere else unsafe just because you think I don't want you here."

He seemed so sincere. She hardly knew what to make of it, of him. She was trying so hard to fit him into the only box she understood, but he was constantly bursting free of it.

"I appreciate that. I'm still deciding for sure. I was thinking I could let you know by the end of the week."

This time his smile was forced. "Sure. Of course. I'll see you this afternoon."

He pinned her with one last long stare and then slipped out the door, closing it softly behind him. It was the right thing to do. Leaving. So why did it cause this knot to tighten in her stomach?

She sighed and turned back to the sink. Picking up the next glass, she gently washed it in the soapy water, rinsing it before adding it to the drying rack.

Everything was a confusing jumble in her head. Especially when she thought about how much she wanted to kiss him again. Before meeting James, she would have sworn up, down, and inside out that she would never be interested in kissing, touching, or having sex with a man ever again. James was quickly proving her wrong on all three counts.

She had absolutely no idea what to do about that. She couldn't afford to let her heart or her touch-starved body make stupid decisions her mind and soul would have to pay for later. She couldn't—wouldn't—find herself trapped again.

Setting the last dish onto the rack, she released the water from the sink and rinsed out the dirty suds before drying her hands on a kitchen towel. There was no more stalling. She'd given herself a deadline. An unnecessarily long deadline, but a deadline nonetheless.

Glancing at the clock over the stove, she shoved away from the counter and jogged up the stairs to get changed for work. Her door was closed, as she'd left it, and her duffel sat untouched on the floor of the closet. There were hangers on the rod and the dresser was empty, but she hadn't unpacked. What was the point?

She double-checked that the door was locked even though the apartment was empty and wriggled out of the leggings and tank she slept in and into jeans, tugging her Black Orchid shirt over her head. Quickly folding her clothes, she set them back inside her bag and pulled out the plastic bag she kept toiletries in.

Crossing into the bathroom, she brushed her teeth and ran a bit of product and some water through her hair to refresh it. She'd definitely need a wash day soon. Another reason to figure out her next move sooner rather than later.

Returning everything to her bag, she stared down at it. She'd taken it with her when she'd left for work yesterday out of habit more than anything else. But it's not like it was any more secure in her car where she usually stashed it than it was up here in her room.

Her room. She rolled her eyes, annoyed with herself, and hoisted her bag onto her shoulder. Three nights of decent sleep and she was thinking like a crazy person. Nothing here was hers except the things she kept neatly packed in her duffel. Not the room, not the space, and certainly not the man. It was dangerous to want things she couldn't have.

Carrying it down the stairs, she set it by the door and checked the clock one more time. If she had the minutes to spare, she'd make a second cup of coffee and enjoy it while she stared out the window at the busy street below. The life that teemed in Philly's streets reminded her so much of where she grew up.

She hadn't been back in almost a decade, and still the loss of it sat heavy on her chest. There was nothing for her there either. An empty house that had long since been reclaimed by the bank and auctioned to the highest bidder. Her mother's and grandmother's things were sold to strangers.

She'd wanted to grow old in that house once, to settle down there with a good husband and raise a family. She'd released that dream at the tender age of twenty-five, knowing she'd never be allowed to go home again.

When she finally got out, she thought about running there, but the fear she'd be tracked to a familiar place had warred with the shame of where she'd been, and she'd stayed away. Skirting around it as close as she dared but never touching it. Even in her wildest dreams, she'd given up on ever seeing it again.

Shaking herself out of the memories of a past she could never quite bury, she quickly stored the dishes in their places and gave the counter one final wipe down. It was almost ten, and she needed to hurry if she was going to be out of the parking lot before Addy pulled in.

Addy had a habit of showing up about thirty minutes before her shift to double-check pantry inventory and start her first pot of coffee of the day. The woman drank so much coffee Delaney was amazed she didn't shoot off like a bottle rocket by the end of the night.

Grabbing her purse off the counter, Delaney made her way to the door. She wasn't leaving, driving around for an hour, and coming back because she wanted to lie. It was just that she had a right to her privacy, same as anybody else.

So if Delaney wanted to pretend she wasn't staying in the spare bedroom in her boss's apartment while she debated whether she should give into the burning want to kiss him again or leave town, then that was her prerogative.

But leaving the door unlocked behind her reminded her she had a decision to make and not a lot of time to make it.

Chapter Sixteen

On Friday, James pulled up to the gate guarding the Callahan estate and punched in his code. The wrought iron opened on silent hinges, and he drove through the spindled trees and around the circular drive, parking behind Aidan's truck.

Letting himself in through the open garage, he followed the sound of voices back to the family room and poured himself two fingers of scotch from the minibar in the corner of the room. No kids for tonight's dinner. The next generation of Callahans were all safely tucked in bed upstairs or at home with their nannies.

He stood at the fringe and sipped his drink. The family had seemingly exploded overnight, with his cousins all finding their women, getting married, and having kids. It was nice to see, even if he occasionally found himself wondering what his life might look like now if Maura hadn't been stolen from him.

He'd spent months dealing with the bitterness that simmered in his chest when he thought about everything they'd gained and everything he'd lost. None of it was their fault. He could hardly punish them for it. So he'd settled into a different rhythm with them instead.

"What are you doing over here all by yourself?" Viv wondered, setting an empty glass on a tray and shifting to stand beside him.

"Just watching and observing. Are you glowing?"

Viv's mouth quirked up at the corner, but her eyes narrowed on his face before she gestured to her husband across the room. "Aidan told you, didn't he?"

James blinked big, innocent eyes at her. "Told me what?"

Laughing, Viv gave his arm a gentle shove. "He's the worst at keeping secrets, that one. My penance for demanding complete honesty, I guess."

"Your secret is safe with me," James assured her.

"What secret?" Evie refilled her wineglass and joined them. "The one that you're pregnant?"

Viv cut a sharp look at her husband. "Aidan! Did you tell the entire family? Or just these two?" She hooked a thumb at James and Evie.

"We all know you're pregnant," Brogan replied.

"I did not tell them!" Aidan insisted when Viv gave an angry squeak. "Well, I told James. But in my defense, I was sleep deprived."

"What's the point of my party now?" Viv sighed. "I'll have to cancel."

"Why?" Libby was curled up on the couch next to Brogan. "We like parties."

"How did you guys even figure it out?" Viv grumbled.

Aidan held his hand out to her, and she crossed the room, stepping into his arms. "You're not drinking right now, princess. They're not idiots."

"That's how I put it together. You didn't order wine when we had lunch the other day."

Viv frowned at Evie. "I don't *always* order wine."

"You're Italian," Evie replied, as if that simple fact invalidated Viv's entire argument.

"She's not wrong." Libby grinned into her own glass of Pinot at Viv's frustrated huff. "Congratulations, by the way."

Aidan laid his hands on his wife's stomach and grinned. "Thank you."

"Who else has a secret they want to share?"

"James is dating again," Aidan supplied.

"That's not a secret." James took another sip. "I'm sure half the syndicate knows by now."

"Definitely old news, but quite the hot topic among the single ladies, I'm told."

James rolled his eyes, eager to talk about anything else but his love life. Especially since the only woman he wanted right now was currently very off limits and sleeping in his guest bedroom.

"Where are the rest of us?" James wondered.

"Cait was picking up something for Evan's birthday party, and Declan is grabbing Sean from the airport. They should be here any minute," Evie said.

As if on cue, he heard the echo of voices drifting down the hallway before all three of them appeared in the doorway.

"Just the people we were waiting for." Evie turned her face up to Declan's for a kiss. "How was the flight?" she asked Sean.

Sean crossed to the minibar, pouring himself a shot of whiskey and downing it with a hiss before answering. "I fucking hate that thing."

"See!" Evie jabbed a finger in the air. "We need to get rid of that damned helicopter and get a jet."

"So you've said a million times," Declan replied as a maid stepped into the room to announce dinner was ready.

"It's happening," Evie assured him.

Chuckling, James followed the family into the dining

room and waited for them all to take their usual seats before sliding in next to his father.

"So." Declan turned to Sean once dinner had been served. "What's the update from New York?"

"I'm close to a final deal with McConnell. He assures me Fahey and O'Neil are both on board, but I'm going to set up a meet with all three. I don't think I can get him below 10 percent, though."

"What was the floor?" James wondered.

"Seven." Declan tapped his fingers on the table. "I'm willing to go ten, but I don't want it to look like he got the upper hand."

"If I let him open the negotiations, he'll go high. My guess would be fifteen."

Evie nodded. "But if we open at seven and they counter at fifteen, ten allows us to meet in the middle and save face. On both sides."

Sean inclined his head. "Exactly. Once they've agreed to let us run guns through the boroughs, we'll have to establish a base up there. Warehouses, men, living quarters. Driving convoys back and forth would be an unnecessary risk."

"I've been looking at some properties," Aidan said. "James and I found a few that look good in Queens, a couple others in Brooklyn. I'm not keen on telling them exactly where the warehouses are. A 10 percent cut of sales is all they need to know about the business we do. But if we could get them to draw up some territory maps to make sure we're not surrounded by street gangs or something, that would help us narrow down our search."

"Logistics-wise, I've got a solid team of about twelve guys I'd recommend sending up there. I can put together another team if you think it's necessary. A couple have families, so you'd want to decide if it's a permanent relocation or not."

Declan nodded at James. "Is the training program going to

net us enough people to replace them and not leave ourselves spread too thin?"

James saw his father shift in his seat. Sean hadn't been as vocal a dissenter as Mick Donahue about women joining their ranks, but they shared the same mind on it.

"Absolutely," James assured him. "I haven't attended any of the self-defense classes Evie and Reagan have been giving, but we've got at least twenty solid candidates who would do great work on the front lines."

"More who could provide backup or get a job and work on the inside somewhere," Brogan added.

"The self-defense classes are going well. I wouldn't put any of them on the front lines, but we're talking with maybe about a dozen women who are interested in some inside jobs. Several interested in being nurses," Evie added with a wistful smile at James.

"I had some wives approach me at a baby shower Viv and I went to last weekend," Cait added. "They asked me if I thought this was a good idea considering what happened to Finn." Cait twisted the wedding band she still wore around her finger and shared a look with Viv. "I think they were surprised by my answer."

"Which was?" Libby prompted.

"I told them this life asks a lot of all of us. Whether we sit at home and wait for our men or we go out and fight alongside them. We never know when we might be asked to sacrifice something we wished we could hold on to. But the choice would always be theirs."

"I think she convinced more than a few mothers to give their daughters the choice to decide for themselves," Viv said.

"Reagan will love knowing that's probably why attendance at Wednesday's class was so high." Evie reached across the table to take Cait's hand, squeezing it gently. "Thank you."

"It occurred to me that more people on our side isn't a bad thing." Cait smiled.

They finished dinner, chatting through the logistics of establishing a second base of operations in New York. If all went well, they'd set their sights on Boston, but Declan wanted to give it time. Boston was more volatile than New York, with more turf wars among the Irish there. He didn't want to risk wading into the mess until they knew this would be a viable and manageable revenue stream.

James had no doubt establishing this arm of the syndicate and creating a solid presence in New York would go well. The fact that Declan was willing to respect the city's mob bosses rather than going in guns blazing like any other asshole might do went a long way to establishing a relationship.

Creating tension and upheaval would interrupt the flow of money. For everyone. And Declan rarely allowed much to interrupt the flow of money into Callahan coffers. They weren't looking to rule New York, merely establish a base there and see what happened.

It was close to midnight when James left Glenmore House and decided to do some last-minute checks on inventory stock at their warehouses. They were delivering several big shipments over the weekend, and he wanted to do one last check before going home. And maybe a small part of him was hoping Delaney would be asleep by the time he got there.

She hadn't made any other mention of leaving, and he hadn't broached the subject either. He didn't want her to go, even though he knew he couldn't have her if she stayed. He selfishly wanted her to stay. He couldn't help it.

Every time she laughed or he caught her smiling at a customer or heard her teasing Addy or Clara, he toed a little closer to the line he promised himself he wouldn't cross. The line that stood between him wanting her from a distance and having her underneath him in his bed sobbing his name. It was a finer line than it should be.

Checking his watch, he locked up the last warehouse and headed back toward the Orchid. It was nearly two in the morning. In the time it would take him to drive across town, the pub would be closed and cleared of customers and the kitchen would be clean and quiet, waiting for tomorrow's busy Saturday rush.

As expected, the parking lot was empty save for Delaney's SUV, and he parked in his usual spot, letting himself into the kitchen and using the single light to make his way to the stairs. He locked the lower door and trudged up in the dark.

The upper door was locked, and he fumbled with his keys before he finally felt it slide home and the lock give way. He heard the faint rumbling of a laugh track when he opened the door, the flashing blue lights of the TV reflecting off the door of the microwave.

Closing the door and flipping the bolt into place, he scanned the living room. Maybe Delaney had left the TV on like she did at the motel. Something to ease her nerves over being alone.

He crossed to the living room to find the remote, pausing at the sound of her low chuckle followed quickly by the laugh track on the TV. Okay. Not asleep. Awake and cuddled up on his couch watching a sitcom, apparently.

Not wanting to scare her, he crossed back to the front door, opening and closing it with a little more force to announce his presence. When he turned back, he saw her head and shoulders above the cushions, and then the TV went dark.

"Hi." She turned to face him when he stopped beside the couch. "I couldn't sleep, and I wasn't sure when you'd be back, so I made some popcorn and...sorry."

"Sorry for what?"

She pushed off the couch and stepped around him to carry the bowl of popcorn into the kitchen. He leaned against the wall, one hand shoved into his pocket, and waited for her to explain.

"For taking over your living room." She dumped the popcorn kernels into the trash and immediately washed the bowl, setting it in the rack. "Besides, I should get to bed anyway."

"Delaney," he said softly, shifting when she stopped next to him at the bottom of the stairs. "You're allowed to use anything in the common areas of the house you want. You don't need my permission. As long as you stay here, what's mine is yours."

She looked up at him, and his eyes were drawn to the amber flecks in her own when they caught in the low light. He made the mistake of dropping his gaze to her lips, his mouth instantly watering at the sight. He wanted to do exactly what he'd been thinking about doing since that first time in the kitchen. He wanted to taste her again.

He shifted forward at the same time she did, and their bodies brushed, her forearm against his stomach, his against her hip. She smelled good. That was the only coherent thought he could string together. Her gaze locked on his mouth, and he barely swallowed the moan that bubbled up.

"Delaney."

"Yes?"

"I want to kiss you."

Her eyes darted up to meet his, and he saw surprise in them but also want. At least he hoped it was want. He wouldn't touch her if she said she didn't want it.

"Okay." Her voice was soft and breathy, and it made his knees weak. He wondered what she'd sound like with his tongue gliding over her skin.

"I don't want you to think that I'm doing it for any other reason than because I want to."

She inched closer until there was barely any space between them; her gaze remained steady on his. "Okay."

He slid his hand slowly around her waist, pressing against the small of her back to bring her body flush with his. She fit so perfectly that it seemed impossible.

"This isn't part of my master plan to get you to stay. You can leave whenever you want."

"James? Shut up and kiss me."

He didn't need any more invitation than that, bringing his lips down to meet hers and groaning when her arms instantly wrapped around his neck. She used him to steady herself as she pushed onto her tiptoes, and he braced her with his other hand on her hip.

It would be effortless to lift her into his arms and guide her legs around his waist, to carry her up the stairs and lay her down exactly where he wanted her—in the middle of his king-sized bed.

Instead he focused on the feel of her body against him, the long, lean lines of her, and the swell of her breasts as they pressed against his chest. Her breath came in shallow pants that frayed the edges of his control, so he focused on her tongue and the way she teased it over his lower lip, sighing when he slid his against it.

He let her set the pace and the pressure, content to drink her in and savor her for as long as she would let him. When she finally broke away, her dark brown eyes were cloudy and her lips swollen. It made him want to dip his head for another taste, but he didn't.

She slowly lowered herself to the floor and took a small step back. He hated feeling the cool air on his skin where her body had been. He searched her face to see if he could find any regret there; instead her mouth lifted into a small smile.

"Goodnight, James."

"Goodnight, Delaney."

He sagged against the arm of the couch while she jogged up the stairs. He waited until she closed her bedroom door and locked it before turning off the rest of the lights and following her up. Her light was still on, and he lingered for a second before turning and heading to his own bedroom.

Closing the door, he leaned back against it. The line he wasn't supposed to be crossing was fading more and more by the minute. And he wasn't entirely sure he cared enough to ink it back into place.

Chapter Seventeen

D elaney bolted up in bed, frantically looking around for the noise that had woken her. Another low rumble reverberated through the room. She rubbed her hands over her face. Just a truck driving by on the street.

It was an unfamiliar sensation, being jerked out of a sound sleep, because she hadn't let herself sleep that deeply in such a long time. She was used to being half alert, ears straining for even the slightest hint of danger. Even before she'd run, she could never let herself truly relax. It always seemed to hurt less when you were constantly prepared for it.

Twisting to look at the clock, she jolted. It was almost ten. So much for her plans to get up early and take a long, hot bath while James was out doing whatever he was doing this morning. She was sure he'd wake her up moving around, but she'd been too wrapped up in her dream to hear him.

Maybe because her dream had been about him. His hands on her waist, his lips against hers. Her dream had taken them farther than the kiss they'd shared in the living room the night before. He'd pressed kisses over her skin while his hands skimmed up under her shirt.

He'd groaned when she'd tightened her grip on his hair and guided his mouth to her breast. Then he'd rewarded her with a slow circling of his tongue over her nipple through the thin cotton of her tank top. Even now, she could feel them pebbled and aching at the memory of his mouth. The imagined, entirely fictional memory of his mouth.

She slid out of bed and crossed to the bathroom. Unwinding the scarf she'd tied around her head, she ran a bit of product through her hair and used her fingers to fluff out the curls. She rubbed moisturizer into her skin and, for the first time in a long time, thought about buying a little makeup to wear.

The idea felt ridiculous. Makeup was just one more unnecessary thing to haul around when she left again. Unless she didn't leave. She'd promised James an answer by tomorrow, and she was no closer to deciding one way or another. Well, that wasn't entirely true. She knew what she wanted to do; she just wasn't sure it was the right choice.

She wanted to stay, wanted to kiss him again, wanted to allow herself more. It would be easy; he'd weakened her defenses. Not with brute force, but with trust. He was constantly handing her the control, reminding her she could stop whatever happened between them at any moment, that all of it was her choice.

It had been so long since she felt like any of that was true, but she felt that way with him. He could be manipulating her, making her feel safe so when he pounced she was too stunned to see it coming, too dependent to leave. But even as she tried to paint him with that brush, it wouldn't stick. She knew the signs now. He didn't have any of them.

Hopping into a pair of jeans and pulling her Orchid t-shirt on over her head, Delaney stared down at her bag on the floor of the closet and slowly slid the door closed. Decision made, her heart thumped in her chest.

It felt both heady and terrifying to stay. It could be fine, or it could all go horribly wrong. She wouldn't know which one until she was in the thick of it. But she wasn't a doe-eyed co-ed anymore. She'd take it one day at a time and not look beyond that. It's not like she was looking for happily ever after. She didn't believe in them anyway.

Jogging down the stairs, she grabbed a banana from the bowl and peeled it on her way down to the pub. She was cutting it close, but she had a few minutes to spare before Addy showed up. Maybe she'd run to the store and grab that makeup. She was out of practice, but it couldn't be that hard to relearn some old tricks, could it?

The noise didn't even register until she tugged open the lower door, and then the sound washed over her. The pumping bass of Addy's music. Shit. What the hell was she doing here already? If the music was going, that meant she'd had at least one cup of coffee.

There was no way to sneak out from this spot unless she got lucky and Addy was in the walk-in. Even if she was busy in the freezer, Addy had definitely seen Delaney's car in the lot when she pulled in. Shit, shit, shit.

She didn't expect to keep this secret forever. Then again, she hadn't really known she'd be in Philadelphia much longer until a few minutes ago. Desperate to hear something over the noise, Delaney thought she could just make out the distinct whoosh of the walk-in door opening.

Perfect. She tugged open the door separating the stairs to the apartment from the rest of the kitchen. If she hurried, she could rush past the freezer without Addy being any the wiser that she was there. But she'd miscalculated.

The noise wasn't Addy going into the walk-in. She was coming out. And when she saw Delaney standing at the bottom of the hidden stairs, the door slowly swinging shut behind her, her mouth fell open.

"It's not what it looks like." Delaney silently kicked herself. The lamest line in the history of the English language.

Addy jerked as if Delaney's words had yanked her out of some kind of trance and carried the bowl she'd filled with ingredients into the kitchen, setting them on the counter. When Delaney followed, she reached over and violently pressed the button on the Bluetooth speaker to silence the music.

"It's none of my business what it looks like."

"Addy—"

"Really," Addy interrupted, neatly lining up her ingredients on the stainless steel table. "You're two grown adults who can do whatever you want in your free time."

"We're not sleeping together."

Addy's hands stilled, then reached for the beef she'd brought out from the walk-in, dumping it into a clean bowl and adding seasonings to it. Delaney was sure Addy didn't believe her, and that thought caught on something inside her.

This woman was the closest thing she'd had to a friend in a very long time. Clara too. She didn't want either of them to think less of her. Another attachment she hadn't allowed herself in what felt like forever. Worrying about what people thought of her.

"Morning!" called Clara's singsong voice from the hall. Jesus, why was everyone so early today? Clara appeared in the doorway and frowned. "What's wrong?"

"Nothing," Addy said quickly.

Delaney sighed when Clara's frown deepened. "If you'll let me, I want to be honest with you both."

Clara stepped further into the room, looking from Delaney to Addy and back again. "Be honest about what?"

"About why Addy saw me coming down from James's apartment this morning.

Like Addy's had done, Clara's mouth fell open. She

pivoted and disappeared into the pub. Delaney wrapped her arms around her middle and squeezed. She hadn't anticipated this being the hardest part of deciding to stay. When Clara returned with a barstool, Delaney couldn't help but shake her head.

Clara set the stool down in the middle of the kitchen, hopped onto it, and gestured at Delaney. "Go on."

"Last Sunday night, I was attacked in my motel room." She reached up to brush her fingertips over the rough scab of her healing cut. "I got back from my closing shift, and the manager and some other guy, probably a junkie, were waiting for me inside."

Clara gasped, and Addy stopped forming burger patties to listen, so Delaney continued. "They would have raped me —or worse—given half the chance. When I got away, there was only one place I could really think of to go."

"And of course James offered for you to stay," Clara said.

Delaney nodded. "In his spare bedroom." She glanced over at Addy, who had resumed her work, carefully placing formed burgers onto neatly cut parchment squares. "I should have left the next morning, but nothing else felt..."

"Safe?" Clara offered.

"Yeah. Nothing else felt as safe. I've been looking for somewhere else to stay, and I even considered leaving Philly completely. Heading down south where it's warmer, maybe."

"You're leaving?"

Delaney looked over at the hint of disappointment in Addy's voice. So she might be shocked or disapprove, but Addy didn't hate her. That was nice to know.

"No. I decided to stay."

"With James?"

Delaney tried to decide how to answer. She didn't want to stay anywhere else, but she was going to see if she could figure out how James felt about a roommate before making any concrete plans. It was true that nothing else felt as safe as he did, but there was something more there too. Something she wasn't sure she was ready to admit to herself, let alone these two women whose friendship she had come to value.

"Do you like him?" Clara wondered.

"Of course. He's a nice guy, a good boss, very fair."

"No." Clara shook her head. "Do you *like* him?"

Delaney felt heat flood her cheeks. "Well, I... I mean..."

Clara chuckled. "I'll take that as a yes. Despite what some people"—Clara shot a pointed look at Addy, who ignored her—"have to say about workplace romances, I think it's great. James *is* a nice guy, and he hasn't really been with anyone since his wife died. You two might be good for each other."

Delaney chewed on the inside of her cheek. She'd have to digest that bit of information later. "I don't think it's that serious. We haven't slept together, and I don't even know if he's interested in going that far."

"He's interested," Addy said matter-of-factly.

"Agreed." Clara bobbed her head. "He's always making eyes at you when you're not looking. If he hasn't kissed you yet, he's plain stupid. He has kissed you, though, hasn't he?" Clara squealed when Delaney nodded. "I knew it! And?"

Delaney blinked. "And what?"

"Oh, come on," Addy said. "Even I want to know how it was."

"It was..." How could she even convey that the way James kissed her calmed her nerves and ignited a fire inside her at the same time? "It was unexpectedly incredible."

"Are you going to bang him?"

"Jesus, Clara. Maybe that part is actually none of your business."

Clara dismissed Addy with a flip of her hair. "You didn't seem to think so when you were giving me a play-by-play of your hot night with that couple you picked up in a bar."

Addy sighed. "That was a hot night."

"Exactly." Clara turned back to Delaney. "So. Are you? Going to sleep together?"

Delaney was saved from having to answer by the sound of the exterior door slamming seconds before Mike appeared in the doorway. He looked at all three women, head slightly cocked like he was trying to figure out if they were gossiping about him or something unrelated.

"Anything interesting?"

Clara shared a knowing look with Delaney and Addy before sliding off the stool and lifting it with both hands. "No. I'll go over bar stock with you if you buy me lunch."

Mike held the swinging door between the kitchen and the dining room for Clara. "I always buy you lunch."

The door closing muffled Clara's reply, but Mike's laugh carried through and made Delaney smile. If those two weren't sleeping together, she'd be very surprised. Suddenly aware she was alone with Addy again, the smile dropped from her face, and she twisted to study the woman.

"I didn't expect any of this to happen. Your friendship is important to me, Addy, and I don't want to do anything to jeopardize it while I'm here."

"You say that like you might up and leave at a moment's notice."

Delaney swallowed hard. "I just never know where life is going to take me. I try not to look too far ahead."

Addy shaped the last patty and set it on a parchment square. She stacked the raw burgers and set them into a prep container, covering it with plastic wrap. She looked up at Delaney, the bright blue of her hair turning her green eyes to turquoise.

"James deserves a little happiness after everything he's been through. And I suspect you do too. Just be careful with each other. Because happiness can turn to regret in a blink."

Chapter Eighteen

James circled the training area where women had paired off and were practicing a series of self-defense moves. One combo after another until their opponent was on the floor. Then they switched off and started over. It was easier now, when their opponents were roughly the same size and strength level. Eventually he, Brogan, or Holt would play the attacker and finesse their form and strength.

It was easy to spot the ones who'd been practicing at home or doing the strength training exercises they'd given them. They moved faster, smoother, and with more direct purpose than the others, who seemed to flail about and hope their punch landed.

"Jade. If you leave your arm like that, your attacker is going to snap it in half. Closer to your body," he barked across the open space.

Jade immediately adjusted her arm and went into her next move. He watched her finish her set. Her lack of practice was evident in her sloppiness. She pivoted too slowly or made contact with the wrong part of her partner's body. If she couldn't get it right on someone about her height, she'd never get it on an attacker who would tower over her.

"Stop." He paused next to the pair of them and waited for Jade to brush her hair out of her eyes. "You're too slow."

Jade gave an exasperated huff. "I'm trying to remember all the steps."

"You don't need to remember all the steps. You only need to remember the next one. You're not answering a test question. Let your body remember the steps one at a time as you need them rather than wasting precious minutes making a list before you even begin."

James gestured at Jade's partner to move back. "If someone attacks you from behind, they're not going to wait for you to remember all the steps to get away before they drag you into the dark alley to rape you."

Without warning, he spun until he was behind her, wrapping his arm around her neck but not squeezing. "I'm a foot taller than you, my arm is around your neck, you're alone. What do you do first?" She hesitated. "Stop thinking," he commanded, tightening his arm around her neck to ramp up her adrenaline. "What's first?"

"Step forward with my left leg."

"Good." He started to drag her backward to throw her off balance. "And then?"

"Drop my right shoulder"—her body lurched as she moved—"and spin away from you." She shoved at his chest with both hands hard enough that he stumbled back a step. "Push you away from me."

"And run like hell." He grinned. "Very good. Even the smallest hesitation gives the other guy the upper hand. And that's the last thing we want him to have. Run it again."

He watched them run the sequence through twice more, correcting form for both of them. Jade was already doing better on the second pass. She just needed to get out of her own head.

"Thanks for filling in today," Reagan said once the students had filed out and it was quiet. "Evie had a last-minute thing she had to take care of with Declan."

"Not a problem. Pub is closed today anyway, and I don't mind ignoring all the paperwork I have to catch up on. I'll have to see if Brogan can keep me out of jail for tax evasion."

She laughed. "The syndicate has done worse things to avoid prison. I'm surprised I haven't seen Addy or Clara at one of these classes, though. Seems like it's something at least Addy would be into."

Reagan tugged her hair free of its ponytail and ran her fingers through the red strands to smooth them. She looked so much like Maura when she had her hair down.

"Addy's mentioned wanting to come a couple times. I honestly wish I could get Delaney into a class like this."

"The new girl you hired?"

"Yes." James helped Reagan tidy up the mats they'd laid down for sparring, stacking them against the far wall. "What's that look?"

"No look. I just think it's interesting." She waited for a beat before asking, "Aren't you going to ask what's interesting?"

"I have no doubt you'll tell me."

Reagan snorted. "What's interesting," she replied, empha-sizing the word, "is the fact that you hired outside the syndicate."

"There's nothing interesting about that." James straight-ened and shoved the last mat into place. "Declan hires outside the syndicate for his restaurants all the time. And plenty of people in Philly are looking for work."

"Uh huh. And in the year you've been open, you've never hired one of them. I have seen literal strangers walk in off the street to ask if you're hiring, and you always tell them no."

"So?"

"So." Reagan tilted her head to study him. "What was different about her?"

Absolutely everything. That was the problem.

James shrugged. "She helped me out in a pinch when Maizy flaked, and she was good at her job." He saw her cross her arms over her chest out of the corner of his eye.

"And that's the only reason?"

"Does there need to be another one?"

He turned away from the neatly stacked mats, hoping she'd drop it. She followed him at a jog to where they'd left their stuff, slipping on her coat and easing her hair out of the collar so it framed her face.

"How's dating going?"

"That's quite the segue."

"Is it?" Her smile was wide and innocent. He didn't believe it for a second. "Didn't you go out with Aisling Donahue a few times?" she continued. "How'd that go?"

"It was fine." He pulled on his jacket and headed for the door. "She's nice."

She followed him into the parking lot. "But you don't like her. At least not enough to get serious."

"Maybe it's because she's a cop." He reached up to tug her hair when they paused between their parked cars. "Feels too much like dating my sister."

Reagan swatted his hand away. "I am not a cop. I am a nerd who works with cops." She paused, her eyes searching his face. "I think it's good you're moving on. Healthy. And I think you should do that with whoever makes you happy."

Was she saying what he thought she was saying? Probably. Reagan's brain always seemed to work three steps ahead of everyone else's.

"And what if there are consequences for that?"

She waved a dismissive hand in the air. "You know me. I've always been more of an ask for forgiveness instead of permission kind of woman."

He watched as she climbed behind the wheel of her sedan and navigated out of the parking lot. He stood there, considering Reagan's words, until the wind bit through his jacket. He was ready to move on. That's why he'd started dating again. But he hadn't really expected happiness. At least not the kind of happy he'd had with Maura.

It wasn't even something he considered a possibility until he met Delaney, until she tugged at him in ways only one other woman ever had. He didn't quite know what to make of it. Or why the pull he felt was so strong.

He hadn't really understood it with Maura either. He'd just never had a reason to question it before. Never had an invisible barrier that would have prevented them from taking any kind of relationship as far as they wanted it to go.

He'd long since given up pretending he didn't want Delaney, didn't want to run his hands over every inch of her, didn't want to discover what kind of sounds she'd make while he was inside her. He couldn't pretend he didn't want to know every single thing about her even though he couldn't return the kind of honesty he craved. But what he wanted might not matter anyway.

She was asleep when he got home the night before, and he'd momentarily avoided her final verdict on whether she was planning on leaving, either Philadelphia or his apartment, he wasn't sure. Considering it was barely three in the afternoon, he didn't anticipate he'd get off so easy today.

Which meant getting too hung up on what might or might not make him happy seemed useless when all of it was wrapped up in a woman who could very well be gone in less than twenty-four hours. If she was even still there when he got back.

In an effort to drown out the voices in his head, he cranked up the radio and got lost in navigating the after-school traffic, starting and stopping behind buses depositing kids in front of apartment buildings and at the end of streets lined with rowhomes.

When he finally pulled into the parking lot, his fingers tightened on the steering wheel. Her car was still parked in its usual space. So she hadn't left. At least not yet. Stopping by his office on his way to the stairs, he grabbed the stack of paperwork he really needed to finish and tucked it under his arm.

He'd been considering hiring someone to do all this paper pushing bullshit. He'd stubbornly wanted to learn how to do it himself just to say he knew how, but he really hated it. Had from the very first moment. Tonight, however, it would be a welcome distraction in case the worst happened.

The upper door was locked, as it always was since she'd moved in, and he deftly unlocked it in the pitch black. Almost all the lights were on, and he wondered if Delaney did that to chase away the gloom of the day or because she was alone— or both.

He turned a few off on his way to the stairs, wanting to change after trading punches and fixing elbows and stances for most of the afternoon. When he neared the base of the stairs, he heard the music for the first time.

It wasn't a song he recognized; he didn't listen to much blues, but that wasn't what struck him. It was her voice. The clear alto rang out over whoever was singing on the track. She knew all the words, and she knew them well. And fuck. It was the most amazing thing he'd ever heard.

Not wanting her to stop but not wanting to scare her either, he made as much noise as he could on the stairs. He knew the minute she registered his presence because she stopped singing and turned the volume down.

When he crested the stairs, she surprised him again. She was playing pool by herself. Balls spread out on the felted tabletop, cue in hand as she slipped her phone into her back pocket.

"Hi. I hope it's okay that I... Hi," Delaney amended when he raised a brow, a smile pulling at the corner of his mouth.

"I didn't know you could play. I would have challenged you to a game days ago."

She smiled, a full genuine smile, and it erased a little more of that line he was trying so hard to keep in place. "I worked at a bar once before. When it was slow, we were allowed to play pool. Since it was in the middle of nowhere, it was slow a lot. I had a lot of time to practice." She hesitated. "Want to play?"

"Yeah. Rack them up, and I'll get changed real fast."

He heard the click of balls as he disappeared around the corner and into his bedroom. Locking the door behind him, he crossed to the closet and shoved all his clothes to the side, pushing against the flat surface of the wall until it depressed and slid away. He keyed in the number for the safe and pressed his finger to the biometric scanner.

When it opened with a whirring click, he lifted his gun and holster out of the waistband of his jeans and set them inside. Closing the safe and then the hidden door, he shuffled his clothes back into place and pulled on a fresh shirt.

Shit like this was exactly why he should keep his distance from her, not pull her closer. Problem was, he didn't seem to be able to help himself.

Chapter Nineteen

Delaney reset the balls with the triangular frame. Asking James to play pool had been an impulse, but she was grateful for the buffer. She still needed to tell him her final decision, and she'd do it better, gauge his reaction better, if her hands were busy.

She heard him coming down the hall and hung the frame on a peg on the wall. The black t-shirt he'd changed into exposed the bottom of a tattoo on the inside of his left bicep, and her fingers itched to explore it.

She loved tattoos. The artistry and the permanence of inking something important to you onto your skin. She had a small tattoo on her hip she'd gotten in college. After being forced to cover it up with makeup for so many years, she was afraid she'd grow to hate it. In the end, the tattoo and its memory had helped her escape.

"House shoots first?"

James shook his head as he dusted the tip of his cue. "Ladies first."

Moving around to the head of the table, Delaney placed

the cue ball and considered her shot. "Should we make a wager?"

"Loser makes dinner?" He raised a brow when she grinned. "Unless you can't cook, in which case I've got ten bucks."

She laughed. "It's been a while, but I can cook. Dinner it is."

Bending at the waist, she lined up her shot and sent the white ball careening into the colorful triangle. She loved the heavy cracks as the balls crashed into each other and zigzagged around the table. She sank one stripe and two solids and quickly glanced up at his face to check his mood. He was smiling.

"Woman. You could have fleeced me for cash."

Delaney laughed and circled the table to find her next shot. "But you're a surprisingly good cook, so this works out for me too."

She felt his eyes on her as she bent and sent the yellow ball into the corner pocket. This was going to be fun. She'd forgotten what it was like to have actual fun with a man without spending the entire night wondering what casual comment or gesture he might be upset about later.

She missed her next shot, the red ball ricocheting off the side pocket and bouncing off the opposite edge. She straightened, leaning against her pool cue. James bent over the table to line up his blue striped ball to the far corner, and his smooth shot was at odds with the electricity that sizzled through her when he spoke.

"I like knowing you'll still be here at dinnertime."

She barely registered his ball finding its pocket because she couldn't take her eyes off him. There was something utterly mesmerizing about his light blue eyes and dark brown hair, the permanent shadow of stubble on his jaw. She'd allowed herself to wonder more than once what that stubble would feel like as it trailed across her skin.

"I guess I owe you an answer. I tried to wait up for you last night, but I was exhausted."

"I was way later than I intended." He frowned. "Sorry. I should have called or something."

"Why? You don't answer to me. I'm only a houseguest."

"You're not *only* anything," he mumbled.

She blinked, unsure if she'd heard him correctly or she'd hallucinated the whole sentence. She wanted to ask him what he meant by that, but she couldn't bring herself to. "It's your turn," she said instead.

Missing his second shot, he leaned back against the red brick wall and waited. The way he watched her, his eyes tracking her every movement, should set her on edge. She knew what it was to be studied so the person could use whatever they thought they saw against you later. But it never felt like that with James. Instead it felt like he was committing everything about her to memory.

"So." He waited for her to line up, take her shot, and sink it. "You've decided?"

"Yeah. I think I have." She took a deep breath to steady herself. "I want to stay in Philadelphia."

His body jerked slightly, but he didn't move from his position against the wall. "Philly's a nice city."

"It's growing on me."

"Please tell me you're going to stay somewhere better than that shitty motel."

She shuddered. "I am absolutely not going back to that place."

She bit the inside of her lip. Maybe the next part of her plan was too forward. He'd been generous. She shouldn't expect to be able to stay with him. Except being here with

145

him was the only place that felt right. Even if she couldn't explain it.

"I was actually wondering if…"

His fingers tightened on his pool cue, but his tone was light. "If?"

"If you wouldn't mind a roommate?"

"A roommate." Without breaking eye contact, he snapped his cue into the holder attached to the wall and moved to stand in front of her. "You want to stay here?"

She lifted a shoulder in what she hoped was a casual gesture, but she wasn't sure she quite pulled it off with the way her heart was pounding. "It feels safe here. I can chip in for rent or do all the cooking. Or you can fire your cleaning service, and I'll clean once a week."

"That won't be necessary. Are you sure it's a good idea, though?"

There it was. The rejection. The proof that she'd read far too much into his willingness to put up with her and her mess.

"You're right. Maybe it's not. I don't want to impose or be in the way. I'll start looking for something right away. I'm sure there's something I can afford that's not dangerous or whatever."

James stepped just close enough that she had to tilt her head back to look up at him. His blue eyes had darkened, and she couldn't name the emotion that swirled in their depths, but it had something warm humming under her skin.

"That's not what I meant."

She swallowed hard. "What then?"

"All I can think about when I'm in the same room with you is how I want to kiss you. It's getting harder and harder to stop thinking about that."

"Maybe I'm thinking about that too." Feeling bold, she laid her cue down across the felt. "Maybe I can't stop thinking about your hands and your lips and that noise you make in the back of your throat when I press against you."

He took another step closer, and her ass hit the edge of the pool table. "As soon as I start thinking about kissing you, I can hear your little moans and sighs in my head, and then my brain wonders what other kinds of sounds you make. I don't know if it's a good idea to cross that line and find out."

Her eyes dropped to his lips, and every reason she'd listed in her head since meeting him about why she absolutely, positively could not get involved with this man was suddenly impossible to recall.

"Why not?" Her voice was a whisper.

"Because we can't uncross it." His breath fanned over her lips as he slowly, finally, pressed his body against hers. "Because I want to keep you safe."

"You make me feel safe." It was the truth, foreign as it was. "I want you to kiss me, James."

He hesitated for a fraction of a second before his mouth was on hers, his tongue teasing her lower lip while his arms circled her waist. He made that growling sound deep in his throat when she arched in his grip, her breasts dragging against his chest. She really did love that sound.

Uncrossable line or not, she wanted him, and she was tired of not letting herself have what she wanted. She'd been so careful for so long. Why couldn't she be reckless just this once?

She tilted her head, sighing when he immediately trailed his lips over her jaw to her earlobe, tracing the shell of her ear with the tip of his tongue. Working her hands under his t-shirt, she skimmed her fingernails over the lean muscles of his back.

Pushing his shirt up his torso, she stilled when he leaned away. "James. I want to cross the line with you. Even if you want me to leave after."

"Delaney, if we cross this line, I can guarantee that you leaving will be the last thing I want."

She tugged his shirt all the way off and tossed it on the floor. Leaning in to press a kiss along his shoulder, she sighed when his fingers caressed the bare skin of her hips, dipping into the waistband of her leggings.

"Cross the line with me, James."

Before she'd even fully formed the words, he lifted her up onto the edge of the pool table and stepped between her legs. His lips trailed hot kisses down the side of her neck while his hands worked her shirt up over her stomach and breasts. His mouth left her skin long enough to pull the shirt free and toss it on top of his own before he was touching her again.

He tasted her like a man starved, lips and tongue swirling from the base of her neck to her shoulder. He bent to press a kiss to the top of her breast while his fingers worked the catch of her bra, and she gasped. Immediately he slid his fingers away from her bra, and his touch slowed.

The sudden shift caught her off guard. Had he changed his mind and didn't know how to extract himself? No. He was still touching her. This time he was kissing his way across her shoulder, his hands tracing gentle circles over her back. She wanted more from him, more heat, more fire, more urgency.

Griping his face in her hands, Delaney brought his mouth to hers, capturing it in a searing kiss and shivering at his guttural groan when she nipped at his lips and tongue. There it was, that rushing electricity she craved from him.

He palmed her breasts through the fabric of her bra, and she arched against his touch. She ached to feel his hand against her naked skin, but he made no move to undo her bra. Releasing his face, she reached behind her back and undid the clasp herself, quickly discarding the thin fabric.

He paused, his eyes raking down her body, and for the

first time since giving into this impulse, she felt self-conscious. Like maybe she was as undesirable as she'd always been told, that sleeping with her really was a chore. James didn't hesitate in dispelling that notion, taking one nipple in his mouth and swirling his tongue across it while reaching up to gently pinch and tug the other one.

She gasped again, and his touch immediately changed, softened. He pulled back a second time. She moved his hand back to her breast, and he squeezed it gently, rolling her nipple between his fingers. When he bent to take her nipple into his mouth again, she understood. He was trying to learn her, what she did and didn't like or want. The idea that he even cared at all had tears pricking her eyes.

"James," she whispered, and he stilled again. "That feels good. Don't stop."

She shuddered when he increased the pressure, using his teeth on her breast, dragging his palm against her swollen nipple. He skimmed his hands down her sides and over her hips, hooking his thumbs in the waistband of her leggings, waiting until she lifted her hips to work them down over her ass and off her legs.

She should feel exposed, but his gaze heated her, his eyes roaming every inch of her naked body, and she wondered how she didn't catch on fire from the intensity of it.

James trailed his fingertips up the inside of her thigh, scratching lightly with his nails. "I want to taste you."

"Yes. Please." She sucked in a sharp breath when he immediately went to his knees. "Here?"

He glanced up at her, his eyes cloudy with lust, then back over his shoulder at the leather chairs behind them. "You'd rather the chair?"

"No. Yes. I mean…" She tried to gather her thoughts while he stared at her with those eyes, his fingers rubbing tight circles higher and higher up her thigh. "I don't want to mess up the pool table."

His grin was wicked. "The pool table can be cleaned. And I will enjoy knowing I had you on it."

"Will you?" Her breath caught in the back of her throat.

"Mmm." He spread her legs wide so she was forced to brace herself on her hands and kissed her thigh. "I promise you I will."

He held her gaze while he extended his tongue and dragged it up her slit. She hissed when he flicked it against her clit once, twice, three times.

"James," she groaned when he wrapped his lips around her clit and teased his fingers over her pussy.

"You're better than I imagined."

He slid one finger inside her, curling it up to drag against her g-spot, and she groaned. But he didn't slow this time, didn't stall. Instead he increased the pressure of his finger inside her and used his other hand to draw circles over her clit.

"How can I be better than you imagined?" She could barely get the words out as a second finger joined the first. "Nothing's happened yet."

"Nothing?" He increased the pressure against her clit. "I can feel your pussy clench down on my fingers every time I touch this spot right here." He grazed it inside her as he pumped in and out, and she squirmed. "Your hips rock when I pinch your clit like this."

She whimpered low in her throat when his fingers tightened around her clit, and her hips lifted off the table.

"Delaney?"

His fingers moved like a piston inside her, and she couldn't stop her hips from matching his rhythm, breath catching in the back of her throat when his fingers tightened on her clit again.

150

"Hmm?"

"I want to feel you come."

"Oh God."

"Can you do that for me?"

He curled his fingers inside her, the tips catching against that sensitive spot while his mouth replaced his pinching fingers, licking and sucking at her clit.

"Yes," she whimpered. "Fuck."

He pushed her closer and closer to the edge of control with his lips, his tongue, his fingers. He begged her to come undone for him, and when she did, she sobbed his name.

He stood up and settled between her thighs but didn't move to touch her again, waiting for her to set the pace. "More?"

She nodded. "More. I want to feel you inside me." She wouldn't normally be so bold, but caution couldn't penetrate the lusty haze in her brain.

James instantly scooped her up off the pool table and turned for the hallway. "Your room or mine?"

"Yours." She pressed her lips to the column of his throat. "I think your bed is bigger."

"And it's got condoms."

Grinning, he turned toward his room and shoved the door open with his shoulder. It was simple, like the guest room, but she could see little touches of him. A collection of watches on top of the dresser, a framed photo of a woman and a little boy, a big TV hung on the wall.

He set her down on the edge of the bed and worked his button and zipper open. She dragged her tongue over her lower lip as he tugged his jeans and boxers down his hips.

"I haven't been with anyone in a long time," she confessed. "Not anyone I wanted to be with anyway."

He frowned, but he didn't press her for an explanation.

"We don't have to do this. I can eat you until your eyes cross instead."

She laughed, her heart flip-flopping in her chest. "That is such a tempting offer. Maybe later. Right now, I very much want you."

James reached into the nightstand and pulled out a condom. "We only go as fast or as slow as you want, Delaney. Always."

She reached for the packet when he ripped it open and delighted in his low hiss and the subtle thrust of his hips when she slid the condom down his length and stroked back up.

"Let's start with slow and see what happens."

He eased her back on the bed and covered her body with his. She sighed at the weight of him, at the feel of his lips caressing the skin of her shoulder. She arched against his chest when his hand cupped her breast. It felt almost foreign to have a man touch her to elicit her pleasure and not his own.

Still, as much as she enjoyed it, as much as she wanted him, she couldn't stop her mind from drifting somewhere darker, somewhere forbidden, somewhere where she'd been unable to stop the man from climbing on top of her and doing whatever he wanted to her body. Her breath shuddered against James's ear, and he stilled.

He pulled back to look down at her, and all at once, she felt shame and embarrassment wash over her. He was not her tormentor; she couldn't imagine him ever doing those things to her. She couldn't tell him. He'd never want to touch her again, and it felt like too much, like too deep of a look inside her soul.

"I need to see your face," she whispered.

He didn't hesitate, rolling so he was on his back and she was positioned above him, her thighs straddling his hips.

152

When she shifted, she felt the brush of his length against her core, and she bit back a moan. The freedom to move, to see him, to be able to touch him as much or as little as she wanted, whenever she wanted, lifted a weight from her shoulders.

His hands caressed the tops of her thighs, and his fingertips traced over the shape of the tattoo on her hip, the one he'd been too busy to notice earlier. She felt herself slowly slide back into her body, felt the lust for him lick low in her belly.

Eyes never leaving his, she reached down to grip the base of his shaft and position his cock at her entrance, slowly sinking down onto his length. She felt his hands slide around to grip her ass, fingers digging in hard, but he didn't move, didn't lift her up and down or try to control the pace.

"I was right," he panted.

She leaned down to press a kiss to his lips, groaning at the way he felt as she moved. "Right about what?"

"You are far better than anything I could have imagined." He squeezed her thighs. "Take what you want from me, Delaney."

She sat up, bracing her hands against his chest, and lifted her hips until he slid almost all the way out of her and then sank slowly back down onto him again. He leaned up to capture her nipple in his mouth as she found her rhythm, fingernails digging into his chest as his lips and teeth and tongue worked over her breasts.

He ground his hips against hers with every downward thrust, and the pressure on her clit sent shock waves through her. "James," she pleaded. "More."

He gripped her hips and thrust up into her, swallowing her gasp with his mouth as his fingers dug into her skin. His thrusts were slow but hard and deep, and each time the friction against her clit made her shiver.

"Yes. Please."

She couldn't form full sentences, but he seemed to know exactly what she needed, punctuating her words with each thrust of his hips. But he let her stay on top, let her maintain control and drive his movements. She felt herself being shoved closer to the edge with each grinding thrust of his hips, each rock of her own, but this time she wanted to take him over the edge with her.

"James." His breath was hot against her cheek. Her hands braced on either side of his head. "I want you to come with me. I'm so close."

"Yes," he hissed in her ear.

She matched him thrust for thrust, desperate for her own release, desperate to feel him lose control. When he drove inside her with one last hard jerk of his hips, she tipped over the edge, stars clouding her vision, and her name was a strangled gasp on his lips when he flew with her.

Delaney collapsed on top of him, panting into the crook of his neck while she floated back down to earth. His hands slid up her back to her shoulders and down again, soothing, caressing, exploring.

"Am I dead?" She felt his laugh against her cheek. "If I'm dead, I've never been happier."

"Then we're both dead." He twisted to press a kiss to the top of her head. "Are you okay?"

Pushing up onto her hands, she studied him. "I'm the best I've been in a long time. Is this going to make me staying here weird?"

He twirled one of her curls around his finger. "Why would it be weird?"

She turned her head to press a kiss to his palm, smiling when he cupped her face. "In case I want to do that again."

"Do you? Want to do that again?"

"I think I do. A lot."

"Then it's definitely not weird." He sat up, wrapping his arms around her back and holding her tight against him, groaning when she wrapped her legs around his waist. "But I need to make one thing very clear first."

Her heart leapt into her throat, and she instinctively leaned away from him. So much so that he loosened his hold on her. This was the moment he laid down all his expectations, all his rules.

"Sex is not a condition of you staying here."

She jerked in his arms. That didn't even come close to what she thought he was going to say.

"Sex or no, you can stay here as long as you want. No rent, no cleaning. Just a safe place for you to live. Understood?"

"You mean that."

He sighed. "Of course I do. I want you to want me in your bed, Delaney. If there's ever a moment when you don't, we'll figure that out. Okay?"

She nodded and that flutter in her chest only he gave her beat a little faster. "Okay. James?"

"Yeah?" He brushed her hair off her face, tracing her jaw with his fingertips.

"Round two?"

Chapter Twenty

Rolling onto his side away from the harsh midmorning light burning through the window, James clutched the pillow he wished was Delaney to his chest. They'd come up for air to have dinner and finish their game of pool, though he'd barely been able to keep his hands off her long enough for her to win because she'd been playing in one of his t-shirts. The hem barely skimmed the tops of her thighs.

After beating him, they fell back into bed. But she hadn't stayed, and he hadn't pushed her. No matter how much he wanted to wrap around her and hold her all night long, he'd never push her.

She was running from something. She was scared, and he'd be damned if he ever gave her a reason to be scared of him. He'd much rather take his time and earn her trust, even if he didn't deserve it.

Giving up on falling back asleep, he shoved out of bed and slipped into the bathroom for a quick shower. She still hadn't stored any of her things in the bathroom. There were no bottles of shampoo or soap on the empty shelves in the shower, no makeup palettes on the sink, not even a tooth-brush in the medicine cabinet. He wondered if that would change now that she'd decided to stay.

Against his better judgment, he wanted her with him, and now that she was, he wondered if it was a mistake. Not just because he'd given in to everything he'd been trying to hold himself back from for weeks, but because he couldn't afford to have her this close for God knew how long. How was he supposed to keep his life a secret from the woman who lived across the hall?

He couldn't tell her about the syndicate, couldn't explain his late-night activities or why he might occasionally come home with blood on his clothes or the fact that there was a gun safe hidden in his closet. He couldn't let her see that he never left his apartment unarmed. Not even to work in the pub.

Turning off the water, he ran a towel over his head and chest and then wrapped it around his waist. He couldn't even introduce her to his family. Not that introducing her to his family was a thing he should be worrying about at this stage. He'd only known her for a month, only spent one night with her, but it would simply never be a possibility he could entertain.

At some point, he would have to let her go, and the only thing between now and that inevitable conclusion was how long he decided to torture himself with her. But that was a problem for another day. Maybe it was better knowing it wouldn't last forever. He could focus on enjoying whatever time they had together for as long as they had it.

He pulled on a pair of jeans and a long-sleeved shirt and padded barefoot down the hall. He could just hear her stir-ring as he passed her door and decided to leave her to her morning routine. They could save any awkwardness for breakfast. He felt like omelets today.

The shower rushed to life overhead as he pulled ingredients from the fridge and started chopping them. A bit of leftover pepper, ham, and some mushrooms. He poured them into a hot pan and let them cook while he cracked eggs into a bowl. Whisking them with salt and pepper, he heard the shower stop and the click of her bedroom door closing.

He was just pouring eggs over melted butter when she appeared at the top of the stairs. Her fingers toyed with the sleeves of her sweater as she made her way into the kitchen, her tell for when she was nervous or uncomfortable.

"This first omelet is all yours. Unless you want something else."

"No. I love omelets." She offered a thin smile. "Thanks."

He couldn't stand the way she looked at him, like she might bolt at any second. For the first time, he wondered if she regretted last night. He kicked himself. She'd told him she wanted to stay, that she felt safe here, and the first thing he'd done was give in to his own desire to fuck her. What an idiot.

"Are you okay? With…" Jesus, how did he even say it? "With everything that happened last night?"

She skirted the kitchen island and pulled the bread from the pantry, crossing to the toaster and adding two slices. "Yeah, last night was really great."

Something in her tone made him think that wasn't the whole of it, but he couldn't tell if she needed space or to be pulled close.

"I'll understand if you don't want to stay anymore after that. I can help you find somewhere else."

She stared into the toaster, and the silence stretched between them like a chasm. He slid the omelet he was making onto a plate as her toast popped up, and she jumped.

"Do you want me to leave?"

Her voice was so quiet, but he could hear it clearly, her need for reassurance. He laid a hand on her shoulder and ran it down the length of her arm, linking his fingers with hers and pulling her toward him. She wouldn't meet his gaze, and he cupped her cheek in his free hand, waiting until her eyes met his.

When they did, he leaned down and captured her lips in a kiss that was slow and soft and demanded nothing. She slid her arm around his waist, her hand fisting the shirt at the small of his back, and pushed up onto her tiptoes. He growled low in his chest, and she pulled away, a half smile teasing her lips.

"That's the sound you make," she murmured. "The one I love."

"I can't help it when you do that." He kissed her lips again quickly and released her. "I don't want you to leave. But I don't want you to regret us having slept together either."

"I thought you might regret it," she admitted, buttering her toast and setting it on the plate.

"Please. My only regret will be if we never do it again."

She laughed as he poured his own eggs into the pan and swirled it gently with a spatula. "Okay, well, I'm glad we cleared that up."

"Me too." He added bread to the toaster for himself, then shuffled the rest of the chopped vegetables on top of his gently cooking eggs. "You're always welcome in my bed. For sex or for sleeping or whatever else."

She paused with her fork halfway to her mouth, then nodded, taking the bite. "I'll keep that in mind. Is it okay if I make dinner tonight?"

"Of course. I really do have to catch up on a verifiable fuck ton of paperwork today." He gestured to the pile he'd left on the edge of the counter. "But I could go to the store this afternoon."

"Oh, no. My treat. I refuse to live here for free, so you're going to have to let me do a lot more cooking." She speared up another bite of egg. "But you're in charge of the omelets. This is delicious."

He grinned and plated his food, grabbing his toast out of the toaster when it popped up. "This was an easy one to master."

"Where did you learn to cook like this?"

"I taught myself after my wife died." He let the pang in his chest appear and subside before speaking again. "I lost myself for a few months after her accident, and her sister set me straight. You've met Reagan."

Delaney tilted her head. "The redhead, right?"

James nodded. "She's a very no-nonsense kind of person. Showed up at my house one day telling me to get my shit together because Maura would be embarrassed for me. She was right. So I did. Get my shit together, I mean."

"And part of that was learning how to cook?"

"Yeah." He chuckled and shook his head. "I was on a first-name basis with the pizza delivery guy. It was kind of a wake-up call."

"I'm sorry about your wife. I...I read about her."

He raised a brow. "Did you?"

She dipped her head and quickly took a bite of toast, chewing and swallowing before replying. "Before I started working at the Orchid. I, ah, googled you."

"I figured as much." She visibly relaxed. "You mentioned something about me being remarried when you met Reagan."

"Right. Subtle like a hammer. That's me."

"Oh, I don't know. You seem pretty mysterious."

He paused to see her reaction and watched the shutters slowly come down. He had no right to poke at her when he could never reciprocate a level of honesty any deeper than what Declan allowed to be printed in the papers. She rose from the table and carried her empty plate into the kitchen, setting it and her silverware into the dishwasher.

"I'm going to get out of your hair for a few hours. Let you get to all of that paperwork. Do you mind if I get a real coffee pot? Something small I can keep on the edge of the counter. Or in my room so it's not in the way."

"Delaney. You don't have to keep a coffee pot in your room. The only reason I don't have one is because I hate hot coffee. Not because they're forbidden."

"Okay. Thank you." She collected her purse from where she'd hung it by the door when she came downstairs and slipped into her jacket. "Is there anything you need from the store?"

"No, I'm good."

She smiled before disappearing down the stairs to the pub, and he scrubbed a hand over his face. Carrying his dishes into the kitchen and slotting them in the dishwasher next to hers, he sighed. What in the fresh hell had he gotten himself into?

Chapter Twenty-One

He stared at the message on his laptop screen. *No records match your search.* He'd been moving in circles ever since arriving in Indianapolis. Amy Parker was too common a name, and having no other details besides her name and photo, he was forced to comb through every single records database he could access, trying to match what he found with the pictures he had.

When he wasn't holed up in his hotel room tabbing through page after page of what felt like every Amy Parker this side of the Mississippi, he was flashing a brand new missing persons flyer at restaurants. Knowing she had a penchant for waiting tables, he started with the restaurants close to motels.

If she needed to get her car fixed, she probably wouldn't work somewhere that required a lot of driving. But Indianapolis was a big fucking city with plenty of motels, and he'd still only been to a fraction of the places that fit his criteria. She was a needle in a haystack unless he could get his hands on a broader database to search.

He put a call into a contact who could access some kind of

dark web database he didn't really understand, but it would give him a direct line to search for all her information. If she wasn't still in Indianapolis—and if he had to guess, she probably wasn't—he'd need more than confirmation that she'd been here to find her somewhere else. A social security number or a photo of her driver's license.

With that information, he could find her anywhere in the country, assuming she used the same details anywhere she got work. And why wouldn't she? She'd been gone long enough to start feeling comfortable, so comfortable she ran her mouth to the people at the bar and led him here.

He should have tried to get more details out of the guy, but the man was already suspicious, and he didn't want to shut him down completely. Which meant for now he was stuck sifting through these damn databases on his own while he waited to hear from his contact about that broader access.

At a knock on the door, he slid his gun off the edge of the desk and pushed out of the rickety office chair. Crossing to the peephole, he peered through it, then tucked his gun in the waistband of his jeans and pulled out his wallet.

"Got a pizza for—"

"Yeah, yeah. That's me."

He shoved bills at the gangly kid in his ugly orange and black uniform and slammed the door in his face. Shutting his laptop with a frustrated snap, he set the pizza box on top and bent to retrieve a can of Coke from the fridge. He popped the top and took a long pull.

Propping his legs up on the edge of the bed, he turned on the TV and fished a slice of pizza out of the box. He flipped through the limited channels while he chewed. Not even a football game on in this dump. Not that there'd be a good game to watch in this neck of the woods anyway, but anything would be better than *I Love Lucy* reruns.

He left it on a local news station and listened to the sexy

weather girl report that tomorrow's weather was going to be more of the same. Cold as fuck and windy. Christ, how did anyone survive up here?

His phone rang, and he grabbed it from on top of the dresser, swallowing the rest of his slice with a swig of Coke.

"Hello."

He strummed his fingers on the arm of his chair while he listened to the angry squawking on the other end. Clients really had very little patience for this part of the process. They somehow all thought just because they wrote a big check, they'd get every answer to their burning questions in a blink. Investigations took time. They took skill. They couldn't be rushed.

"I've tracked her to Indiana. Indianapolis," he said in response to the next question. "I'm still determining where she went next."

A pause. "Well, in my estimation, she likely stayed for a bit and got a job." He rubbed his temple. "I can appreciate that you think she was a lazy bitch, but she wouldn't have lasted this long without some cash, so she would have had to get it from somewhere." He rolled his eyes and sucked his teeth. "Even if she was spreading her legs for it."

He clenched his jaw and barely managed to keep his cool at the shouted insinuation that he was incompetent because he hadn't found her in a city with a population of nearly a million people. Correction. Hadn't found her *yet*.

He interrupted the long-winded rant by loudly clearing his throat. "I assure you I am doing everything I can to find her. I've started a canvass of local businesses and should have access to more digital records shortly." More screaming. "I'm doing everything I can. I'll call you when I know mo—"

The call ended with a series of monotonous beeps, and he tossed his phone onto the bed. Fucker. He was beginning to remember why he so rarely took jobs like this. People with this much money made his teeth ache. Entitled little shits too lazy or too privileged to do their own goddamn dirty work but didn't mind telling him how to do it.

It wasn't as if he wasn't looking. If he had to stay and show her picture to every goddamn business in Indianapolis, he would. Because that's what the client was paying him to do.

When his phone rang again, he scowled. If the prick was calling him back to yell some more, he wouldn't hold his tongue this time. He swiped his phone off the edge of the bed when he saw the readout and pressed the button to accept.

"That was faster than I expected."

"I used it as an excuse to get out of some dumb party the old lady wanted to drag me to."

He chuckled, grateful he'd never tied himself down with a woman. He liked to fuck them and leave them. Even better if he left them black and blue. "Well? Did you get me what I needed?"

"Yeah. I sent it to your secure email."

He pulled up his inbox and clicked the link his contact had sent him. It brought up pages of Amy Parkers, but it was easy to filter them out by age, race, and other identifying factors he could use to narrow it down. Perfect. If she'd worked on the books in Indiana, he'd be able to find her here. If she hadn't, well, that was a different story.

"I really appreciate this. Can anyone tell if I've been using this thing?"

"No. It's untraceable. But the more specific you can be, the better results you'll get. It's not a magic bullet."

"I'll start broad and go from there."

"You do that. If you can't find whoever you're looking for in there, then what?"

"Then they either worked for cash under the table or that fucker in Michigan gave me bad information."

165

His contact chuckled in his ear. "For that guy's sake, I hope he didn't."

He disconnected the call and started keying in broad filter parameters. He'd already wasted too much time in Indiana searching for this bitch. If the barman had given him bad intel, he'd take his happy ass back to Michigan for a little chat. The man would be lucky if anyone found him still breathing.

Chapter Twenty-Two

"I hate football," Addy grumbled, sliding the last burger of the night on top of a second patty and adding another slice of cheese. She shoved it under the broiler to melt and turned to plate up the remaining fries.

"I could live forever and never watch another game again and not be mad about it," Clara agreed.

"At least they all finally left," Delaney pointed out, munching on a now cold mozzarella stick. "I'm surprised James left us to fend for ourselves on a night this insanely busy."

Addy and Clara shared a look that Delaney had come to think of as their Top Secret Glance. Whatever they knew about where James was, they wouldn't share it with Delaney. It was a look that didn't use to bother her.

She had her own secrets. What did she need to know about his? Except the more time they spent together, the more he touched her, the more she saw who he really was as a person, the more she wanted to know everything about him. The more she wanted him to know everything about her.

But she couldn't risk that. It seemed almost laughable for

the thought to enter her mind at all when she couldn't even bring herself to fall asleep next to him. She wanted to. Every morning when she woke up cold and alone in her bed across the hall, she told herself James wouldn't hurt her no matter how vulnerable he found her.

But repeating that like a mantra in her head in the light of day did nothing to stop the anxiety that crept up her spine when it was dark and just the two of them in his big bed. It couldn't stop the way the panic tightened her throat at the memory of big hands wrapped around it.

She'd tried to sleep next to him two nights ago. It felt perfect to have his arm wrapped around her waist, her head pillowed on his bicep, his breath deep and steady against her bare shoulder. But despite her heavy eyelids and her body begging for sleep, she hadn't been able to let go, hadn't been able to stop thinking about all the times her vulnerability and trust had been used to hurt her.

In her heart of hearts, she knew James would never do that to her. For reasons she couldn't explain, she trusted every part of him, even the secret ones, but she couldn't make her brain catch up. She couldn't convince it he wasn't a threat in the dark.

"One double cheeseburger, no onions." Addy's voice jolted Delaney out of her thoughts as she slid the burger into a cardboard container and added fresh fries, passing the box through the window to Clara. "You sure you don't want anything before I clean up?"

"Yeah." Delaney waved away Addy's offer. "I have some leftovers upstairs, but honestly I'm so exhausted I might just crash."

"You should go up." Clara gave Delaney's shoulder a gentle nudge. "We'll finish up here."

"Are you sure?"

Clara gave a curt nod. "You worked a double, and it was a

madhouse today. I'm sure. I'll just sit here and eat this burger while I watch Addy clean."

"Thank you," Addy replied sarcastically. "That's very noble of you."

Clara took a big bite of her burger. "What can I say? I'm a good friend. Go," Clara said to Delaney, pointing to the door.

"Okay. I'm going." Delaney wrapped an arm around Clara's shoulders and squeezed. "Thank you. I'll see you both on Wednesday."

"Not me," Clara said. The new girl is officially flying solo, and I get a three-day weekend. You'll have to let me know how she does."

"I will," Delaney promised. "Night."

They started poking at each other before Delaney even made it all the way across the kitchen, and she shook her head as she climbed the stairs. Locking the door behind her, she looked first at the fridge and then toward the loft. She should eat something. If she didn't, she'd wake up nauseous and irritated with herself. Not the best way to start a morning.

Crossing to the fridge, she pulled out the leftover stir-fry she'd made the day before and put it in the microwave to warm. Her stomach growled when she opened the door, and she briefly eyed the table before carrying her food into the living room and sinking down onto the couch. She'd seen James eat on the couch several times, so she didn't think he'd mind, and it was so impossibly soft.

Turning the TV on for noise, she tucked into the stir-fry. It was better fresh and still needed some sesame oil to finish, but she was too hungry to be that picky about it. She flipped through the channels until finally settling on a sitcom she used to watch with her mom a million years ago and let the episodes she'd long since memorized soothe her while she ate.

Eyes still closed, Delaney tried to place the noise echoing through her room. It didn't sound like the usual traffic that drifted up from the street or the muffled noises James often made in the kitchen when he got up before she did. Gripping the blanket around her, she buried her face into the pillow and froze.

It wasn't the cool satin she was used to sleeping on to protect her hair. It was cotton and felt eerily similar to the pillows on the couch. Had she dragged one upstairs with her last night? The blanket felt thinner than usual, softer too.

She tried to remember the events of the night before, but the last thing she remembered was eating dinner in front of the TV. She heard the noise again, a faint rustling sound, and opened her eyes.

She wasn't upstairs, locked safely behind her bedroom door. She was on the couch, curled into a ball under the blanket that normally lay draped over the armchair in the corner.

The TV was off, the black screen reflecting the light from the sun that shone through the windows, and the dish she'd expected to find on the coffee table from her dinner last night wasn't there. The rustling returned, followed by the sound of the top clicking closed on the lid of the trash can, the clink of a bottle. No doubt James pulling one of his iced coffees out of the fridge.

She pushed slowly up to a sitting position, running her fingers through her hair before securing it in a thick ponytail on top of her head. She'd deal with that later. Once her heart stopped hammering against her rib cage. A reward for avoiding a panic attack over falling asleep on the couch and leaving herself exposed all fucking night.

Not ready to turn around, she folded the blanket with

trembling fingers and draped it over the back of the couch. When she did finally pivot toward the kitchen, James was standing at the island smiling at her, his eyes traveling over her face like he was taking her in.

"Hey, you. Good morning." He pointed to a box in the center of the island. "I brought breakfast."

"Are you just getting in?"

"No." He shook his head and took a swig of his iced coffee. "I got in very late last night—more like very early this morning—and you were asleep on the couch. I didn't have the heart to wake you, so I covered you up with the blanket and let you sleep."

He reached into the cabinet for two plates and set them on the counter. "When I woke up, you were still out, so I went to meet my cousin to handle a little business and brought back some of the best donuts in Philly."

He'd come in not once but twice, and she hadn't woken up? How could that be? She'd slept on high alert for years, her body and her brain constantly scanning for imminent threats. Her ears always perked for the slightest whisper of a sound.

It was hard to remember a time when she would have let herself relax so completely, sleep so deeply that she wouldn't hear someone come into the room. Hard to remember a time when she hadn't barricaded herself behind a locked door in order to get even just a few hours of sleep.

Tears pricked her eyes at the realization. It was like something cracked open inside her, and she could cry from the relief of it. It had been so long since she'd felt well and truly safe. James had given her that, and he didn't even know it.

"Are you okay?"

She looked up at him and smiled. "You let me sleep."

"You say that like you're surprised."

Closing the distance between them, she stopped in front

of him and laid her hands against his chest. "I am. You're always surprising me." She glanced over his shoulder at the open bakery box. "I love donuts, by the way."

"Good. I wasn't sure what you liked, so I got one of everything."

"I don't discriminate against donuts."

He chuckled, then sobered, reaching up to cup her cheek. "You sure you're okay?"

"I'm sure. But I want one thing before breakfast."

"Coffee?"

She shook her head. "This."

Sliding her hands up his chest and over his shoulders, she laced them behind his neck and pulled his mouth down for a kiss, groaning softly when his hands instantly gripped her hips and pulled her tight against him. He reached down to squeeze her ass, lifting her onto her tiptoes, and she nibbled his bottom lip in response.

He growled against her lips and turned them so his body pressed hers against the counter. She teased her tongue against his, shivering when he ground his hips into hers.

"I should have brought donuts home a long time ago," he said when she tilted her head to press kisses along his jaw, dragging her teeth over his earlobe, his fingers digging into her ass in response.

"I just realized something," she said, tracing a line down the column of his throat with her tongue.

"Tell me." His hand slid up her side, his fingertips brushing against the underside of her breast.

"I've never had sex in a kitchen before."

He cupped her breast and squeezed, and she hissed. "Never?"

"Never."

"We should fix that." His fingers deftly undid the button of her jeans, dragging down the zipper. "Right now."

"I agree."

They tore at each other's clothes. Him shoving her jeans and panties down her thighs, pressing kisses along her hip as he helped her out of them, her yanking his sweater over his head and throwing it somewhere behind her. Her Black Orchid shirt was followed quickly by her bra, and while his tongue circled her nipple, she seriously considered buying some sexier bra and panty sets.

"Why do I always end up naked before you?" she panted as he lifted her onto the counter.

He sucked her nipple, pulling back until it fell out of his mouth with a pop. "Because I love to look at you."

She ran her hand over the front of his jeans, squeezing the length of his cock through the fabric and making him groan. "I like to look at you too."

"Well, don't let me deprive you."

He dragged his thumb over her nipple, making her shiver while she undid the button of his jeans and worked down the zipper. Pushing his jeans and boxers down over his ass, she wrapped her fingers around his cock and stroked him from base to tip, sighing when his fingers tightened on her nipple.

He leaned in to press a kiss to her breast. "The condoms are upstairs. Don't go anywhere."

She watched him toe off his shoes and socks, shoving his jeans and boxers all the way off before sprinting for the stairs. She barely had time to think before he was in front of her again, holding up a condom between them and panting softly —from need or his race upstairs, she wasn't sure.

She gave him another long stroke, noting how he gripped the counter when she touched him, and then worked the condom down his length. She loved knowing she could please him as much as he pleased her. That he wanted her as much as she wanted him.

His fingers found her clit while his mouth worked her nipple, and she gasped, her hands tightening in his hair.

"Tell me what you want, Delaney."

She dropped her head back with a groan when he scraped his teeth over her nipple, his fingers applying more pressure against her clit. "I want you."

"Tell me."

"I want you to fuck me, James."

Her voice was a breathy sigh she hardly recognized, and his fingers left her before being replaced with the head of his cock. He traced it up and down her slit before slowly sinking inside her, his lips trailing across her shoulder as he ground his hips against hers.

She wrapped her legs around his waist, bringing his mouth up to meet hers as he pumped in and out of her, hips thrusting hard, fast, his tongue teasing over her lower lip.

"Yes," she sobbed when his fingers found her clit, and he didn't slow his pace.

"You're so pretty when you come for me, Delaney. I want to watch you come."

His fingers worked furiously over her clit, his cock pistoning inside her until she clenched around him and crested the wave of her orgasm. But he didn't stop, continuing to fuck her, easing her toward the next peak with his lips and teeth on her skin, his fingers on her sensitive clit, his cock pounding into her.

"James," she pleaded, her fingernails scoring across his back until he hissed. "I need... I want..."

"I know..." he said through gritted teeth. "Come for me again, and I will."

She shuddered at his words, at both the command and the promise in them. When he dipped his head to take her nipple into his mouth, she gasped, rocking, grinding, arching against him until she couldn't hold back, her release swamping her until she was dazed and spent with it. She wrapped around him, holding on tight until his body went taut and he gave himself over to her.

"I'm sure I'm not the first person to tell you this." He flicked his tongue against the side of her neck. "But you are perfect."

"You actually are the first person to tell me that. And thank you."

He leaned back, tracing his fingertips over her cheekbones and along the curve of her jaw. "Impossible. I'll have to make sure to tell you every day to make up for it."

She laughed, cupping his face in her hands and giving him a quick kiss. "I think the once is enough."

"Not even close. I want to take you upstairs and keep going, but I'm drowning in meetings today."

"I can wait."

He kissed the tip of her nose. "Let's clean up, and we'll have donuts before I have to leave again."

He lifted her off the counter and set her gently on her feet, scooping up their clothes on his way to the stairs. She trailed behind him, admiring his ass as he climbed, but instead of turning into her room to get changed, she followed him into the bathroom, smiling when he turned to look at her over his shoulder while he turned on the shower.

"Showering together is a great way to conserve water."

"Well." He reached for her hand and pulled her close, nipping her chin. "We wouldn't want to be wasteful."

Chapter Twenty-Three

J ames wanted nothing more than to stay home, naked, with Delaney all day, but he had to satisfy himself with making her come twice more in the shower.

He expected it to be a long one today. They were moving the bulk of their product up to the New York warehouse. A move he'd been preparing to make for weeks. Today was not the day to be distracted by thoughts of Delaney's thighs wrapped around his waist or how her fingers tightened in his hair when he tongued her nipple.

Declan and Evie were busy with a real-world event all day they couldn't get out of. Not ideal, but Aidan and Brogan were running point from Brogan's tech lair at Glenmore House. The word from his father in New York was that all systems were go.

James decided to separate the shipment in two and send them on different routes with plenty of cover. There would be three men in each truck, plus four supporting cars per caravan. Excessive, maybe, but he didn't want to leave hundreds of millions of dollars worth of weapons vulnerable to an attack.

Over the course of the last week, they strategically leaked multiple dates for the caravans, and the chatter Brogan monitored hadn't raised any alarm bells. They didn't have as many ears to the ground in New York, but that was changing. Declan had already been approached by bosses in other boroughs looking to make a deal. New York was going to turn out to be a very profitable investment.

The warehouse where they were loading the first shipment was buzzing with activity when James arrived. He'd chosen the men for each team with careful precision, and Declan had approved his choices for those who would remain behind in New York and oversee operations for at least six months before they reevaluated.

He checked the inventory against the list someone handed him while it was loaded into a moving van. There was no room for error today. Errors making this transfer had the potential to get someone killed or cost the syndicate millions. He didn't intend to be responsible for either one.

When his phone rang, he dug it out of his pocket. Aidan.

"Hey. Everything good?"

"Yeah," Aidan assured him. "No problems on our end. Chatter's quiet. We still on schedule?"

"We are. Last few crates for shipment number one are being loaded, then I'll do a briefing and send this group on their way. On time if not early."

"Perfect. I'm keeping Declan updated. We're still a green light."

"Great." James stepped out of the way as the last stack of crates was moved into the truck. "I'll call with another update once they're off. Let me know if anything changes."

Disconnecting the call, James shoved the phone back in his pocket and reconciled the last of the inventory. Once it was all loaded and the door secure, he waited for the men to gather and quiet before speaking.

177

"You're the first group, and you'll be taking route A to the warehouse. I've programmed two alternative routes in case shit goes down, but the word from Aidan is everything is quiet. Your orders are to drive straight to the warehouse in Queens—no stops—unload, and guard the place in shifts until the second shipment arrives later tonight. My father will oversee your arrival."

He shuffled the papers in his hands. "Car assignments. Three men in the truck, four men in each car. Two cars in front, two cars in back. The closer you get to New York, the less certain our position is. We'll keep the lead car updated, and it'll be your responsibility to update everyone else on your team. Questions?"

When no one spoke, he nodded. "Good. Let's roll out ahead of schedule, then."

He stood in the mouth of the warehouse's loading bay doors and watched them pull out of the gravel lot. Anticipation and nerves twisted in his gut, but he'd done all he could to make sure today was a success. Once the second load was gone, all he could really do was monitor from home base.

Roughly half of each team would stay behind in New York to establish a base presence there, with the entire operation overseen by Sean, who seemed more than happy to get out of Philadelphia. James had never been close with his father; the physical distance hadn't changed much. Sean still talked with Declan more than he did with his own son.

And as much as James might want to, he couldn't go with them anyway. Someone had to stay and take care of the business in Philly. He had four deliveries on the schedule this week alone. More product arriving next week for a new client Aidan landed the week before. Crime never slept.

Closing up this warehouse and locking it down tight, he drove to the next one. This one was just as active. The second team was scheduled to leave at the same time the first team made their initial hourly check-in.

"The rest of our guys get off okay?" Liam O'Sullivan hefted a box and slid it into the back of the truck while James scanned his supply list.

"Yeah. Ahead of schedule. No issues reported so far."

"My brother said the training sessions are going well." James's eyebrows shot up, and Liam shrugged. "We had a beer the other night."

Holt and Liam were at odds about nearly everything, including allowing women in the syndicate ranks. Listen to Holt tell it, and Liam sided with their father on everything simply to gain favor and hope to be named heir to the O'Sullivan line over his older brother.

The O'Sullivans preferred to choose an heir from each generation rather than it naturally falling to the first-born son. It made the competition between brothers more than a little cutthroat.

"I didn't realize you and Holt were on better terms since your last fight."

"It probably helps that I'll be staying behind in New York for a few weeks. He'll have time to work Pop onto his side."

James snorted. "You know Holt has only ever viewed taking over as head of the family as a duty. You're the one who sees it as a prize to be won."

Liam's jaw clenched. "That's because it is. It always has been."

"Maybe," James agreed. "But you're the one who chose to ruin your relationship with your brother over it."

The men finished loading the last of the crates into the back of the truck and checked their own personal weapons. James tried to keep the shipments as even as possible, but this one had some bigger guns along with ammo because it was pre-sold to one of Sean's contacts. They'd officially close the deal in a couple of days, which meant this shipment arriving safely was critical.

Triple-checking inventory, monitoring the loading, and checking in with Aidan and Brogan for updates kept him busy until the sun fell behind the trees rimming the property and the air chilled. They needed to pick up the pace if they wanted to stay on time.

With the last of the crates finally loaded, he handed out car assignments and gave them the same spiel. He was just about to send them off when his phone signaled, and he motioned for them to wait when he saw Declan's face flash across the screen.

"What's up?"

"Second team left yet?" Declan's voice was tight, and James straightened.

"Not yet. Problem?"

"Maybe. Niko Ivankov just showed up at this event to inform me his father would like me to know about a possible ambush."

"An ambush? By who?" The group standing around him all jerked to attention. "I haven't heard anything from the first team."

"He was light on the details. Apparently the Russians in New York want to test me. They reached out to Ivankov for assistance."

James swore under his breath. "How long ago did they do that?"

"I don't know. For his sake, I hope it was only today, or he'll be down another finger—or worse." James heard the lethal threat in his cousin's tone. "I've already notified your father, but I want you to put the first team on alert for any kind of Russian interference. I want all my product to arrive safely in New York, James."

"Absolutely. We might want to have Brogan expand his

monitoring. See if he can find his way into some databases in New York to keep an eye on things."

"Yes. Aidan is already on that. I'm stuck at this fucking thing a bit longer before I can bow out without causing a scene. Keep me posted." Declan didn't wait for a response before disconnecting the call.

"Looks like New York's Bratva haven't learned it's best not to fuck with the Callahan syndicate," James said. "Rumor is they might be attempting an ambush. I don't have any more than that," he added over the questions.

"My father's aware in New York, and I'll put the other team on alert. They should be making contact for their first check-in any minute. Which means you need to roll out and watch your six."

"We could delay by a day or two," one of the Gallagher cousins suggested.

James shook his head. "That only gives them more time to plan and strategize, which might be exactly what they're hoping for. There's no other way to get the product there under the radar, and splitting it into smaller shipments only makes for more targets and divided resources."

"We could take the longest route, throw them off," Liam suggested.

"Yeah," James agreed. "I think that's the new plan. Plus I want the cars around the truck in a diamond. One in front, one behind, one on either side. You'll have a better view that way. Check in every thirty minutes instead of every hour."

His phone chirped as the men split off toward their assigned vehicles—an incoming call from the first team—and he swiped the pad of his thumb across the screen.

"Hey, we've got an issue. I need you to—"

"We're being tailed," Maguire said.

"Fuck," James muttered. He didn't need to ask if Maguire

was sure. Their men were trained well enough to spot a tail. "For how long?"

"About twenty minutes. Two light-colored SUVs. New York plates."

"What's your location?" He secured the warehouse while he listened to the answer. "Why are you still so close?"

"Because I've been leading these fucks in circles as far out into the middle of nowhere as I can. I wanted to confirm before I reported in."

"Okay. Good. Keep circling them. I want to make sure we're covered from retaliation in New York before we take them out, but I'm on my way and calling in another team. I can be there in less than thirty minutes."

James jumped into his car and gunned the engine, peeling out of the parking lot. "Maguire, get your second lead car to break away and come up behind them. We'll flank when backup gets close."

"Copy."

The line went dead, and James punched in Declan's number. "We've got a problem. A tail on the first shipment." Declan bit off a curse. "New York plates, so I'll hazard a guess it's not Philly Bratva. Two SUVs. Maguire is leading them through the middle of nowhere. I'm heading up there to intercept and calling in backup."

"Do it. I'm wrapping it up here. I'll call Sean."

James dialed Aidan to have him rally the team on standby and floored it once the call was done. He would not have his carefully orchestrated plans derailed by some Russian cowboys from New York who wanted to test the power of the Callahan syndicate. If they wanted to play with fire, they were going to get burned.

Philly's streets gave way to suburbs as night fell, and James whipped past shopping malls and chain restaurants. A text from his father let him know the Irish in New York were more than happy to slap the Russians back into place and even happier to have the promise of Callahan firepower to do so.

When the road signs signaled he was close, James called Maguire and put him on speaker. "I'm almost right on you, and backup is about five minutes behind me. You good?"

"Yeah, they're idiots if they haven't realized I'm drawing them out."

"Let's hope they're idiots then," James replied. "How do I get to you?"

"If you're in the town, take a left at the sign for the park and follow that road. We're about two miles up."

"Make sure it's nice and secluded. None of them leave alive."

"Perfect," Maguire said.

Headlights flashed in James's rearview as he sat in the turn lane, and he honked his horn once. As soon as he turned onto this road, he knew they wouldn't have any trouble here. These Russians either thought it was their lucky day isolating the caravan or they'd made them. Either way, bullets would fly, and the Bratva assholes would never see home again.

The longer he drove, the denser the trees became, and James spotted the taillights from the caravan when he crested a hill. He sent a single-word text to Maguire and sped up. *Go.*

The lead car turned first and then the truck. Another car came from the opposite direction, flashing its lights, and James recognized the SUV as one of theirs. The two cars riding at the rear turned with the truck along with the two silver SUVs.

James kicked up gravel when he swerved onto the narrow road and lurched to a stop behind the SUVs. Syndicate men poured out of the cover cars at the same time the Russians did, and he ducked down against his Porsche when shots rang out. Popping up, he took aim over the hood and fired, watching the Russian closest to him drop to the ground.

In less than five minutes, all ten Bratva soldiers were dead at their feet, and not a single syndicate man had so much as a graze wound. James jogged over to the bodies, irritation warring with satisfaction in his chest.

"Load them back into their SUVs and drive them to McGee's," James ordered, stepping back when his men swarmed the vehicles. "You"—he gestured to the original team—"get back on the road. My father is expecting you. You shouldn't have any more problems, but if you do, he's your first call."

James stood in the dark while the men rushed to follow his orders. When it was finally quiet, he slipped his gun into the holster at his back and retrieved a small shovel from the trunk of his car, using it to cover up the blood soaking into the gravel from where the bodies had dropped.

Dousing the shovel with bleach and wrapping it in an old towel, he set it back in the trunk of his car and dialed Declan.

"Threat neutralized. Our men are back on the road. Based on what I'm hearing from Dad, we shouldn't have any more issues with the Bratva."

"I'm hearing the same. Good work today, James."

Tossing his phone onto the passenger seat, he drove home. He wanted a shower, a cold beer, and Delaney. In that order. Shit. Delaney. He looked down at his shirt, his hands. He wasn't covered in blood—this time—but he was dirty from digging, and since it was her day off, she wasn't likely to be out, allowing him to sneak in and store his gun in the safe before he saw her.

She didn't normally push him for information. She hadn't asked a single thing about the late nights he'd been keeping lately even though he could tell she wanted to. Still, this one would be hard to explain if she asked.

The light over the stove was on when he let himself into the apartment, but he didn't hear the TV, and the rest of the first floor was dark. It was unusual for her to be here and not have all the lights on. It was late, and her car was in the parking lot, but maybe she'd gone out with Addy or Clara to a movie or something.

He climbed the stairs, eager for that shower, but his gratitude for the privacy was short-lived when he saw the light spilling out from her room into the hallway. She must have heard him coming up because she met him at the doorway, her eyes traveling up and down his body.

She opened her mouth, but no words came out. Finally she dragged her gaze up to his face, but her body was in shadow from the light haloed behind her. He desperately wanted to know what she was thinking.

"Rough day?"

He barked out a laugh before he could stop himself. "You could say that."

She nodded slowly as if trying to piece together his long absence with his disheveled appearance. Or maybe she was listing out all the reasons staying here with him was a terrible idea. He could hardly blame her for that.

"I made some pasta for dinner. Why don't you take a shower, and I'll bring you a plate?"

"That sounds great."

When she pushed onto her tiptoes, careful not to touch him as she pressed a kiss to his lips, he held his breath.

"Are you hurt?"

"No," he whispered.

"Is anyone you love hurt?" He shook his head. "Good. You grab that shower, and after you eat, maybe we can go to sleep early. If you don't mind your bed being a little more crowded tonight."

She amazed him. He hardly deserved her. He wanted to

scoop her up and carry her into the shower with him, but he simply leaned down and brushed his lips against hers once, twice, a third time.

"Are you sure you're okay with that?"

Delaney smiled. "I'm sure."

She lingered a bit, and he thought she might finally ask him where the hell he'd been and what the hell he'd been doing, but eventually she stepped around him and padded barefoot down the hallway. He watched her go, and the tightness in his stomach spread up to his chest.

He wanted to be honest with her. He wanted to come home and tell her about his day and the bastards that had almost cost them more than a dozen lives and millions of dollars. He wanted to tell her everything about him. And he couldn't.

For now she was content not to ask questions, but he knew it wouldn't always be that way. Every day he watched her claim a little bit more of her confidence. At some point, she'd be brave enough to demand answers, and when that day came, he'd have to let her go. He already knew it would be one of the hardest days of his life.

Chapter Twenty-Four

Delaney brushed a fingertip over the dangling gems on a silver charm bracelet and watched them sway and catch in the light. Addy and Clara had insisted on coming to this craft fair after lunch, and since they rode together, Delaney was a captive audience.

Stalls were packed into the empty convention space and created wide rows for people to wander and browse. It was a beautiful array of all types of creative art, but it was busy. While she wasn't as uncomfortable with the crowd as she might have been a few months ago, this many people in an unfamiliar place made her nervous.

When a group of college girls approached the booth, she moved on to the next one with its brightly colored skeins of yarn stacked in boxes to look like a rainbow. Her grandmother tried to teach her to knit one summer, but Delaney had grown frustrated making lopsided dishcloths and uneven scarves, quickly giving up.

No matter how much her grandmother encouraged her to keep practicing, Delaney refused. At fifteen, she had far more interesting things to do with her time. Like flirting with the boy who lived three floors down from her grandmother's apartment and spending too much time on the phone with her friends.

Now she wished she'd spent that time sitting with her grandmother to watch her soaps in the afternoon or learning how to make one more family recipe or listening to stories about how her grandparents met.

She sighed. At least she had those memories. The one thing no one would ever be able to take from her. She might have lost her home and the people who loved her thanks to her bad choices, but she would always have the memory of her mama's laughter or her grandma's sweet potato pie.

"Hey!" Addy said, popping up beside her and making her jump. "Do you crochet or whatever?" she asked, gesturing at the yarn.

"No. My grandmother tried to teach me once." Delaney's smile was sad. "I was very bad at it. What did you buy?" She eyed the bag in Addy's hands.

Addy held it up with bright eyes. *Minuit Noir* was printed in bold letters on a pale pink background next to the silhouette of a woman. "Come see. You have to buy something."

Without waiting for a response, Addy gripped Delaney's hand and dragged her through the crowd, around a cut-through, and down the next aisle, stopping in front of a booth the size of two normal spaces. Inside were racks of lace negligees and satin corsets and colorful bra and panty sets.

Delaney frowned. "I thought this was a craft fair. Where everything is handmade."

A woman approached them, her black and gold braids piled high on her head in an elegant bun. "Everything here is handmade by me. I can also do custom sizing. Would you like a bra fitting?"

"She would," Addy said, giving Delaney a nudge forward.

Delaney shot a look at her friend, who only smiled, and followed the woman behind a curtain. Stripping off her t-shirt, she suddenly felt very uncomfortable in her cheap cotton bra. The woman pulled a measuring tape out of nowhere and deftly wrapped the cold plastic around Delaney's rib cage, noting the measurement and mumbling it to herself before repositioning the tape and taking a second, then a third measurement.

"You'd be a three-six in our sizing. But I would recommend something custom if you wanted a body suit or corset." The woman smiled. "Well, corsets are always better bespoke. Did you want to try something on?"

"Ah. Maybe just a bra. Or two," Delaney added.

"Do you care what color?" Delaney shook her head. "Perfect. I have a few I think would be beautiful with your skin tone. Be right back."

The woman slipped out and left Delaney alone in the stall. She didn't need a new bra. She had two that fit her just fine. Sure, they were nothing that would inspire sonnets, but they got the job done, and so far James hadn't complained while taking them off her. Something he did often enough.

That thought made her smile—*he* made her smile. The more she was with him, the more she wanted to be. He never pushed, never demanded, never asked for more than she was able to give. Even when she was ready to take the step to sleep in the same bed with him, he was patient. Always checking in to make sure she was comfortable or had what she needed.

Three nights ago, she'd woken from a nightmare to find him staring down at her, stroking her face, whispering that she was okay, that she was safe. Her normal instinct would have been to run, to not show any weakness that could be used against her later. Instead she curled into his side, breathed in the familiar scent of him, and let the heat of his body lull her back to sleep.

He was a gift, she was sure of it, and she'd started to let herself wonder what it would mean to stay in Philadelphia for the long term. She'd been on the run for so long that she never imagined she'd feel safe enough to settle anywhere. What would it look like to stay with him and maybe make a life together? Was it possible, knowing everything she'd run from? Would he even want that?

From the other side of the curtain, a soft knock dragged her out of her thoughts. "I have a few options for you in a few different styles." A hand appeared with hangers dangling from a finger. "I'm running a buy one get one promotion today, so if you buy the bra, the matching panties are free. Let me know if you need any help!"

Delaney took the bras, and the hand was gone again. She ran her fingers over the lace and satin and hung them on a hook secured over the curtain rod. She slipped the first one over her cotton bra but felt silly, contorting herself to remove her regular bra and then adjusting the cups and straps.

It was beautiful, with delicate embroidered detailing around the cups and a tiny satin bow between her breasts. The deep sapphire reminded her of James's eyes when he first woke up, and that reason alone made her want to buy it. She checked the price tag and winced a bit. Not as bad as she was expecting, but more than she'd spent on a bra in a long time.

She had the money, though. Living with James had allowed her to save up quite a bit, and with her mind straying toward sticking around Philadelphia for a while instead of running again, she could afford a little splurge.

Slipping off the blue satin, she traded it for red lace, and her eyes went wide. This one brought out the golden undertones in her skin, and she absolutely glowed. A must buy. She didn't even care about the price.

After trying on each one, she decided to buy the blue, the red, and a hot pink number with plunging cups and an adjustable strap. That one was both sexy and surprisingly comfortable.

Stepping out of the changing stall, she saw Clara and Addy talking at the mouth of the booth. When they spotted her, they smiled. Addy gave a wiggling cheer when Delaney pointed at the bras she was buying.

"You are a bad influence," Delaney said when she joined them, her purchases wrapped in baby pink tissue paper and tucked inside a paper bag.

"You love it," Addy said. "Besides, tell me the bra doesn't feel like a cloud is holding your tits."

Delaney laughed. "You got me there. It was so soft! And the fit was great too. What's next?"

"I was just telling Addy about a jewelry stall back that way." Clara pointed over her shoulder. "There's this pendant I need someone to talk me either into or out of. Then after that, I think I'm ready to go home."

"Sounds good to me."

Delaney trailed after them, content to people watch while their heads were bent close together in conversation. Quickly sidestepping a vendor spraying unsuspecting people with an acrid-smelling essential oil, she bumped into a man with blond hair and a neatly pressed white button-down.

For a split second, her heart lodged itself in her throat, and with every sense on high alert, she braced to run. Then he turned, his frown melting into a smile before a woman tugged his hand and led him in the opposite direction. Not who she thought it was. Why would it be?

If it had been him, though, she was prepared to run as fast as she could and never look back. She would never let herself get sucked back into his world again. She'd rather be dead.

Delaney took deep, steadying breaths, scanning the crowd

for Addy and Clara. Spotting Addy's bright blue hair, she jogged to catch up with them, rubbing her sweaty palms on the thighs of her jeans while she fought to control her breathing.

"Okay." Clara picked up a velvet bust and held it up for both of them to inspect the pendant hanging around the neck. "What do we think?"

It was big, probably about the size of a quail's egg. Diamond shaped rather than the oval Delaney had been expecting. It was pretty, but it didn't really seem like Clara's style.

She was trying to figure out how to let her friend down gently when Addy blurted, "You'll hate that after five minutes of wearing it."

Clara sighed and set the bust down on the table again. "The more I stare at it, the more I know you're right. But I want something shiny. I need shiny so I feel better about being alone on Valentine's Day."

Addy rolled her eyes. "Who the hell cares about Valentine's Day? Be your own valentine, for fuck's sake."

Clara pouted. "I care about being alone on Valentine's Day." She picked up a pair of earrings and held them up to her ear while she studied herself in a little stand mirror. "What about these?"

"Now those I like," Addy agreed. "You should get those. But not because of Valentine's Day."

Delaney's eyes scanned the crowd while they squabbled about the commercialism of a made-up holiday commemorating the horrific death of a martyr. She'd find it funny if her heart wasn't still pounding.

It could have been him. But it wasn't. And she was tired of living like this, always looking over her shoulder, wondering if he might have put all the pieces together and be on his way to claim her, to drag her back to hell disguised as a million-dollar mansion.

For the first time in a long time, she felt normal, like she didn't have to constantly gauge every threat. She wanted to be free. Really free. Not the kind of freedom she bought herself when she ran. That freedom was filled with never staying in one place for more than a few months and constantly worrying he'd show up out of nowhere and kill her this time. That freedom felt more and more like its own kind of prison.

But getting out felt impossible, insurmountable. In some ways, running had trapped her. It had been worth it then, when she couldn't imagine ever wanting someone else.

She tried to imagine a life where she could stop waiting for the other shoe to drop, where she could have love and commitment and tomorrows. It felt like too big a reach. Especially when the man she wanted that with had his own skeletons.

Whatever she might want, she knew enough to know that you couldn't build any kind of real life on secrets.

Chapter Twenty-Five

With an exasperated huff, James shoved the last piece of paperwork into a file drawer and slammed it shut with his foot. He had finally tamed the mountains that had been towering on his desk for weeks.

With their men and their weapons safely settled in New York and a lull in their sales here at home, James had more than two minutes to himself for the first time in a long time. Even Delaney was out with Addy and Clara, not that he viewed her as anything but the best kind of distraction.

They'd settled into a nice routine since she started sleeping in his bed. He liked having her there and not just because of the sex. Falling asleep with his nose buried in the nape of her neck and waking up with her head on his chest and her arm wrapped around his waist was something he hadn't let himself have in so long.

His mind had started fucking with him, dreaming up ways he might actually be able to keep her. Wondering if it was possible to bring his cousins around, to include her in his life without putting the family and the syndicate at risk. It wasn't likely.

Which is why he shoved the thought from his head no matter how many times it popped back in to torture him. It didn't matter what he wanted. His first duty was to the family, and if that meant letting her go to keep the family safe, to keep Delaney safe from him, then that's what he would do. When the time came.

But that time wasn't here yet. And until it was, he would enjoy her. They would enjoy each other. For however long they could.

Dropping back into his chair, he swiveled toward the computer and keyed up the website where he placed his weekly grocery order. Prices had gone up slightly, but not enough to eat into his comfortable profit margins.

He double-checked the order against the list Addy gave him and added a few more things for the garnishes he liked to keep stocked at the bar before hitting submit. They were set on liquor, but his usual supplier was running a sale, so he stocked up on his best sellers and added a couple of new beer samples to his order.

The door to the kitchen squeaked open and let in a rush of cold air down the hallway just as he submitted his order, and he turned toward the door in time to see Delaney standing in it. Her smile wrapped around him. She'd been smiling and laughing more in the last week than the entire time he'd known her.

"Did you three have fun?"

"We did." She held up a pink bag. "I even bought stuff."

"Clothes?"

A wide grin split her face. "Well, I can definitely wear them." She crossed the small space and stopped in front of him. He reached up to pull her into his lap, and she pressed her lips to his cheek, whispering against his ear. "I'll model them for you later."

He plucked the bag from her hands and peeled apart the layers of tissue paper to reveal satin and lace. He barely bit back a desperate groan.

"I'm going to hold you to that."

She nipped his chin and then eased back to survey the cleared desk. "You've been working hard today, it looks like. Last time I saw this place, there were papers up to here." She held her hand out over the desk.

"I don't think it was quite that bad." He adjusted her hand. "More like here. But yes, I did. I deserve a break."

"I'm happy to distract you."

He tightened his arm around her waist when she ran her fingers through his hair, her fingernails scratching along his scalp. "I want to take you out." She jerked in his lap. "On a date."

"Really? Why?"

"Because I think it would be fun spending time with you outside the walls of this building," he said. He couldn't say he thought he was falling in love with her. It was too soon and too cruel. "And I'll enjoy knowing you have something in this bag on under your clothes."

Humming low in her throat, she leaned in and pressed a lingering kiss to his lips. "I'm in. But only if you promise to peel it off me later."

He scoffed. "What kind of fool do you take me for?"

Her laugh was quick and bright. "What did you have in mind?"

"There's this new axe throwing bar Mike was telling me about."

"Axe throwing." She tilted her head, her fingers playing in the hair at the base of his skull, but he couldn't read her expression. "Is it a good idea to mix axes and alcohol?"

"I asked Mike the same thing. He said they have a drink limit." He nuzzled her neck. "I'll protect you."

"Of that, I have no doubt. Especially because you're always carrying a gun," she said after a beat, watching him closely.

His body went rigid, and his fingers flexed on her thigh. "What?"

"At the small of your back," she replied. She tried to keep her voice light, but there was something in her tone.

"And how do you feel knowing that?"

Delaney shifted in his lap, the bag crinkling when she reached up to cup his face. "Different than I expected. You aren't like anyone I've ever met before. You'll never know how grateful I am that of all the places I could have stopped for a drink that night, I wandered into the Orchid."

"I'm glad you did." He captured her lips in a kiss, sighing when she moved to straddle him. "I think we have some time before this place opens." His lips skimmed her throat.

"We should really make the most of it."

James lifted her onto the desk and eased between her thighs, taking the bag from her hands and setting it on the floor. "I have been thinking about doing this all day."

"Making out with me in your office?"

He slid his hands up under her shirt, pushing it up over her breasts and tugging the cups of her bra down so he could feast on her nipple, grinning when she sighed and tightened her fingers in his hair.

"Fucking you on this desk. Hard, fast, rough. But only if you—"

"I want that," she interrupted, reaching for the fly of his jeans and undoing it enough to slip her hand inside, cupping him. "I want you. Hard, fast, rough." She gasped when his teeth found her nipple. "Show me how much you want me, James."

Groaning softly when she squeezed him, he pulled her to her feet and turned her in his arms, drawing her back against his chest and grinding his cock against her ass. Running his hands under her shirt, he palmed her breasts, dragging the pads of his thumbs over her nipples and leaning down to whisper against her ear.

"I love the sounds you make when I touch you."

He slid his hands down to the waistband of her jeans, flicking open the button and dragging down the zipper. He used one hand to work the denim over her hip while he slid the other inside and grazed her clit with his fingertips.

"That one might be my favorite," he whispered when she gasped. "That husky sound in the back of your throat. I wonder what other sounds you might make when I fuck you from behind."

She whimpered softly when he braced her hands on the desk and worked her jeans down around her thighs. "That's a good one too."

Sliding open the top drawer of the desk, he pulled out a condom.

"You always keep those in your desk?"

He laughed as he freed his cock and slid the latex in place, fingers tracing across her hip and down to her pussy to rub against her clit. "Hoping I'd get to live out this fantasy right here. With you. You're in control, Delaney," he said, his cock brushing against her slit and making her groan.

"Yes. Don't stop."

Before she even finished the sentence, he sank into her to the hilt, her hips jerking back against his. "You are exquisite," he breathed. "Hard, fast, rough?"

James waited until she nodded before sliding out and slamming back home again, gritting his teeth at the way she clenched around him. She made him want everything he shouldn't when she gave herself over to him, when she trusted him with her body. But he didn't want to think about that now.

He only wanted to think about the way she moved with him, her hips grinding against his with each thrust, her body vibrating when he drew rough circles over her clit and squeezed her nipple between his fingers.

He wanted to hear more of her panting moans as his teeth dragged across her shoulder while he fucked her. He wanted to feel her shatter in his arms and sob with relief so he could relentlessly push her toward another peak until he was satisfied that no one else had ever made her feel the way he did.

It was selfish, but he wanted to imprint himself on her memory so when this was over, she'd always remember him. Long after she moved on, he wanted her to think about him and smile at the memory of the way he touched her, the way he made her feel.

When her body went taut and her back bowed, he wrapped his arm around her waist to hold her in place while he pounded her through her orgasm. "That's so good," he groaned in her ear. "Come for me just like that."

His fingers strummed her clit, unrelenting, his cock sliding in and out of her as she convulsed around him.

"James," she whimpered, and it only made him want her more. "I want…" She shuddered when he pressed hard against her clit, hips grinding against her ass. "I want…"

"I know," he whispered when she couldn't find the words. "Come for me again, and I'll come with you."

"Yes," she hissed, rocking back into him with each deep, hard thrust.

He cupped her breast as she started to shake, tweaking her nipple and making her groan. She always came so much harder the second time, and he loved every fucking second of it.

Keeping a steady pace with his cock and fingers and teeth,

he drove her toward the second peak until she screamed his name and then followed her over, arm cinched tight around her waist while he lost himself in her.

"Oh, wow." Her breathing was ragged, and he felt the rise and fall of her chest under his palm. "How do you do that to me?"

James pressed a lazy kiss to her shoulder and sank into his chair, pulling her into his lap before they both fell over. "A careful analysis of what drives you out of your fucking mind."

She laughed and leaned her head back against his chest. "You're an awfully quick study."

"You"—he nibbled her earlobe—"are my favorite subject."

"Maybe we should stay home." Delaney squirmed in his lap while he traced the shell of her ear with the tip of his tongue. "We could study some more."

"Let me take you out. I want to." It surprised him how much. "But don't expect to get much sleep tonight."

"Mmm," she murmured. "I have a great boss. He'll understand if I'm a little late for work tomorrow."

Grinning, James set her on her feet and tugged her jeans and panties back up over her hips before giving her ass a squeeze. "Lucky you. I still want you to wear something you bought today. But don't tell me which one. I want it to be a surprise."

"Deal." She leaned down and pressed a quick kiss to his lips before scooping the bag off the floor and jogging upstairs.

He listened to her go, scrubbing a hand over his face. Taking her out into public was a risk. Addy and Clara knew, and Reagan might have suspected, but as far as he could tell, he hadn't become the subject of syndicate gossip. If he wanted to keep it that way, they should really stay home instead.

But he didn't know how much longer they had together.

How much longer she would notice things like him coming home covered in dirt and carrying a gun everywhere and not ask questions. The minute she did, he'd have to end it. If he had to ultimately lose another woman to this life, then he deserved to have a little taste of normal with her before he had to let her go.

Chapter Twenty-Six

He waited in the back corner of the parking lot, his truck wedged between the dumpster and a wooden fence separating a back patio area belonging to the restaurant next door from the lot. He'd been sitting there for hours, slumped down in his seat, pretending to be asleep but carefully watching the back of the building.

There was only one other car in the little employee lot, and the last server had left about thirty minutes ago, so he didn't think he'd have to wait much longer. He was determined to get the answers he came for.

After spending several more days in Indianapolis talking to restaurant owners and narrowing his search in the database, he couldn't shake the feeling that this son of a bitch had given him the runaround. Call it a hunch or a gut feeling or whatever the fuck, but he couldn't ignore the sensation that he'd been had.

Abandoning Indianapolis, he'd spent two days driving through a snowstorm to find his way back to Ann Arbor and then another two days sitting on the restaurant to make sure he could identify the guy's car and some kind of regular hours. He must be the owner because he'd been there open to close both days and was the only one who never left to take a break.

The client had paid his monthly invoice and told him to do whatever was necessary to find this girl as soon as possible. He intended to do just that. Starting with getting some real answers out of this guy. And if the man didn't have any fresh information, at least he would feel better for taking his frustrations out on someone.

The back door opened, and light spilled out over the pavement. He sat up straighter and tracked the man's path over the roughly plowed lot toward his vehicle. The newer Jeep was parked under a security light, but the parking lot was shielded from the street by a privacy fence and a couple of shade trees.

"Hey there." The man whipped around, keys held out in front of him like a weapon. Then recognition lit his eyes, and he relaxed a bit. His first mistake. "Remember me?"

"You're the guy looking for his sister, right?"

"That's right." He shifted to block the man from view of anyone who might wander past the narrow opening to the lot.

"Any luck down in Indianapolis?"

Without warning, he lashed out with a sucker punch to the gut, cracking his neck with a satisfied grin when the man doubled over and wheezed.

"I think you and I both know I didn't find anything."

"What the fuck, man? I told you maybe she didn't want to be found."

He reached down to grip the man's shirt and hauled him back to a standing position. "I remember. But see, I got a hunch you weren't being totally honest with me about her." He shoved another fist into the man's stomach. "My hunches are usually spot on."

"You're insane," the man sputtered. "I told you everything I know about her."

The next punch connected with the man's jaw and had his head snapping back violently. "Unfortunately for you, I don't believe you. What's her name?"

The man swayed on his feet and then made a half-hearted attempt to rush him, but his grip was weak, and he could tell the motion made him dizzy. He brought his knee up into the man's groin, and he made a strangled sound in the back of his throat before dropping to the ground.

He crouched down and gripped the man's hair, lifting his head out of the dirty snow. "You hippie freaks can't even fight back around here. Now. We can do this the easy way or the hard way. I'll enjoy myself no matter what you choose."

"Fuck you. That girl is scared, and now I know why. I'm not telling you shit."

Pushing to his feet, he kicked the man in the stomach once, twice, three times, and the pitiful whimpers that drifted up from the ground were like music to his ears. There was a time to gather information and a time to employ brute force. Christ, he missed using his fists to find the details he wanted.

"You sure that bitch is worth all this?"

"I'm sure." The man coughed. "If this is what you're willing to do to me, I can only imagine what you'd do to her if you actually found her."

He was down, gripping the man's throat in an instant. "So you *were* holding out on me." He squeezed until the man gasped. "You ready to die to keep her secret? She's not worth the sacrifice."

"Go to hell."

He squeezed harder, enjoying the way the man's lips and then his nose and then his whole face turned blue. "How about I kill you and root around in your little shithole of a bar and find the information I want myself? Then you'll be dead, and she'll be mine. A win-win for me."

The man rolled onto his stomach and tried to push to his feet, but he shoved him back down with a boot. Bracing his gloved hands on the Jeep for leverage, he rammed his foot into whatever body parts he could make contact with. He listened to the sounds of wheezing pleas and grunted protests and cracking bones, kicking long after the man stopped moving.

Out of breath and aware he couldn't linger too much longer if he didn't want to get caught, he crouched down next to the man and patted his pockets until he found a set of keys. Dragging the body out of the yellow beam of light and wiping the blood off his boots in the snow, he jogged across the parking lot and tried the different keys until he found the right one.

Not wanting to draw attention to the place, he let the dim security lights lead him to a door marked Office Staff Only and tried more keys until it finally swung in. It was tidy, a desk pushed up against the far wall with three tall file cabinets lined up in the opposite corner.

He closed the door behind him and turned on the light. He'd left the guy bleeding, if not dead, at the edge of the parking lot, so he prayed this guy didn't have hundreds of employee records in these damn cabinets. They were unlocked, a blessing, and he slid open the top drawer of the one closest to the desk.

Old menus and coupons and other useless crap. The next three drawers in this cabinet held more of the same. The second cabinet looked like financials. Purchase orders, receipts, tax shit. He didn't have time to comb through W-2s. He needed employee files.

In the bottom drawer of the third cabinet, he struck gold. File folders neatly arranged in alphabetical order with employee names written in bold Sharpie. He pulled the first one all the way out and flipped it open. Right on top was a photocopy of their driver's license. A slow grin spread over his face. Fucking bingo.

Slipping the folder back into the drawer, he quickly leafed through the rest. He grew more irritated by the second until he found her near the very back. He pulled the folder from the drawer and laid it open.

A Nebraska driver's license. Clever bitch. These weren't just fakes; they were good fakes, expensive ones, and with forgeries like these, there was no way she was working under a different name in every state.

He had her now. As soon as he had visual confirmation, he'd call his client. Or maybe he'd take a few days and play out some of the fantasies he'd spun in his mind on these long, lonely nights on the road. Then his irritating prick of a client could have her.

Tucking the folder under his arm, he switched off the light and locked the office door behind him. He backtracked down the long hallway to the rear door and poked his head out to make sure the parking lot was still empty.

Seeing no one, he jogged quickly back to the Jeep and shoved the keys back in the guy's pockets. Definitely dead. Served him right for getting in the way.

Now that he had what he came for, he needed to get the fuck out of here. The lot didn't have cameras, but that didn't mean he wanted to hang around and wait for someone to spot him a few dozen yards from a dead body. Climbing into his truck, he drove slowly onto the street and around the corner.

He wanted to get as far away from Ann Arbor as possible before he was forced to stop and sleep. Pulling into a rundown gas station, he bought maps for both Illinois and Ohio and some shitty coffee before filling up at the pump.

Tank full and burned coffee scorching his insides, he reached for the file folder on the seat and flipped it open to her picture. She'd changed her hair, and her smile wasn't as bright or as innocent as the ones he had of her. But she was as beautiful as ever. He traced a finger over the outline of her cheek.

"I'll see you soon, Delaney Williams."

Chapter Twenty-Seven

The bar was busy for a weeknight but not crowded, and James kept her hand firmly in his as they wound past groups of people already flinging axes at walls. Delaney smiled when he helped her out of her jacket. It wasn't a gesture she was unfamiliar with, but she knew he wasn't being kind with the expectation of repayment.

"Can I get you guys something to eat or drink?" The waiter had short, spiky blond hair and a thick black choker necklace that seemed at odds with his red and black plaid shirt.

James gestured for Delaney to order first while he hung their jackets on a peg. Another refreshing thing about him. He didn't insist on ordering for her.

"I'll have a rum and Coke, please."

"I'll take your winter lager."

"Tap or bottle?" The kid sounded bored.

"Bottle. Want anything to eat?" James shot a look at Delaney. She chewed on her bottom lip. "Anything you want," he added, reading her hesitation.

"Cheese fries?"

He grinned. "With extra bacon."

The kid nodded and scurried off, and James pulled her in close for a kiss. "You sure you don't want something else?"

"Maybe later. As a reward for not killing myself with an axe."

He chuckled. "I won't let you kill yourself. Besides, the guy showed us how to duck."

"A basic but useful skill." He reached for the axe secured in a holder on the wall and held it out to her. She waved him away. "Oh no. You first. If you live, I'll try it."

He stepped up to the line painted on the floor and lifted it over his head, the metal glinting in the light. With one fluid movement, he heaved the axe at the bullseye on the far wall, and the blade lodged into the wood with a thwack.

"Shit, that was satisfying. Okay." He tugged it free from the wall and brought it back to her. "Your turn."

She hopped off the stool positioned behind a long, thin table at the back of their lane and took the axe from his hands.

"If I chop off a toe or something, you're responsible for sewing it back on."

"Don't be silly. I'll take you to see Doc."

Delaney peeked over her shoulder at him, scrunching her nose at his winning smile before turning her attention back to the weapon in her hands. She tightened her fingers around the base, trying to remember the instructions from their practice session when they first arrived.

Hold it low on the handle with both hands but don't grip it too tight. She relaxed her fingers, lining up her thumb the way the instructor showed them. Bring both arms back over her head, swing forward, release.

The axe hurtled toward the wall but struck it with the back of the axe and not the blade, falling to the floor with a sad clang. She stuck her lip out in a pout, then tried to suck it in while James immediately went for the axe, grinning at the look on her face.

"Aww, don't pout, beautiful. You released it too high."

"I don't even know what that means!"

He stopped next to her and demonstrated. "Your grip was good. Not too tight. But you let it go up here." He held it up so the back side of the blade was parallel with the top of his forehead. "You want to release it when it's here." He moved it down until he held it straight out in front of his body. "Not too high and not too low."

He moved behind her, wrapping her fingers around the handle and whispering against her ear. "You're very cute when you pout." Planting a quick kiss on her cheek, he stepped back.

She took a deep breath, relaxed her shoulders, swung the axe over her head, and lobbed it at the wall again. This time it bounced off the wall and skidded to a stop about halfway down the lane.

"That was a little too low." James bent to retrieve the axe.

"It's like the Goldilocks of axe throwing," she grumbled.

"Is someone competitive?" James teased.

"No!"

"I wouldn't have thought so based on our games of pool, but maybe you are. Or maybe it's because I can't distract you the same way here that I do at home."

She felt heat flood her cheeks, and he gave her a wicked grin. "I'm *not* competitive. I just don't like to be bad at things."

"You're not bad at it," he insisted, nodding at the waiter when he set their drinks down. "You're still learning."

"Uh huh. Your turn."

He raised the axe. Throwing it again, he hit the bullseye almost dead center.

She huffed out a breath. "Have you done this before?"

"Nope. I guess I have good hand-eye coordination."

She took a sip of her drink, eyeing the axe when he held it out to her. "Okay. Still learning."

Delaney held the axe out in front of her body to remind herself exactly where she needed to release it. Right in front. Just the right spot. Like Goldilocks. She always hated that story. What kind of brat sleeps in all the beds and eats all the food in a stranger's house?

Shaking the thought from her head, she hefted the axe into the air, blew out a slow breath, and threw it. It barely caught the edge of the outer ring, but it landed with that oh-so-satisfying thwack the way James's two had, and she jumped up and down, pumping her fist in the air.

When she turned back to face him, he was watching her, smiling wide, and her insides melted. In all her years, she'd never had someone look at her in a way that made her melt like that.

"See? Practice!"

She retrieved the axe from the wall and hung it back in its place when the waiter brought their cheese fries and set them between their drinks. Rounding the skinny table, she reclaimed her stool and popped a fry into her mouth with a groan.

"Cheese fries are one of the most underrated foods on the planet."

"A favorite of yours?" he wondered.

"The best. I basically lived off these in college." She paused with a fry halfway to her mouth and braced herself for the litany of questions that usually accompanied a statement like that. Questions she wasn't prepared to answer.

"I never went to college myself," he said instead. "But there was this diner my cousins and I would go to when

Declan finally got his license. They had the best bacon cheeseburgers I've ever had in my life."

"Can't go wrong with a good bacon cheeseburger." She chewed the fry slowly, trying to think of a question she could ask that wouldn't prompt an inquisition into her past. "What made you want to open the pub?"

He smiled, but it was edged with sadness. "Maura always wanted to open one. She used to design menus and floor plans for it in her spare time."

"How come you never did it when you were married? Sorry, that's none of my business."

"No." He linked his fingers with hers and brought her knuckles to his lips. "It's a fair question. Truth is, we weren't married all that long. She was killed the day after our wedding." When Delaney gasped, James squeezed her fingers. "A freak accident."

The way he said it made her wonder if there was more to the story, but she didn't want to pry. It wasn't her place.

"I bought the building on what would have been our first wedding anniversary." She nodded. "Yeah, you might know that if you really did google me. It was something they loved to include in all the articles."

"I think it's sweet. To remember her that way. Is it…" She bit her lip, unsure how to word her question or if she should even ask it.

"Is it what?"

"Is it weird to have me there? In a place you built to remember her by?"

James cupped the back of her neck and drew her in until their lips were a scant inch apart. "No. It's not weird." He kissed her long and deep, teasing his tongue along her upper lip. "I think Maura would have liked you. A lot. Why? Is it weird for you?"

"To be honest, I don't think about it much." She grimaced. "That sounded callous."

"No, it didn't. You didn't know her. She and I existed long before I met you." He took a swig of beer. "What's the hardest lesson you've ever learned?"

"That's a deep question for a first date."

He chuckled and swiped a fry through the pile of sour cream on top of the fries. "Would you rather me ask where you grew up or how many brothers or sisters you have or something?"

Absolutely not. She plucked her lower lip with her fingers while she considered his question. The hardest lesson she'd ever learned. She dragged her eyes up to his face.

"People will always show you who they are. It's best to believe them the first time."

The silence sat heavily between them, punctuated by the soft thud of axes hitting their targets and cheers from the other lanes as players won and lost their games.

"I don't know who hurt you, Delaney. But I never will. You're safe with me."

Tears pricked the corners of her eyes, and she slid off her stool to stand between his legs, cupping his face in her palms. She didn't need him to say it out loud to believe it, she believed in actions more than words, but the fact that he would offer it up made her wonder if they really could have the more she'd started to let herself want.

"I know. I couldn't have stayed if I didn't believe that deep down. You're a good man, James Callahan." Something flashed in his eyes, but he masked it quickly, and she frowned. "Maybe you don't believe me, but you are. What-ever else might be true about you, you're good, and that's what I care about."

She pressed a soft kiss to his lips, sighing when his arms

came around her waist and held her close. He made her want to unburden herself, to spill out all of her secrets and see if he would still want her.

She ached with it, but she knew some secrets you couldn't come back from. No matter how hard you tried.

Chapter Twenty-Eight

J ames sat alone at the conference table in the basement of Reign, pen tapping against the stack of papers in front of him. They were supposed to be going over the inventory list for the next set of shipments due to arrive at the docks in less than forty-eight hours. Aidan had closed another big deal, one that promised a long and fruitful partnership with a European contact.

Then there was the revised logistics to go over for New York. Their first two sales in the city had gone off without a hitch. Still, James didn't want a repeat of their initial move. He hoped to speak to Declan about setting up a system to deliver product directly to New York rather than to Philadelphia and have to truck it.

It would be a much more extensive plan to ensure them the same setup they had at home. More men on the ground in New York so they could strategically place them at the harbor to receive shipments and make sure paperwork was doctored or eyes looked the other way when necessary. They had all that in Philly. They'd have to build it in New York.

He looked up when lights flashed on in the main room,

and minutes later, Declan strode in, followed shortly by Aidan. Both of them looked a little pissed off.

"Rough morning?" James wondered as Declan dropped into his chair with a groan.

"A Russian rat who didn't want to talk," Aidan said.

"Took all night to persuade him," Declan added. "Sorry to keep you waiting."

James waved away his cousin's apology. "Was he involved in the hit on our caravan?"

"Indirectly. He was apparently sharing information with the Russians in New York."

"That he was getting from where, exactly?"

"His own asshole," Aidan supplied. "It was pure dumb luck they found us. They were aiming for one of our leaked times and got stuck in traffic."

"Still." James twirled his pen around his fingers. "I don't like the idea of the Russians colluding between New York and Philly."

"Neither do I. Ivankov has a week to root out the cancer from his own organization, or I'm going to do it for him. Brogan is watching. Now tell me what we're moving this week."

James slipped his quickly scribbled notes out from the stack and scanned them. He'd burn them later, but it always helped to jot it down, even if it was in an unreadable short-hand to anyone off the street.

"Six shipments being staggered over two days. Three go to Aidan's new Belgian friend, two to a repeat customer, and one to a low-level drug lord in"—he squinted at his notes—"Pittsburgh."

"Not that low level if he's buying from us."

"Trust me," Aidan interjected. "He's a poseur hoping to buy himself some street cred by waving around a bunch of AK-47s. I'll be surprised if he's still alive a week after delivery."

Declan snorted. "Everything handled then?"

"Yep. Crews established, and since some of them are new to working together, we're running drills later this week to make sure everyone knows what the fuck they're doing."

"Good. How are the training classes coming? I'd like to put more men on the ground soon. People," he corrected.

"They're going well. Another month at the outside, and I'll have a group ready for you for low-level stuff. Security, patrol, shit like that. Brogan has some incredible shooters he'll want to keep working with. And Holt and I have pegged about eight we want to train for deliveries and special ops."

"All right. I talked to Sean. New York seems solid, but they'll want another delivery soon."

"About that." Both Aidan and Declan looked up at him, and he shifted in his seat. "I think we should establish a bigger base up there. Have product shipped directly to New York for New York deals."

Declan leaned back in his chair, steepling his fingers in front of him. "That would be quite a base."

"I know. It would require eyes and ears at the docks and probably in a few other paper pushing places. But we start making regular convoy shipments from Philly to New York, and we only open ourselves up to more attacks. They won't succeed, but that doesn't mean they won't try. Shipping directly to New York eliminates that risk for us."

"And it establishes a firmer base of power in the city."

"Which makes us look even better to potential buyers," Declan added. "All right. Draw up some preliminary plans for me to look at based on our setup here. I trust your father to run it there the way you're running things here, so it should be an easy thing to wrangle."

"Done. I can have something drafted before our next meeting. I've also heard from a few men interested in making

New York a permanent placement. If we decide to stick it out for the long haul."

"We'll definitely be maintaining a presence there for the full year at least. You have names?"

James slid a list out of the stack and across the table to Declan, who nodded as he read. "Yeah. These make sense. They're all eager to make names for themselves. Gallagher surprises me, but then again, his brother just got married. I'm good with these. Include them in your plan, and we'll discuss it again."

Declan's phone signaled, and he pushed out of his chair, fingers flying over the screen, responding to whatever message he'd received. "I've got to run. Good work, as always. Aidan. Tonight at—"

"Seven. Yeah."

With that, Declan left in a hurry, and James shuffled his papers back into a stack, making a few notes on the list of names for relocation. When he looked up, he caught Aidan staring at him.

"Can I...help you with something?"

Aidan cocked his head. "I was just curious how things are going with you. We haven't had a chance to hang out in a while."

"Having a wife and kid will do that to you."

"You been out on any more dates recently?" Aidan pushed to his feet, and James followed suit.

"With Aisling Donahue, you mean?" James replied, deciding to play dumb.

Aidan shrugged. "Just in general."

"Cut the cloak and dagger bullshit, Aidan." James grabbed his coat off the back of his chair. "If you have something to say, say it."

"Did you enjoy axe throwing the other night?"

Shit. James forced himself not to react. "Axe throwing?"

"I assume that's what you were doing when I saw you walk out of that bar. With your arm wrapped around a woman who looked an awful lot like your only non-syndicate employee."

James allowed himself a momentary sigh of relief. At least it hadn't been some other member of the syndicate who saw them. If it had, gossip would already be flying, and that would be even worse than the interrogation he was getting from his cousin right now.

"Oh, right. It was fun. Thanks for asking."

He wasn't going to offer up any more than that. If Aidan wanted to know, he could ask. His cousin didn't disappoint.

"That's all you have to say for yourself?"

"Despite what you may believe, I don't have to ask permission from you or anyone about what I do in my personal life." James stepped into the main part of the basement and started for the stairs.

"So you're fucking her."

"Among other things. Lucky for both of us, none of it is any of your damn business."

"It's the syndicate's business, James. And you know that, or you wouldn't be so defensive about it."

"Delaney doesn't know anything about the syndicate or my role in it. The family is fine. The secret is safe. The syndicate lives to rule another day."

Aidan was silent as they navigated around the cleaning crew mopping the floors and crossed the parking lot to their waiting vehicles. James was praying he would drop the whole damn thing.

"What the fuck are you doing, James?"

"I'm enjoying her while I can."

Aidan crossed his arms over his chest. "You're getting too close. I know you. I saw how you were with Maura. It's too similar. You're falling for her." Aidan cursed at the look that crossed James's face. "You already have. Declan will never go for this. It's too big a risk."

"I'm not asking Declan to go for anything," James gritted out. "I'm handling it."

"And if she finds out?"

"She won't." James didn't bother letting Aidan know Delaney already suspected something was up. She just hadn't asked the right questions yet. "I've been doing this for a long time, Aidan. I know how to be careful."

"How do I know you're not going to do something stupid over this woman?"

James clenched his hand into a fist at his side. "After every goddamn thing we've been through, now is when you decide not to trust me?"

"It's not that I don't trust you—"

"Bullshit. That's bullshit. You of all people should know we can't help who we fall in love with." James shoved a rough hand through his hair. "I'm doing my best to have as much of her as I can for as long as I can. And I'm prepared to lose her when the time comes."

"You should never have let it get this far in the first place."

"Fuck off, Aidan. I hope this life never takes from you what it took from me. I made a choice with Delaney, and as much as I probably should, I don't regret it."

Aidan jerked open the door of his truck and climbed onto the running board. "You're walking a fine line here, James, and if you're not careful, you'll burn everything we've worked so hard to protect to the ground."

"Don't worry," James spat, unable to keep the bitterness from his voice. "The only person who'll get burned in the end is me."

Sliding behind the wheel, Aidan jerked his door closed and peeled out of the parking lot. James stared after him, clenching his jaw until it ached. He'd known from the start how this was going to end, how it had to end. That didn't mean he had to fucking like it or that he owed his cousin an explanation for his choices.

Finding Delaney happened as unexpectedly as losing Maura. He didn't ask for either one, but he'd be damned if he wouldn't allow himself to grip onto at least a few moments of happiness while he had it.

His loyalty to the family and the syndicate would always win out over everything else, even if it meant losing another piece of himself. James knew Aidan wouldn't say anything, at least not yet. But he also knew he didn't have much time left with her. It was slipping through his fingers too fast. Soon, whether he was ready or not, he'd have to let her go.

Chapter Twenty-Nine

The smell of bacon and coffee teased her out of sleep, and Delaney rolled onto her back, arching off the mattress to stretch. They'd gone on a date, a real date, and the world hadn't exploded. In fact, it was the most fun she'd had in a long time. James made her feel like anything was possible. It was a heady feeling, even if it was constantly at odds with her past and its secrets.

Rolling out of bed, she reached for the hoodie she'd stolen from him and tugged it on over her tank top, padding barefoot down the stairs. He was in the kitchen flipping something on the stove while coffee hissed into the pot, his own iced coffee open at his elbow.

He heard her and turned, and the smile he gave her warmed her right down to her toes. Then his eyes traveled up and down her body, from her headscarf to her feet and back again, and she shivered with it.

"Good morning." She leaned up on her tiptoes to brush a kiss across his lips, stealing a piece of bacon off the plate.

"Morning, beautiful. Breakfast is almost ready if you want to fix yourself some coffee."

She turned toward the pot and noticed the big bouquet of peonies in the middle of the kitchen table. Pouring coffee into a mug and adding a spoonful of sugar, she watched James plate the eggs he was frying and bring them to the table along with the bacon and some sort of potato and veggie hash.

"What's the occasion for those?" She set her mug down and bent to inhale the bouquet's delicate floral scent. Peonies were one of her favorite flowers, but she didn't remember ever telling him that. "They're so beautiful."

James wrapped his arms around her from behind. "Beautiful flowers for a beautiful woman."

"Flowers just because? That's very sweet of you."

He pressed a kiss to the side of her neck. "Not just because. You didn't think I'd forget your birthday, did you?"

"What are you talking about?" She smiled as his lips continued to trail over her jaw to her earlobe. "My birthday isn't until…"

Delaney froze, and her heart pounded painfully in her chest. Her birthday wasn't until September. Delaney Williams's birthday was in February. She squeezed her eyes shut and tried to come up with something, anything to say. James hadn't released her, but he was very, very still, and she was afraid of what she might see on his face when she turned around.

"You're right," she replied, infusing as much sunshine into her voice as she could. "I can't believe I forgot." She turned in his arms and chanced a look at his face. It was an unreadable mask. "Thank you for remembering. And for the flowers."

He smiled, but it didn't quite reach his eyes. "You're welcome. Let's eat before everything gets cold."

Delaney sank into the chair James held out for her and let him add food to her plate, but the silence between them was thick. This was the moment. The perfect time to confess everything, to lay it all on the table and see what came next. She knew she could trust him with her body, with her safety, but could she trust him with her secrets?

"Busy day today?"

"Yeah," he replied. "I've got to teach a self-defense class and then meet Aidan for a few things. You're working, right?"

She nodded. "Just the afternoon shift. I'm off around six. I didn't know you taught self-defense classes."

He flinched, refusing to meet her gaze when he spoke again. "Reagan teaches them, really. Sometimes she asks me to help out." He opened his mouth and closed it again. "Well, I should probably get going."

Delaney didn't know what to say to stop him when he shoved back from the table and carried his plate to the sink.

"I wasn't sure if you would want to go out tonight or stay in, but maybe..." He took a deep breath before continuing. "Maybe we could stay in and...talk."

Delaney's heart plummeted into her stomach, and she swallowed around the lump in her throat. Talking meant questions. Was she prepared to answer them?

"Okay."

"Okay," he repeated. "I'll see you tonight."

He retreated to the door, stuffing his feet into his boots and slipping into his jacket, all without glancing in her direction. When the door closed behind him with a gentle click, the silence was deafening.

Appetite vanished, Delaney pushed her plate away and stared at the flowers artfully arranged in a cut glass vase. She would have two choices tonight, lie to his face or tell the truth. She didn't feel prepared for either one.

Delaney cruised through her shift on autopilot. It was steady but not slammed, with customers who tipped well and didn't linger too long. A perfect day in the restaurant industry. She clocked out at six on the dot and climbed the stairs with heavy steps. She'd seen James head up nearly an hour ago, so she knew he was waiting for her.

Sometime around two, she decided to tell him the truth. The whole of it. Every nasty, unflattering, uncomfortable detail of it. Telling him wouldn't put her in danger; she believed that wholeheartedly. He would never betray her. Oddly enough, it wasn't the danger she was afraid of—it was his rejection.

All day she played scenarios in her head where she told him the truth, bared her entire soul to him, and he decided he didn't want her anymore. That she was too much trouble. If that did happen, it was at least something she was prepared for.

The lights were on when she let herself in, but he wasn't in the kitchen. She hung her jacket on the hook by the door and kicked off her shoes. The apartment was eerily quiet. Maybe he slipped out again and she missed it. Then she heard his feet on the stairs.

Turning slowly, she offered him a half-hearted smile. He looked about as nervous as she felt. But she had to push through this. He deserved to know the truth, and if freedom was something she really wanted, this was as good a place to start as any. She couldn't be free and have secrets.

"Delaney, I—"

"Wait." She swallowed, rubbing a hand over her chest to calm her furiously beating heart. "I have something I need to tell you. Can we sit?"

They moved to the couch, and he surprised her by sitting close enough to touch if they wanted. That seemed like a good sign.

"I don't really know how to say this. I've never told anyone this story before. Just…please don't interrupt me until I'm finished. Okay?"

He nodded, and she took a deep, steadying breath.

"I'm married. Technically. Legally." She looked down at her bare left hand. "We met when I was in my last year of law school. He came to speak at my university, and I was…smitten. After his lecture, he caught up to me in the hallway and asked if he could take me out to dinner." Delaney shook her head.

"I immediately said yes. He was older, smarter, widely published, very well known in the criminal litigation field." James shifted at that, but she pushed through. "He charmed me. Took me out to fancy restaurants and bought me expensive gifts. I guess you'd call it a whirlwind romance. We'd only dated about six months, most of it long distance, when he proposed."

She shifted to tuck her legs underneath her, scooting back when their knees brushed. "I only had about three months left until graduation when he asked me to marry him, but he insisted I drop out. Said I'd be too busy planning the wedding to study for exams and swore up and down I'd finish school later and take the bar, and we'd be this elite, high-powered couple."

Her laugh was bitter, and she rubbed at the crease that formed between her brows. "I should have said no, but he made so much damn sense, and every time I even hinted at waiting until after I graduated, he twisted my words and made it sound like I didn't want to marry him. So I finally agreed and dropped out, and we moved to his family estate in New Orleans."

Snow began to fall outside, and she fixed her eyes on the swirling ice crystals, gripping her hands in her lap to anchor herself in the present moment. "It only took him three months to hit me the first time."

James swore under his breath, and she gripped her fingers tighter. "I was chatting with friends about graduation and saying I was bummed I couldn't even be there to watch them walk, but he didn't want to go. I promised to watch the live stream and call them later. He was livid and said I was trying to make him look like the bad guy. When I told him he was being ridiculous, he backhanded me across the face." Delaney rubbed her cheek at the memory.

"He apologized. He always apologized, but he never stopped. He just got better at hitting me where no one could see the bruises. One night, after we'd been married about three years, I laughed at a joke one of the partners at his law firm told at a party. When we got home, he accused me of sleeping with the guy. He almost killed me."

James reached for her hand and laced their fingers together, but he didn't speak, and she was grateful for that. She might not be able to get through the rest of it if he did.

"I went to the police after that. I knew he was friends with the superintendent, but I was covered in cuts and bruises. I figured they'd have to take me seriously. Instead they put me in an interrogation room and called him to come pick me up. They never even took my statement. He broke my arm that night and had one of his doctor friends make a house call so he wouldn't have to take me to the hospital."

She rubbed at her wrist, which still ached when it rained. "I started figuring out how to get away from him after that. I didn't trust women's shelters not to hand me back over to him the way the police did, so I saved up whatever money I could get my hands on and started plotting how to disappear."

"And how did you?" he whispered.

"I pretended to sleepwalk. I used to when I was younger

but hadn't in years. If he made me take a sleeping pill, I'd pretend to swallow and then spit it out and act like the pills made the sleepwalking worse. It took me months to establish a pattern of regular sleepwalking, and in the last few weeks, I started actually leaving the house."

"I don't understand."

"We lived on the bayou. The bayou means alligators. I wasn't sure it would work, but he wouldn't let me drive myself anywhere, and I wasn't allowed to leave the house without permission. I'd wander a little closer to the water each time I did it. On my last night, I stashed a bag behind a tree. When I walked down to the water, I left a piece of my ripped nightgown at the water's edge, grabbed my bag, and ran."

She finally dragged her eyes back to his face. He was staring at her with a look so intense it made her shiver, but she couldn't tell what he was thinking. When she tried to pull her hand from his, he held her fast and pulled her closer until their knees touched.

"How long ago was that?"

"A little over a year. I keep an eye on the news reports from that area. He assumed exactly what I wanted him to. They searched for my body for weeks."

"It wasn't suspicious that they never found anything?"

"Not really. Alligators don't tend to leave much behind. Eventually he had a funeral for me, played the grieving husband for the cameras." She snorted. "He was always good at that part. Faking it for his image."

James was silent for a long time, his thumb rubbing circles on the back of her hand. "When's your birthday?"

Delaney smiled. "September second. Yours?"

"March thirteenth." He paused again, then whispered, "Is Delaney your real name?"

"No," she murmured. "It was my great-grandmother's

maiden name. And Williams was one of the most generic last names I could think of that wasn't Smith or Jones. My legal name is Alice Devereaux. I'm sorry."

His gaze snapped to her face. "For what?"

"For bringing all of this to your doorstep. I didn't want to. I never imagined… I never thought for a second I would stay. That I would feel like this about you."

He reached up to wrap a curl around his finger. "Are you sorry you stayed?"

"No," she said softly, drawing his gaze. "How could I ever be sorry I met you?"

His voice was barely audible when he asked, "So what now? Will you stay in Philly?"

"I don't know." She sighed. "I guess it depends."

"On?" he prompted.

"On whether or not I have a reason to."

"And if you don't?"

Her heart sank at the meaning in his simple question. "Then I'll move on and start over somewhere else. Wouldn't be the first time."

"What if I could help get you all the way out?"

"What do you mean? I am out. He thinks I'm dead."

"I mean out." He pulled her into his lap, pressing his forehead against her cheek, and her heart gave a lazy flutter. "Real freedom. The kind that meant you wouldn't have to spend the rest of your life wondering if he was behind you. Would you want that?"

More than anything. "It's not possible." His arms came around her waist, but she couldn't relax against him. Just because she wanted it didn't mean she could actually have it. "You can't stop him. He's too powerful, too well connected." She shuddered. "You don't know what he's capable of."

"I have a pretty good idea." He pressed a kiss to her jaw.

"Let me help get you out, Delaney. Let me give you your life back."

"If he finds out I'm alive, he'll kill me. He always said death was the only way I'd ever get away from him."

"I would never let that happen. Do you trust me?" She nodded. "Then trust me with this. Trust me to keep you safe."

"Okay. Where do we start?"

Chapter Thirty

I t took him longer than he liked to find her. He made the mistake of starting in Illinois, hoping she'd slip up and circle closer to home, before branching out and checking the other surrounding states. He'd come up empty in Indiana and Ohio but finally found exactly what he was looking for in Pennsylvania.

She was waiting tables at a bar again—her favorite—and he'd been sitting on it for the last forty-eight hours. Normally he would snap a few photos and immediately call his client to verify identity and provide a location, but he wasn't ready to hand her over yet. He wanted some time alone with her first, but she never fucking went anywhere by herself.

She was either with some skinny girl with ugly blue hair, a blonde with big tits, or a dark-haired man that touched her like they were pretty cozy. The first time he saw the asshole put his arm around her, he'd nearly snapped his steering wheel in half.

He couldn't exactly explain why he was so obsessed with her. It wasn't his usual MO, but he'd spent a lot of time looking for her, and he deserved a little reward. It's not like he'd be able to brag about this later to all his friends. Not that he had many friends.

He checked the time on the dash when he saw a shadow cross over the window in the bar's front door and made the snap decision to do something else he never, ever did. Attempt to make contact.

With his body acting independently of his brain, he got out of his truck and jogged across the street. It was empty, obviously; he'd only just watched them unlock the door. He claimed a small two-top table about halfway down the row and waited. He didn't know if she was working today, but he hadn't seen her leave yet either.

The blonde pushed through the swinging door separating the dining room from the kitchen, and he barely hid his disappointment. On any other day, he'd appreciate the sway of her hips and that thick, round ass and the generous handful of her breasts. Today he wanted someone else.

"Hi," she said sweetly, her accent a little less abrasive than the others he'd been listening to for days. "Welcome to The Black Orchid. My name's Clara. Can I get you something to drink?"

"A Coke. Or what do y'all call it up here? Pop?"

She smiled. "We're still serving soda here in Philly. You'll have to go further west for pop. I'll be right back with that."

He gave himself a moment to stare at her ass as she walked away, but then his eyes were roaming the bar. It was a decent place with a lot of wood accents and simple brass fixtures. Simple but expensive and clean.

The blonde emerged from the kitchen again with a glass and a straw in her hand, and he tried to imagine Delaney walking toward him instead. The thought of her smiling at him, greeting him, serving him without knowing he would be her downfall made his dick hard. If only she were here to really fill out the fantasy.

Clara set his drink down on a napkin and gestured to the menu. "You ready to order, or do you need a minute?"

"I need a minute, if you don't mind."

"Sure thing."

"I hope you're not working by yourself today."

She paused in her retreat to the kitchen and tilted her head while she studied him. There was something sharp and measuring in her gaze underneath the customer service politeness.

"Don't worry. There's always someone around to help out. I'll check back on you in a few minutes."

She returned his smile but shot a look at the guy wiping down the bar that had the kid shooting him a curious glance. That girl was sharp. But she was tiny. She'd be easy to over-power if he had a mind to. Lucky for her, he was here for someone else.

The door opened, and a couple of college kids came in and sat at the table right in front of him. They looked like regulars based on the greeting they got from Clara and the way they made small talk. While she was preoccupied with them, he pulled up the photos of Delaney he'd taken with his high-powered lens and sent to his phone.

Her holding hands with the dark-haired man, taking the trash out, laying ice melt down on the front steps, but his favorite was the one he'd snapped of her standing in the window of what must be an apartment above the bar.

Her hair was wrapped up in a colorful scarf, exposing the long line of her neck. Her arms were bare, and the tank top she wore hugged her torso and gave him the perfect view of her breasts. Smaller than Clara's, but he didn't mind that.

He couldn't tell from the photo, but he liked to imagine her nipples poking against the fabric just like he imagined standing behind her, wrenching them until she begged him to stop, fucking her until he was sated. He'd beat off in the shower that morning to the fantasy of tying her up and making her take his cock while she cried.

He wanted to experience the real thing before he was forced to call his client. But he was stuck with the images he conjured up in his head because the bitch apparently walked around with a fucking escort. He hit the lock button on his phone to make the screen go dark as Clara stepped up to his table. Didn't need her to raise the alarm.

"How are we doing over here?"

"Great. I think I'll take a bowl of the stew."

She smiled. "Can't go wrong with that one. I'll bring you out a basket of bread. Did you want anything else?"

He shook his head. "No, that's it for now. Hey," he said before she stepped away. "How late are y'all open tonight?" There was that searching look again. "I think my wife might like this place," he explained. "I thought I could bring her back for dinner if it works with our schedules."

Her eyes dropped to the bare fingers of his left hand, and she nodded but didn't smile again. "We're open until midnight tonight. I'll go put your stew in."

He silently kicked himself as she walked away. This is why it was better to remain a neutral third party. When you got attached to the people you were hunting, you were bound to make mistakes, and he'd made a big one coming in here and asking too many questions from a girl too good at reading strangers.

While he debated whether to leave without the stew, his phone signaled an incoming text. His client wanted an update. He ignored it, and another one came right on its heels. Jesus, the guy was relentless.

"Believe me," he mumbled to himself. "We're both impatient to have her."

It didn't take long for his food to arrive, piping hot and served with a basket of what looked like homemade Irish soda bread. He ate it quickly, burning his tongue, while he tried to ignore the fact that Clara stood at the corner of the bar talking in hushed tones and shooting him furtive glances.

The last damn thing he needed was someone spooking Delaney enough to disappear. According to the records search he'd run, she'd been working here long enough to save up enough money for her to lay low for a good long while. If he lost her now, it could take him months to pick her back up again.

He decided to get out of there as quickly as possible and stop stalling. He needed to shake this weird pull she had over him, call his client, and get paid. Getting paid was all that mattered in the end. He'd hire someone when he got home, maybe someone who looked like her, and satisfy all his fantasies that way. Second best would have to do.

Without waiting for the bill, he dropped two twenties on the table and pushed to his feet. Shoving out into the dreary day, he hunched into his jacket. So far Philadelphia had proved to be warmer than Michigan, but it was still too fucking cold for his thick blood. Maybe that's what it was. The cold had scrambled his brain.

He climbed into his truck and drove back to his hotel, securely locking the door behind him before turning on his laptop and bringing up the photos he'd taken. He composed an email to his client with a couple of photos attached and pressed send.

Before he could even dig his phone all the way out of his pocket, it was ringing.

"Mr. Devereaux. I seem to have located your wife." He kicked back in his chair and couldn't help the self-satisfied grin that spread over his face. "She's been in Philadelphia for a little while now, working as a waitress at a bar and restaurant in the city."

"Do you have more pictures? I want to know everything," Devereaux demanded.

"I'll have all the details for you when you have my final payment. What are your next steps?"

Devereaux was quiet for so long he pulled the phone away from his ear to make sure the call was still connected. "I'm coming up there. We can meet in person for a rundown of the details, and then you'll get your final payment. In cash."

"Cash is great. How soon can you get here?"

"I'll be there tonight. I'll send you the details of where I'm staying, and you can pick me up in the morning. Early."

Devereaux disconnected the call, and he rolled his eyes. He wasn't a goddamn taxi service. The sooner he could hand this bitch over to her husband and get the fuck back to New Orleans with his money, the better. The whole damn job was getting to him.

It didn't matter, though. By this time tomorrow, he'd have the last of what he was owed and be home in his own bed by nightfall. Then he could wash his hands of all of it and take a well-deserved vacation.

Chapter Thirty-One

J ames let himself through the gate of Glenmore House and pulled around the circular drive, parking behind Brogan's Jag. Despite having moved into one of their renovated properties with his wife, Libby, Brogan still did syndicate work from his third-floor lair. That was the family nickname for the syndicate's base of operations for all things tech.

If it could be hacked, downloaded, or erased from existence, Brogan could do it from that windowless room. Which was exactly why James needed his help. Sitting quietly through Delaney's story made James want to hold her as tightly as he could and never let go. But letting go was inevitable. The least he could do was give her true freedom from that asshole of a husband of hers first.

Keying in his code for the garage and entering through the side door, James took the stairs to the third floor two at a time. He wasn't all that keen on informing Brogan of the whole situation with Delaney, but he knew he didn't have another choice. Besides, he was doing all this so he could end things. He deserved some kind of credit for that.

He heard the hum of the computers and the click of keys before he stepped into the doorway. Brogan's broad back was facing the door. His cousin's hulking, muscular frame would look more at home as a bouncer at a club than behind a computer. James rapped his knuckles against the wood.

"Hey." Brogan tilted his head. "I didn't know you were coming to see me today."

"I need a favor. A personal one."

"What's up?"

James stepped into the room and closed the door behind him, ignoring Brogan's answering frown. He wanted this conversation to remain private if someone came home early.

"I have a woman working for me. I need to make her ex-husband disappear."

Brogan's eyes narrowed on James's face. "And why do you need to do that?"

"Because he beat her near daily for eight years until she faked her own death to escape him." James took a deep breath, and Brogan's scowl deepened. "If we were normal, I'd hold her hand through a divorce and pray he didn't kill her. But we're not normal, and I want him to pay."

"Out of the kindness of your heart?"

"No. Because I'm in love with her." He held up his hand even though Brogan made no move to speak. "I know what you're going to say. I've already heard it from Aidan. I need to do this so I can let her go and know she'll be safe."

"And what exactly did you hear from Aidan?" Brogan asked, brows raised.

"That I should never have let it get this far with her."

Brogan bit off a curse. "Well, I fucking hate that."

"That I'm in love with her?"

"That Aidan and I actually agree on something."

James clenched his jaw. He didn't need another lecture. "Are you going to help me or not?"

"What do you need from me?" Brogan asked after a beat.

James closed the distance between them and handed Brogan the paper where he'd jotted the extra details Delaney had given him over the last few days. "I looked into him some on my own. He's as well connected as she says, so we probably can't actually make him disappear. As much as I might want to obliterate him off the face of the fucking earth."

Brogan keyed in the details and brought up several newspaper articles. "Yeah. Too many questions. Plus, I assume you don't want your girlfriend to think you murdered him."

"Correct." James blew out a breath. "I don't want her to think that."

"We could do an accident."

Brogan pulled up a blank window, and his fingers flew over the keys, adding a string of neon numbers and letters that James couldn't decipher. When he hit enter, a series of windows flooded the screen that looked like official records.

"Your boy's an attorney?"

"Criminal defense, yeah. Why? Is that going to be a problem?"

"Shouldn't be. But why's a criminal defense attorney so chummy with the mayor and the superintendent of police? Don't they tend to like the guys who aren't putting criminals back on the street?"

"I don't know. Why don't we ask the mayor of Philadelphia what he thinks about Declan's extracurricular activities?"

Brogan snorted. "Bit different, but I see your point." He sifted through the windows until something caught his eye, and he let out a low whistle. "Well, well, well. This might prove useful."

James moved closer to get a better look at the monitor. "A DUI."

"Multiple DUIs over the last year. Never charged for any of them, though." More typing. "According to internal and unofficial records, there was another one about two months ago. Wrapped his car around a tree. Lucky to have survived. Single car accident, no charges filed. Looks like a drunk driving accident where he isn't so lucky might be your best bet."

James rolled the idea over in his mind. There were multiple ways to stage an accident and make it look real. His main concern would probably be getting in and out as quickly as possible and not leaving any witnesses behind who might be able to identify him. Then again, if Devereaux had a habit of drinking to excess and running his car into things, it wouldn't raise much suspicion if the accident scene looked right. Open and shut case.

The trick would be James getting away for long enough to take care of it without letting Declan or Aidan know what he was up to. It's not like he could take a spontaneous vacation without raising some eyebrows. It would be a quick trip down to New Orleans once he had more information and knew Devereaux's patterns better.

"This woman really that important to you?"

Brogan's question drew James out of his thoughts, and he leveled his cousin with a steely stare. "Was Libby that important to you when DiMarco demanded you hand her over?"

"All right then," Brogan agreed. "Whatever you need to take this fucker out, I'll get it for you. And when you're ready to go down there and end him, I can cover for you."

"Thank you." James shoved his hands into his jacket pockets. "Can you get me some surveillance on him? Is that possible from this far away?"

"Difficult but not impossible."

Heading for the hall, James paused at the door. "And Brogan? Can we keep this between us? I already know how

Aidan feels about Delaney and me. I can't imagine Declan will take the news any better."

"You can't help who you love, James. Even if you don't get to keep them. Something both of my brothers forget when it's convenient. I'll get you everything I can in the next day or two."

James left Brogan to his work and jogged down the stairs. The sooner he could kill this abusive fuck and get him out of Delaney's life, the better. Although part of him wished it didn't have to be an accident so he could make the son of a bitch pay first.

Devereaux deserved every punch, every slap, every bruise, and every broken bone he'd ever inflicted on Delaney. All he'd get would be a death that was far too quick and people saying nice things about him at his funeral. It hardly seemed fair.

In the end, though, James would do what was necessary to set Delaney free, both from her tormentor and from himself. If he had any qualms about letting her go, any ideas about trying to bring Declan around and make him see reason, they died with Delaney's story.

She deserved more than living a life where part of her would always be in hiding, from the cops or any friends she might make outside of the pub staff. She deserved a life she could live out in the open. And he intended to give that to her. By whatever means necessary.

Chapter Thirty-Two

The sky had barely begun to pink when he pulled into the upscale hotel parking lot, and the asshole was late. He didn't fancy playing chauffeur to the guy. He wanted to hand over the information, collect what was owed, and be on his way. He had a late morning flight to catch, and he hated getting to the airport too close to boarding time.

In the dim light of the lamps lining the wide sidewalk, he glimpsed a blond man with a slight build. He looked like the kind of guy you'd expect to be born with a silver spoon in his mouth. Good looking, tall, fit, and completely full of himself.

Devereaux stood by the side of the car for a few minutes before realizing no one was going to jump out and open the door for him. He gripped the back door handle and then changed his mind, climbing into the front instead.

He finished doing something on his phone before finally acknowledging he wasn't alone in the car. "Simmons. I'm eager to hear your good news."

His voice was smooth, his accent familiar, but there was an edge to it that was hard to ignore. The man was revved up at finding her, and that might work to his advantage. After sleeping on it, he'd decided his silence came at a steeper price.

"I've got it all worked up for you in a folder back at my hotel," Simmons said, pulling onto the highway and following the map in his head back to where he was staying. "There's a flash drive with all the pictures I took and a detailed report of the trail I followed."

Devereaux was silent when they pulled into the parking lot, while they waited for the elevator, while Simmons used the keycard to access his room. He said nothing when Simmons handed him the folder and plugged the flash drive into his laptop.

His eyes tracking the page while he read the report was the only sign he was absorbing every bit of information. The heavy silence made Simmons uncomfortable. Other people rarely set him on edge, but this guy gave him the creeps.

"When my sister-in-law told me she thought she saw my wife in Michigan of all places and dressed in jeans, for Christ's sake, I thought she was having one of her episodes. What else could possibly explain why my wife would fake her own death and leave me like that? After everything I've done for her?"

Simmons rocked back on his heels, unsure whether Devereaux wanted a real answer or not. Apparently he didn't, because he kept talking.

"I mourned her. I buried her. I dedicated a scholarship in her name at her alma mater." He clenched the folder so hard it crumpled in his hand and then seemed to collect himself, releasing his grip and taking a deep breath. "You said you had pictures?"

"Uh, yeah." He tapped a key and brought up the images from the drive in a slideshow, stepping back when Devereaux bent over the laptop. "I think she's living above the bar because she doesn't leave the building much. Most of the time when I saw her outside, she was taking the trash out or greeting this guy when he pulled up."

Devereaux's head snapped up, and the look in his eyes was enough to have Simmons taking another step back. "Keep flipping through. He owns the bar. That guy," he said when the dark-haired man flashed across the screen.

Devereaux's taps on the key to advance the slide show grew increasingly more aggressive as he moved through the burst of shots Simmons already knew ended in a kiss. The guy was going to blow a gasket when he saw that.

He sucked in a breath as Devereaux neared the end of the burst, and when he reached it, the man let out a strangled sound and gripped the edge of the desk with white knuckles.

"Were there others?"

"What?" That was not the question he'd expected Devereaux to ask.

"Were there other men she was whoring herself out to?" His voice was low and dangerous.

"Not that I saw her with over the last few days." Simmons scratched at the day-old growth on his chin. "Could be that she had other men, but I don't know how I'd know about that for sure."

Devereaux smacked the screen so hard Simmons thought he might put a hole through it and whirled, green eyes full of madness. "How the hell else would that little slut have survived this long if she wasn't spreading her legs for a man in every damn city? She's going to pay for this."

"How you deal with it is up to you. I don't need any part in that." Even if he might enjoy watching her take that punishment. A lot.

"This kind of disobedience and disrespect for me, for our *marriage*," he continued as if Simmons hadn't spoken, "cannot

244

be tolerated. She'll have to be punished. She brought it on herself."

He muttered the same thing to himself over and over like a mantra. The more he repeated it, the more he seemed to relax until, when he looked at Simmons again, the madness was gone from his eyes, and his face was the same serene mask Simmons recognized from TV.

That was the only reason he'd taken this job—because he recognized the guy from all the interviews he did for cable news as a legal expert and the occasional local broadcast where he represented some other rich fuck and got him off on a legal technicality. Not because he respected his work, but because he knew Devereaux was good for the cash payout.

"Where is she right now?"

He jerked, Devereaux's question dragging him out of the recesses of his thoughts. "At work, I imagine. The address for the bar is in the file."

Devereaux flipped open the folder and haphazardly shuffled papers aside until he had the one he wanted. His lips moved silently as he read through the information.

"How do I get in there? Into the apartment."

Simmons frowned. "How the hell am I supposed to know that? My job was to track and surveil. If you wanted B and E, that would have cost you a lot extra. Besides, you probably don't want to draw that much attention to yourself."

"I didn't ask for your opinion," Devereaux snapped. "I asked you for information." He paused and collected himself. "But you're probably right. Best to try and fly as far below the radar as possible. Is she working today?"

"That would be my guess. She didn't work yesterday."

That murderous look lit his eyes again, but he smoothed it out. "Good. That's good. You did fine work, Simmons."

"I told you I always do."

Devereaux reached into the breast pocket of his perfectly

pressed suit and pulled out an envelope. "I especially appreciate a man who can be discreet."

"About that," Simmons replied, plucking the envelope from Devereaux's hand and peeking at the bills inside. It looked like it was all there, but he'd count it to make absolutely sure. "This has been a long job. It took more time than either of us realized."

"Additional time you've been compensated for."

Devereaux raised a brow in a look so snooty Simmons had to grit his teeth to keep from snarling a response. Fuckers like this really did think the world was at their beck and call.

"What I'm getting at is…if you want to permanently buy my silence, it's going to cost you a lot more."

"Are you trying to blackmail me, Mr. Simmons?"

He shrugged. "Call it whatever you want, but I suspect you don't want folks back home knowing your pretty wife faked her own death and ran out on you or that she's spent the last year running away from your sorry ass either. If you want to keep that between us, you'll need to cough up more cash."

"You're right, Mr. Simmons. I do want to permanently guarantee your silence. And it is going to cost a lot more than either of us realized when we started this."

Devereaux moved so fast Simmons didn't have time to react before the blade of the knife he'd used to cut his steak and eggs at breakfast was buried in the side of his neck. He stumbled forward and slumped down onto the edge of the nearest bed.

Reaching up to touch his neck, his hands came away covered in thick, bright red blood. He couldn't swallow all the way, and when he tried to take a deep breath, it was like he could feel air leaking out from a hole he'd never be able to close.

His fingers danced over the handle of the knife, but he

couldn't make himself grab it. His hands had stopped working properly. The edges of his vision dimmed, and he collapsed onto his back on the bed. For the first time, he noticed a water stain in the corner of the ceiling, and then Devereaux's face filled his vision.

"It's fascinating how much blood can come from such a small cut." Devereaux's eyes dipped down to trace the path the blood made as it leaked from Simmons's neck onto the bedspread underneath. "I used to make a study of how close to death I could take my dear Alice before allowing life to flood back into her body."

His smile was cold. "You won't be so lucky, however." Simmons tried to speak, but every word sounded like wheezing gasps. "No, no. Don't try to talk. You'll just get blood everywhere. It's unsightly."

Devereaux bent to retrieve something off the floor and then was back peering into his face. "You sure are taking forever to die."

He gripped the handle of the knife with a napkin and wiped it off. The motion caused pain to lance through the numbness invading his body.

"Let this be a lesson you take to the grave, Mr. Simmons. Figure out who you're dealing with before you decide to fuck someone over."

Simmons heard the muffled sound of footsteps receding, the soft click of the door closing barely audible over the buzzing in his ears. His last conscious thought was the fact that he was never going to see home again and nobody was alive to miss him.

Chapter Thirty-Three

James didn't need to be at the Orchid to cover Mike's usual opening shift for a little over an hour, so he drove to the warehouse where their biggest shipment of the week had been delivered the day before. Maybe he was a coward, but he didn't think he could face Delaney just yet.

It was quiet. The crew he'd tasked with sorting the crates into smaller shipments wasn't due to arrive until the afternoon, but the manual labor of hauling around heavy boxes was the perfect distraction.

They were stacked in neat rows two tall and in the same place where the unloading crew left them. Grabbing a crowbar from a nearby table, he wrenched off the lid to the nearest crate and made a tally on the inventory list in his pocket.

This sort of work was mindless, checking and tallying. It was why he normally assigned it to someone else these days, too busy for this kind of basic labor. Today he needed it.

His phone rang, but he ignored it, methodically moving down the line of crates and checking each one. Once that was done, he sorted the top crates into piles based on the list Aidan gave him for deliveries.

He'd never questioned this life before. It was family, and family was everything. Now he couldn't help but wonder how much more he would have to sacrifice for the good of the family while everyone moved on with their lives around him.

His phone rang again, and he turned the damn thing off. He needed peace and fucking quiet right now. A minute to screw his head on straight so he didn't have to think about how he was losing someone he really cared about. Again.

What was it Brogan said? You can't help who you fall in love with. Even if you could, he wasn't sure he would have chosen differently. If Delaney was a siren, he'd gladly drown a thousand times over just to spend a few months in her presence.

He checked his watch and, satisfied with the progress he'd made, locked up the warehouse behind him and crossed the parking lot to his SUV. Turning his phone back on, James left for the pub, rolling his eyes at the volley of incoming notifications as it connected to service again.

Hooking the phone up to the car, he called Brogan back rather than listening to his voicemails. His cousin's voice was tight when he answered.

"Where the hell have you been?"

"I was at the warehouse and didn't hear my phone," he lied. "What's up?"

"He's here."

James's fingers tightened on the wheel, and the car jerked in response. "Who?"

"Devereaux. He flew private into Philly last night."

"Shit." Dread settled like a weight in his stomach. "Do you think he—"

"I don't know. But he's been paying a private investigator

a hefty weekly sum for the last two and a half months. My guess is he's been looking. And found her."

"I'm on my way back to the pub now."

"I'll meet you there."

"No. I need to know where he's staying. His movements. Everything."

"I already know where he's staying." James heard the growl of Brogan's engine in the background. "I'm on my way. James? I have to loop Declan in on this, just in case. If we have to kill him, it'll be messy in the press."

"I know. I don't care. I only care that she doesn't die."

James punched the button to end the call and floored it. The image of him holding Maura's lifeless and bloody body flashed through his mind. He would not be too late this time. He had to make sure Delaney made it out alive. And if she didn't, God help the bastard who killed her when James found him.

Her car was still there when he peeled into the parking lot, and he barely missed running into the side of the building when he screeched to a stop. Jumping out, he fumbled his key into the lock at the kitchen door and let himself in to the rage-filled screams of Addy's music.

He didn't acknowledge her greeting wave, sprinting up the stairs to the apartment above. The first floor was empty, and he took the stairs up to the loft.

"Delaney!"

Her bedroom was empty. The closet hung open, but nothing looked out of place. The bathroom and his room were also empty, and nothing looked like it had been disturbed. Pushing back the wall in his closet, he removed two extra mags from the safe and shoved them into his pockets. The only way Charles Devereaux was leaving Philadelphia was in a body bag.

Satisfying himself with one last sweep of his apartment,

he jogged down the stairs and into the kitchen again. Addy's music was off now, her brow pinched with worry.

"Everything okay?"

"Where's Delaney?"

Addy gestured toward the door to the pub. "She was prepping the front of house for opening."

He pushed through the swinging door into the pub and stopped dead. Chairs that would normally be stacked on tables or neatly tucked under them were overturned. The bucket where they put clean silverware to roll into napkins was upended on the bar, the utensils scattered across the surface and onto the floor.

Stepping further into the chaos, James heard Addy swear under her breath. He didn't notice the broken glass until he rounded the bar, but someone had busted in the window on the door and let themselves in. He dropped to a crouch and inspected the droplets of blood dotting the floor. Either Delaney's or the intruder's. James hoped it was the latter.

"How long was she alone in here?"

"Um." Addy shoved her bright blue hair off her face and squeezed her eyes shut, trying to remember. "I don't know. Maybe thirty minutes? She came down after I got here to do prep but before we were supposed to open."

A loud, incessant banging on the kitchen door made Addy yelp, and James glanced up. "That's Brogan. Let him in."

A second later, Brogan joined him, arms crossed over his chest as he surveyed the scene. "What's the timeline?"

"Longest he could've had her is thirty minutes, give or take. He could be anywhere with her in thirty minutes."

"His jet isn't scheduled to fly until tonight. If he's got her, they're still in the city."

James pushed to his feet. "If?"

"He's working with the PI, so it's hard to say if he had the

PI do his dirty work or he did it himself." He gave James a long look. "What's your gut say?"

"That he wouldn't pass up the opportunity to find her and see for himself." Brogan nodded in agreement. "Would he take her to where he's staying? A hotel?"

"It's risky if she didn't go quietly, and it looks like she didn't. But he did rent one. The king's suite."

"Then let's go."

Brogan laid a hand on James's arm to stop his advance to the door. "Declan's not allocating any resources to this. At all. No support on the ground, no cleanup, nothing. You do this, you're on your own."

"I didn't suspect he would." James shook off his cousin's grip. "I'll find her myself, handle it myself, and take whatever consequences Declan wants to dish out once she's safe and this fucker's dead."

"No, you won't." Brogan held up a hand at James's protest. "I'm going with you. Let's start with his hotel. I downloaded the schematics to my phone. Better if we can catch him by surprise and don't have to shoot up the place."

Chapter Thirty-Four

The first thing Delaney noticed when she came to was the smell. That sickeningly sweet scent of cologne that had haunted her nightmares for nearly a decade. The room was dark, but she could just barely hear the distant sound of movement and the low hum of what might be voices.

Unwilling to move too much and draw attention to herself but desperate to get her bearings, she opened her eyes a fraction and tried to make out her surroundings. A bedroom. Or she was on a bed, at least.

The lights were off, and the curtains were closed, but as her eyes adjusted, she noted a TV mounted to the wall and a dresser tucked into the corner. The door to the bedroom was closed, the thin strip of light at the base occasionally interrupted by the shadow of footsteps.

Pushing herself into a sitting position, she winced, fingers moving up to probe at the throbbing ache in her cheek. That's right. He'd shoved her when she refused to go willingly.

She didn't think there was anything else Charles could do to surprise her anymore, but she barely caught sight of his face through the glass of the pub door before his fist was through it and he was reaching in to unlock it. She would have outrun him back to the safety of the kitchen if not for Addy. He was there for her. She didn't want to make Addy a target too.

Delaney had no intention of leaving with him, though. Not when he apologized and pleaded and told her how much he missed her. Not when he demanded and threatened and clenched his fists. He'd gotten impatient with her refusal and moved close enough to shove her into the bar, her body collapsing to the floor in a daze before she passed out.

Slipping off the bed, she crossed to the bathroom. He liked to shave with a straight razor. Maybe he'd left it tucked into his toiletries bag. She'd take that over having no weapon at all. She rummaged through it with trembling fingers. Nothing. Damn it.

She glanced up at her reflection, and the blood in her veins went to ice. He'd changed her clothes, swapping her jeans out for an expensive pair of black slacks and her Black Orchid shirt for a purple cashmere sweater. She hated the color purple. It was his favorite.

Lifting her shirt, she noticed he'd even changed her bra for his preferred brand, La Perla, and her stomach roiled at the realization he'd stripped her naked and did God knew what else while she was unconscious and vulnerable. She braced her hands on the edge of the counter and forced herself to take slow, deep breaths.

She would not leave this city with him. She would get away or die trying. Knowing Charles, she'd be dead either way, and if that was her fate, then she would get to decide the time and the method. She would never be his victim again.

Leaving the bathroom and crossing to the bedroom door, she took a steadying breath before opening it. He was sitting at the table on the far side of the room with his phone pressed to his ear, food spread out on the table before him. He sat with his back to the window, and she studied his profile. The defined outline of his jaw, always clean shaven, the elegant slope of his nose, his high, aristocratic forehead.

No one would disagree that the man was handsome and elegant, sophisticated, even. But it was everything underneath the facade he presented to the world that made him a monster.

She would never forget his full lips twisted into a sneer while he sent her sprawling to the floor with a well-timed backhand to the face. Or his long fingers wrapping around her throat and squeezing until she couldn't breathe. Or his green eyes snapping from warm to deadly in an instant. It was always impossible to predict which imagined slight would set him off.

Ending his call, he glanced up and saw her. His smile was quick, but there was no warmth in it. There never was.

"Oh, good. You're up." He said it like she was taking a nap and not like he kidnapped her and dragged her here against her will. "I've ordered some lunch for us. Come sit."

She stood rooted in place, crossing her arms over her chest. "How did you find me?"

"Sugar." There was that million-dollar smile again. "I told you I would always find you. We're meant to be together."

"Are we? Then why did you try to kill me so often?"

"Don't be ridiculous, Alice." Delaney flinched at his use of her old name. "I agree that sometimes my punishments went a little too far, maybe I was a bit heavy-handed, but you pushed me to do that. All you had to do was behave. Now, come here."

Still she didn't move. "Except it was impossible to *behave*." She spat the word. "There was nothing I could have done to be perfect for you. You were always punishing me for things that happened only inside your imagination."

255

The look he aimed at her was one she knew all too well. She was toeing a dangerous line, and he wouldn't put up with her attitude much longer. But she couldn't stop the words pouring out of her. It was like a dam had been broken. If she was going to die at his hand, she had some things she wanted to say to him first.

"You're trying to provoke me, Alice, and I won't have it. You're always trying to make me look like the villain. Come sit down," he barked, pointing at the chair to his right. "We're going to have a nice lunch, and then we're going home. Your friends have missed you. *I've* missed you."

"How are you going to explain it to them? That I'm not dead?"

He frowned, and his mouth thinned into a hard line. "Yes, you did leave me with quite a mess to clean up. I suspect we'll have to say you had a nasty fall and lost your memory."

"That's very cliché."

His eyes flashed, and he pushed out of the chair. "Maybe I should mangle one of your limbs so we really can say a gator got you." She tried to skirt around him when he rushed at her, but he grabbed her by the arm, squeezing it so hard she yelped. "How would it feel to lose a hand? Or maybe we'd have to take it off up to the elbow?"

He traced a finger down the column of her throat. "Give you some good scarring to make it believable. Or I could take a leg." His hand slid down over her ass to squeeze her thigh. "Make sure you can never run from me again."

A fresh wave of nausea swamped her at his threat. He was just crazy enough to do it.

"You know it's impressive, really," she said.

He released her, shoving her away from him. "What is?"

"How well you manage to hide what a complete psycho you are."

This time when he touched her, his hand found her throat,

256

and he squeezed until she coughed. "You've never appreciated how I held your life in my hands every day and chose not to take it. Because I love you."

In spite of herself, she laughed, but it was cold, derisive. "That's not love, you asshole. Not killing someone and calling it love doesn't prove anything but what a miserable excuse for a human being you are."

Charles brought his face inches from hers, and she cringed away from him. "You think love is fucking that pathetic man who owns a pub? Playing whore and housewife in his little apartment while you wait tables like a nobody? I gave you everything!"

"And you made me pay for it every day! James is ten times the man you will ever be. I'd rather work my fingers to the bone than live in your cage."

His fingers tightened on her throat, and she clawed at his skin. She'd been resigned to death at his hand once, but she wanted to see James again. She wanted to feel his arms wrapped around her and hear his voice in her ear. She wanted to fight.

"I'm sorry," she choked out, gasping for breath when Charles loosened his grip.

"Say it again," he demanded.

"I'm sorry." He released her, and she pivoted away from him, eyeing the vase on the low credenza just a few inches away. "I'm sorry I ever met you."

Lunging for the vase, she brought it down against his forehead. When he stumbled back a few steps, she darted for the door, gasping when he recovered fast enough to grab her hair and yank her back against him. He wrapped an arm around her throat again and squeezed.

James had explained how to get out of a chokehold after she told him about Charles, but she couldn't remember all the steps. And even if she did, it still felt like she was miles from the door. She'd never make it in time. Not while Charles was still breathing.

"It took me such a long time to beat that spirit out of you, Alice," he whispered against her ear, fear tightening her stomach. "But don't worry. I remember how I did it the first time. I can do it again."

"I'd rather be dead."

His laugh was low and dark. "Oh, sugar. Death would be too easy. Now, are you going to behave, or do I have to knock you out again?" He tightened his arm around her neck to prove his point, and she nodded.

"I'll behave."

Charles waited a beat but ultimately released her. As he crossed back to the table and took a seat, Delaney went over the options in her head. She could rush him again, try and hit him with something heavier to knock him out and give her time to get out of the room. Or she could play along and wait until they left, lose herself in a crowd or sprint away from him in public when he was less likely to make a scene.

But her problems were bigger than just getting away. As long as Charles Devereaux breathed, she would never be safe. She squeezed her eyes shut and inhaled long and deep. If she really wanted to be free, she would have to kill him.

Turning back toward the table, she took her seat at his right hand, the only place he ever allowed her to sit. He shook out his napkin with a snap and laid it across his lap, staring at her until she did the same. He leaned forward and removed the cloche over her plate to reveal a salad.

"Your figure was different when I changed you out of those God-awful clothes," he explained. "Don't worry. I'm sure I can help you get it back. You liked working with that personal trainer, right?"

"Which one? The woman? Or the gay man you accused me of giving blow jobs to?"

He threw the cloche across the room, and she jerked when it clanged against the wall. "It's hardly my fault you're such a slut. You were when I met you, and that obviously rings true today. Whoring yourself out to Christ knows how many people to survive as long as you have."

"Is that the only way you think I've been able to hide from you for so long? Sleeping with someone else in exchange for protection?"

"Well, I don't remember you being good for much else, Alice."

She gritted her teeth at the insult, eyeing the steak knife next to his plate. "If I was such a whore, why did you marry me?"

"Every bad girl needs taming. You were a fun project for me. Taking you out of your sad life, dressing you up, turning you into something resembling a lady." He gestured down the length of her body. "I did a fine job until you ruined it."

"My life wasn't sad when I met you. You took everything from me."

"I didn't take anything you weren't willing to give me, Alice. Don't forget that. I didn't force you to marry me. I didn't force you to drop out of law school. You chose to do those things. You wanted it."

"I wanted it?!" She shoved back from the table. "I wanted you to beat me bloody for spilling red wine on the carpet? I wanted you to choke me until I passed out because I forgot your mother's birthday? I wanted you to try and kill me because I laughed at your boss's joke?"

"That's enough!" He pushed to his feet, towering over her until he backed her against the wall. "You wanted the money and the status I provided, and if you had learned your place, I wouldn't have needed to lay a finger on you. If you were treated in a way you didn't like, then it was no one's fault but your own."

"You'd like to believe that, wouldn't you? Does it help you sleep at night? Pretending to be the victim when really you're the monster?"

He slapped her so hard her head snapped back and hit the wall. "It seems even after all the lessons I've taught you, you've still learned nothing," he said through gritted teeth. "Maybe it's time for another one."

Sliding his fingers into her hair, he tightened his grip and yanked so hard she sucked in a breath through her teeth, tears forming at the corners of her eyes. He shoved her forward, and she fell to her hands and knees next to the table. She heard the all too familiar sound of his belt buckle and shuddered. His favorite when he didn't want to leave bruises on his knuckles.

She pushed up onto her knees and faced him, watching him tug the leather from the last of the belt loops on his suit pants. He held the buckle in his palm and wrapped the belt twice around it as he stalked forward. She took a deep breath in and slowly released it, her heart pounding frantically in her chest. Either he was dead at the end of this or she was.

He lashed out with the belt, and she jerked to the left, avoiding the blow. Rage lit his bright green eyes. It always made him angrier when she tried not to get hit. But that's what she wanted. The angrier he was, the less calculating, like something snapped inside him, and he could only give in to his most basic violent urges.

Usually when he got to that point, she was too scared and too bloody to fight back. She'd never intentionally goaded him into a rage before. Keeping her head about her as he lost his might be her only chance.

He struck out again, and this time the belt landed across her forearm, pain radiating up to her elbow. She pushed to her feet and dodged the next blow.

"You've forgotten I own you, Alice." He stalked closer.

"That I can do whatever I want to you because you're my wife."

"No," she said with a shake of her head. "Your wife is dead."

This time when he whipped the belt at her, she grabbed for it, yanking him forward at the same time she picked the knife up from the table. He lurched forward onto the blade, and it sank into his chest. On instinct, she pushed it in to the hilt and yanked it back out again.

They both looked down at the blood blooming over his white shirt, and his green eyes were filled with pain when he met her gaze. She wrenched the belt from his grasp and darted away from him when he staggered toward her.

He fell to his knees, his hands reaching up to clutch his chest. When he tried to speak, only a gargled jumble came out of his mouth. She must have punctured a lung. That should make her feel something, but it didn't. Her whole body was numb.

Delaney stood there in shock, looking down at the bloody knife in her hand. Oh God. How was she supposed to explain this? What if no one believed she killed him in self-defense? Someone pounded on the door, and she barely managed to stifle a scream. Unable to hold himself up anymore, Charles fell to the floor and rolled onto his back.

"Room service!" a voice called from the other side of the door, but it sounded familiar.

Backing away from where Charles lay unmoving on the floor, she crossed to the door, turning briefly to peer through the peephole. James. He was here. Sobbing with relief, she threw the door open and launched herself into his arms.

"James. Oh my God." Her breath hitched as she tried to find the words. "I think he's dead. I think I killed him."

Instantly a tall, broad man covered in tattoos was behind

them, and Delaney jolted, her arms tightening around James's neck.

James let the man usher them both inside and set her on her feet in the entryway. "It's okay. This is my cousin, Brogan."

Delaney relaxed against James's chest, watching Brogan sweep around them and crouch next to Charles. He felt for a pulse, inching away from the widening pool of blood, and then shook his head.

In that instant, it hit her, and her legs gave out. Sinking to the floor, her body shook with sobs. "He's gone. He's really gone."

James knelt next to her and reached for the knife, prying it from her clenched fingers. She let him have it and closed her eyes when his fingers trailed over her face, neck, and shoulders, checking for injuries.

"Delaney, look at me." She dragged her gaze up to his face. "Are you okay?"

Delaney looked back at Charles's motionless body and nodded, tears still streaming down her face. "I'm free."

Chapter Thirty-Five

J ames sat on the edge of his bed with his head in his hands. Seven days. That's how long it had been since he'd found Delaney in that hotel room, steak knife clutched tight in her fingers, her husband lying in a pool of blood on the floor. She'd done it. She'd freed herself and come out the other side with only a few scratches and bruises.

Declan was pissed, though. At the relationship, the compromising position James had put the family in by having his name appear in the papers next to the killing of a prominent New Orleans attorney. The Callahan name. That's really what this was about. What it would always be about. Protecting the family's interests.

For the last week, James had been desperately trying to come up with a way to have them both. To keep Delaney in his life and not put the syndicate at risk. Deep down, he knew she wouldn't betray him, wouldn't betray the family. He couldn't say how he knew that. He just did. Convincing Declan of Delaney's loyalty was less certain.

James glanced at his phone when it rang and sent the

caller to voicemail. New Orleans newspapers and TV outlets had been calling for a statement since the news broke. It didn't matter how much he ignored them; they were persistent. All they did was remind him he couldn't have the only thing he wanted. Delaney.

He heard her moving around downstairs. She'd slipped out of bed early this morning before the sun came up. He could tell she knew something was off between them, but she hadn't said anything. It was just as well because he had no idea what he would say to her anyway. How did you push someone away you wanted to pull close?

But he needed to get it over with. Ignoring the inevitable was only going to hurt them both in the long run. She would have money coming in from her ex and his estate as his next of kin. She could use that to start over anywhere in the world. She could be happy. He could let her go if he knew she'd be happy, even if it wasn't with him.

Snatching his phone off the bed and shoving it into his pocket, he dragged himself to the stairs, pausing at the top to study her. The sight of her took his breath away. Her warm brown skin and black curls that coiled around her head and danced when she moved. Her lean dancer's body and long legs and perfect ass.

He'd miss everything about her, from her laugh to how it felt to hold her while she slept. Aidan was right. He never should have let it get this far. He never should have put himself in the position to lose someone else he loved to this life.

Steeling himself, he jogged down the stairs, heart squeezing in his chest when she turned, setting her coffee mug on the edge of the counter and watching him with those amber-flecked eyes.

"We need to talk."

She deflated, the hope visibly draining from her face, and

he hated himself for it. Hated himself for what he was about to do.

"Yeah," she breathed. "That's probably a good idea."

"You're free now. You can start over somewhere new. Use the money from his estate to tide you over for a while. Maybe go back to Chicago and finish your law degree."

Wrapping her arms around herself, she pinned him with a searching look. "What if I don't want to start over somewhere else? What if I want to stay here? With you?"

The words were a knife to his heart; the look on her face twisted the blade. He wanted that. She couldn't possibly know how much. He couldn't have it. This had to be over.

"I don't think that's a good idea. There's a lot you don't know about me." He raked a rough hand through his hair. He could hardly form the words he needed to end this. "A lot you don't want to know. Trust me, it's better this way."

Anger flashed in her eyes, and she took a step closer. "Says who? Why do you get to decide what's best for me?"

"This is what's best for both of us. Please, Delaney," he pleaded. "Just trust me when I say you'll be better off if you leave and make your life far away from here, from me. Be free and be happy."

She laughed through the tears gathering in her eyes, but there was no joy in it. "You were the first person who made me happy in a long time. Before I met you, I didn't think I'd ever be happy again. I love you." Her words were whisper soft, and they nearly broke him.

"You shouldn't." He forced steel into his voice because he was afraid if he didn't, he'd cave and go to her. If he touched her now, he wouldn't be able to let go. "I'm dangerous."

"You'd never hurt me."

He snorted. "There are plenty of ways a man can be dangerous without beating the woman he claims to love."

She took a tentative step forward, and it took everything

265

he had to remain rooted in place. She was fraying the edges of his control.

"You don't have to do this. You have secrets. I know you do. I'll keep them for you. I would never betray you, James."

"This is so much bigger than me. I can't put my family and hundreds of people at risk. Not even for love."

Her breath hitched, but she nodded. "Okay. If that's your choice. I can't force you to want me. I'm not going to beg."

She crossed to the foot of the stairs and paused in front of him. He held his breath and braced himself for her anger, but her eyes were only sad. She skirted around him and jogged up the stairs.

He heard her rummaging through drawers and pulling things out of the bathroom. After weeks of keeping everything in her duffel, she'd finally unpacked, and now she was tossing it all back in again. He felt like he was going to be sick.

Coming back down, she set her bag on the floor as she bent to tie her shoes. When she stood, she studied him for a long moment. "You made me believe in happiness again. You made me feel safe for the first time in a very long time."

Stooping to retrieve her bag, she looped it over her shoulder and settled its weight on her hip. "I spent eight years married to a man who claimed to be good and loved me with his fists. He was a monster. I don't care what you do. Maybe I should. Maybe it's stupid of me that I don't."

Her fingers twitched on the strap as she reached for the door. "But what you do doesn't make you who you are. Not as long as you're good deep down in the ways that matter." The corner of her mouth tipped up in a small, sad smile. "No one understands the importance of secrets more than I do. And yours will always be safe with me."

Delaney slipped through the door, closing it softly behind her, and he rushed for it, gripping the handle with white knuckles. He wanted to go after her. He wanted to stop her and bring her back upstairs and apologize until his voice was hoarse from it. He wanted her.

His phone chirped an incoming message, and he gritted his teeth as he dug it out of his pocket. Declan. Reminding him of a family meeting to debrief over what he'd been calling the 'Devereaux problem.' James stopped himself from throwing the phone against the wall so hard it shattered. Barely.

Moments later, his phone rang. Declan again. Couldn't the son of a bitch let him grieve in peace over this? He let it go to voicemail, but it was silent for a fraction of a second before it started ringing again.

"What the fuck do you want?" he snarled.

James could all but hear the raised eyebrow in his cousin's tone when he said, "Did you get my text?"

"Yes, I got your text. I always do."

Declan sighed. "James, you know I'm only thinking about the family, the syndicate."

"I know. But I trust her, Declan. And I wish you trusted me enough to let that be enough. She understands secrets. She wouldn't betray us."

A beat of silence. "And how do you know she wouldn't?"

"The same way you knew Evie wouldn't. The same way you knew you could trust Libby and Falcone. I just know. Isn't that enough?"

James heard rustling and the hushed murmur of voices over the line. "Bring her to dinner next week. We'll see what we see."

James jerked upright. "What did you say?"

"I want to meet her. Then I'll decide."

The line went dead before James could respond, but he didn't hesitate to grab his keys from the hook by the door and race down the stairs. He prayed she hadn't gotten far. If he hurried, he might be able to catch up with her. To apologize and tell her how he really felt.

When he burst through the kitchen door into the bright light of day, the sight of her SUV still parked at the back of the lot sucked all the air out of his lungs. She was still here.

He ate up the distance between them with long strides. When her head jerked up and she caught sight of him through the windshield, he smiled. By the time he reached her, she'd climbed out of the cab, and he lifted her into his arms, burying his face against her neck and inhaling her scent.

"I thought you'd be gone by the time I got out here."

"Well, what took you so long?"

He laughed and set her back on her feet, pressing her up against the truck and brushing her hair away from her face. "Stay with me."

"But what about Declan? Your family? I know how important they are to you."

"He wants to meet you. We'll deal with him, with all of it, together. I love you, Delaney. Stay with me."

Her smile was wide, and her eyes were bright when she pulled him in for a kiss, long and slow and demanding nothing. "There's nowhere else I'd rather be."

Epilogue

"Ready?"

Delaney studied herself in the mirror in the bathroom, running a hand down the front of her dress to smooth it. She couldn't remember the last time she'd worn a dress. She thought it might help with the nerves that had been building to a fever pitch all week. It hadn't. But it was a pretty shade of red, at least.

Her eyes met James's in the mirror. "No. But let's do it anyway."

His smile was warm when he reached for her hand, lacing their fingers together and bringing her knuckles to his lips. If he was nervous about how tonight might go, he didn't show it. But his steadiness was enough to quell the worst of the butterflies doing loops in her stomach.

They drove away from Center City to the north. She'd never ventured into this part of Philadelphia before. The homes got bigger, and so did the lots, until there was nothing but massive trees lining the road with the occasional gate and a glimpse of a towering mansion beyond.

Billionaire. She knew the word applied. She'd done her

research, after all. But knowing it and seeing it were two different things. Suddenly she felt hopelessly out of her depth. Not just because she was about to share dinner with the city's most powerful crime family—a sentence that still felt strange to roll around in her brain—but because she'd clawed her way up from nothing and these people had everything.

He turned into a driveway and stopped in front of a tall wrought iron gate between two stone pillars. After punching a code into the box, the gate swung open, and he drove through. The house came into view and her breath caught in the back of her throat.

Three stories of stone and glass rose behind a circular drive. Ivy climbed the far side of the house and wrapped around it. It was stunning, old, stately. James had said something about the house being in the family for over a century. She wondered at having that kind of history in a single place.

"They're just people."

She dragged her gaze away from the house to look at him. "They're gods," she breathed, and he chuckled.

She climbed out of the SUV when he did, and he met her at the hood, squeezing her shoulders and then skimming his hands down her arms. "You okay?"

"What if they don't like me?"

"How could anyone not like you?" She cocked a brow. "In the unlikely event that happens, we'll fake our deaths and run away together. I know someone who's had good practice with that."

She laughed despite herself. "That's not funny."

"Then why are you laughing?" He brushed a soft kiss against her lips. "Impress Evie, and you'll be halfway there."

"Which one is she again?" she asked, trailing him up the walkway to the imposing front door.

"Declan's wife."

"Oh, right. The queen," she said, and he grinned, shaking his head.

He let himself in, and there was something oddly comforting about the fact that he felt enough at ease to go in without knocking or announcing their presence. She took a steadying breath and followed him inside. They weren't just people to her. They held her happiness in their hands.

The foyer couldn't be called anything but grand, soaring above them with a beautiful glass chandelier hanging from the ceiling. The carpet was plush and old, original to the house if she had to guess. A beautiful staircase climbed to the second level, and a long hallway led to the back of the house on the left while another branched off to the right.

The house in New Orleans was a shack by comparison, and that gave her a smug sense of satisfaction. She'd traded up in every way imaginable. Assuming they liked her enough to let her stay. Or trusted her.

They didn't really have to like her, even though she desperately wanted them to. But they did have to trust her. That's what tonight was all about. Earning their trust. She would do it. She had to. Because she loved James too much to lose him.

She heard the low hum of voices as soon as they turned the corner to the right of the stairs, and those pesky butterflies started doing somersaults in her stomach again. Pressing a hand to her belly, she gave James's hand a squeeze, smiling when he returned it.

They stopped in the doorway of the living room. Generous leather couches and chairs were arranged in a large seating area. There was a bar cart against the far wall, stocked with bottles of liquor and wine. It took the room a while to register their presence, but when they did, conversation slowly dwindled.

"Just people," he reminded her.

271

A woman with brown curls and an impressive emerald and diamond ring on her finger made her way across the room. She smiled, but her hazel eyes took Delaney in, appraising, calculating.

"I'm glad you could make it. I'm Evie. Can I get you something to drink?"

Well, nothing like starting at the top and working your way down. "I don't really drink," Delaney said. "Alcohol, I mean."

"Water? Tea? Soda?" Evie clasped her hands in front of her and waited.

"Water's fine."

"Good." She looped her arm through Delaney's and turned them toward the hallway. "Come with me."

Delaney shot James a look with wide eyes, and he nodded, flashing her a smile. Evie didn't speak as she led Delaney down the hallway and past a dining room big enough for twenty. But when they stepped into the kitchen, Delaney couldn't help but gasp.

Evie chuckled. "We get that reaction a lot." She crossed to the fridge, and Delaney turned in a big circle, taking in the expanse of marble and gleaming stainless steel. "Still or sparkling?"

"Still, please." Evie grabbed a bottle of water from the fridge and pulled a glass down from the cupboard, filling it with ice. "Your home is beautiful."

Evie smiled, her eyes going soft. "I can't take credit for it. It's been like this for as long as I can remember. But I do my best to carry on the legacy." She held the glass out to Delaney and cocked her head, that appraising look back in her eye. "I read about what happened in the papers. I've heard a little more about it from James."

"And?" Delaney held her breath for Evie's reply.

"And I'm glad the son of a bitch is dead and you were the

one who killed him. It's nice to exorcise our own demons every once in a while."

Delaney nodded. She'd tried to conjure up the guilt she was sure she should feel over killing her husband. But she couldn't. All that ever floated to the surface was relief and a wonderful sense of freedom.

"The world is a better place without him in it. Though his mother disagrees."

"Mothers usually do," Evie said with a small smile. "Ready to head back into the fray?"

"As I think I'll ever be."

"We promise not to bite," Evie said with a chuckle.

They stepped into the room, and conversation faltered again. Being the center of attention made her uneasy, but she was here tonight for James as much as herself, and she wouldn't let him down. These people could trust her because she was trustworthy. All she had to do was show them.

"Delaney, I'd like you to meet the Callahan family," Evie said, pointing around the room as she made introductions. "Brogan and his wife, Libby; Aidan and his wife, Viv; Cait, who was married to Finn; and my husband, Declan."

Her pulse jumped when she met Declan's steely blue stare, but she forced herself to smile. "It's great to finally meet everyone. James has told me so much about you."

Cait crossed the room to wrap Delaney in a warm hug. "Welcome. Don't let the men get to you." Cait cut a look at Evie. "They're very broody."

Pressing a hand to the small of her back, Evie led Delaney further into the room, and James moved to stand on her other side, leaning down to press a kiss to her temple. She relaxed a fraction at his nearness.

"James was saying you went to law school."

Delaney nodded at Brogan. "In Chicago. I didn't finish, though. I still have a semester left."

"Do you want to finish?" Libby asked.

She tilted her head and considered. "I haven't really thought about it, to be honest. Not in years, anyway."

"What kind of law did you study?"

"Criminal defense."

That sent up a murmur around the room and even earned a raised eyebrow from Declan. She hadn't told James much about her time at law school. He hadn't asked yet. They had so much to discover about each other still.

"Would be nice to have a lawyer in the family," Evie said, moving to pick up her glass of wine off a nearby table and stand in front of her husband.

Declan draped a possessive arm around her shoulders and pulled her close. "We've got Daniel Ryan."

Evie shot Declan a look over her shoulder. "He's seventy-two. We'll have to replace him eventually."

"Lawyers are good with secrets," Delaney said, forcing herself to maintain eye contact with Declan.

Declan flicked a glance at James when he shifted closer and wrapped an arm around her waist. "Yes," Declan agreed. "They can be. Can this family trust you with its secrets, Delaney?"

"Absolutely," she said without hesitation.

"And why should we believe you?"

There was a challenge in the question. But she would rise to meet it. "No one understands better than I do that some secrets are life and death. And I love your cousin enough to keep them." James's fingers flexed on her waist, and she leaned into him, into his warmth.

"Love fades."

"Only if you don't care enough to tend it," she replied. "And I care. More than I ever thought possible. I already know enough to go to the cops." Declan's nostrils flared, and Evie raised a brow. "But I haven't. Because doing that puts

James in jeopardy as much as all of you. And I would never do that."

"This life isn't easy," Viv pointed out.

Delaney nodded. "No. I don't imagine it is. But I've lived through worse. This is the choice I'm making. James, this life, this family, if you'll have me. All I'm asking for is a chance to prove myself. We can take the rest as it comes."

Evie looked at Declan, and they shared a conversation between them without words. Declan looked away from his wife, gaze intense and searching. Finally he gave a curt nod, lifting his glass to his mouth and taking a slow sip.

"A chance, then."

Biting back a grin, Evie raised her glass in a toast. "To taking it as it comes."

Everyone murmured their agreement, and conversation resumed as if nothing had happened. Delaney exhaled long and slow, her fingers tightening on the glass in her hand. James shifted her in his arms and reached up to cup her face, brushing his thumb over her cheek.

"You're incredible," he said softly, leaning down to brush a kiss against her lips.

"You make me remember who I used to be. Before everything went off the rails. You brought me back to life."

"You brought yourself back. But you deserve every good thing, Delaney. And I'm going to make sure you have it."

She pushed onto her tiptoes to press her lips to his again, smiling when someone whistled and everyone laughed softly. There was nowhere else she'd rather be, no one else she'd rather have by her side. She'd walk through hell and back to keep him safe, to keep the people he loved safe.

She'd keep as many secrets as it took to have the opportunity to love him until her last breath.

A Note for the Reader

Dear Reader,

From the very bottom of my heart, thank you. Out of all the billions of books available to read you choose mine. After what happened to Maura in Sweet Revenge, I really wanted to give James a second chance at happy ever after. I hope you enjoyed seeing him fall and fight for Delaney as much as I did! I am deeply grateful that you took the time out of your life to come along on James and Delaney's journey.

If you enjoyed this book, I would really appreciate a little more of your time in the form of a review on Goodreads or Amazon or wherever you purchased it.

I couldn't do this writing thing I love so much without you. This is the last book in the Callahan Syndicate Series but I'm not done telling stories yet. Mark your calendars for a brand new series set in picturesque Sicily. Fall in love with the Bianchi family in The Vows We Break coming in February 2023 to Kindle Unlimited, ebook, and paperback.

For sneak peeks, bonus chapters, updates, release dates, and more, sign up for my newsletter at https://meaghan pierce.com/newsletter or follow me on TikTok.

All my love,
Meaghan

tiktok.com/@meaghanpierceauthor

Also by Meaghan Pierce

Acknowledgments

A massive thanks to Cher who is constantly fielding my questions about any and everything and keeping me sane in the process. I don't think you quite understand how much your friendship helps to keep me going.

Many thanks to Serge for his help in naming the lingerie brand. I love when I can toss out random questions and someone always shows up with an answer. The Duke of Yelp to the rescue.

The Group Chat, the ride or dies, the partners in crime. Y'all are it. I'm constantly in awe of how our pandemic friendship has blossomed into this amazing container full of encouragement, memes, GIFs, laughs, and internet hugs that never fail to make me feel better.

To Caoimhe and Paula, my soul sisters. I couldn't begin to express my thanks for your love, support, opinions, real talk, and screenshot evidence when I get too in my own head.

To my betas: Kate, Ali, Jill, Alyse, and Kia. You helped me make this book better and showed me my blind spots. For that I am so grateful.

To my editor, Mo. Thank you times a million for answering all of my stupid questions with grace and a perfectly chosen GIF. And to my proofreader, Holly. Experiencing my book through your eyes is one of my favorite things about the whole process.

Lastly, thank you to all the readers who kept telling me

they needed to know that James was okay and could be happy again. Your investment in his happiness made bringing Delaney to life a cinch. I hope I did it justice for you.

Printed in Great Britain
by Amazon

10592367R00166